IS SAAVIK REALLY SPOCK'S DAUGHTER?

ON WHAT KIND OF WORLD DID TRIBBLES EVOLVE?

WHY DID KIRK GIVE UP COMMAND OF THE *ENTERPRISE* A SECOND TIME?

These are just a few of the questions answered in this great new collection of articles about Star Trek. You'll explore the ways in which Kirk, Spock, Bones, and the rest of the crew have changed, learn more about the *Enterprise*, V'Ger, and the Genesis machine, and catch up on all the latest happenings and past history of Star Trek in—

THE BEST OF TREK® #7

THE BEST OF TREK #7

FROM THE MAGAZINE FOR STAR TREK FANS

EDITED BY WALTER IRWIN AND G. B. LOVE

A SIGNET BOOK

NEW AMERICAN LIBRARY

Cover art by Eddie Jones

SIGNET, SIGNET CLASSIC, MENTOR, PLUME, MERIDIAN and
NAL BOOKS are published by New American Library, 1633 Broadway,
New York, New York 10019

First Printing, June, 1984

1 2 3 4 5 6 7 8 9

PRINTED IN THE UNITED STATES OF AMERICA

ACKNOWLEDGMENTS

Grateful thanks are due, as always, to the many, many people who have helped to make this seventh collection possible:

Sheila Gilbert of NAL, our overworked editor. Sheila is the person we gripe at and complain to; she's also the person her bosses gripe at and complain to. She never fails to be understanding, cheerful, and helpful, and we'd give her a raise if we could. The best we can do, however, is dedicate this collection to her. Thanks, Sheila!

Pat and Bill Mooney, Elaine Hauptman, Leslie Thompson, Christine Myers, Mary Lowe, and the rest of our friends and fans.

Our contributors, without whom there would be no *Trek*. We just could not do it without you!

And, finally, our readers. Thank you for making the *Best of Trek* books one of the most successful and popular science fiction series of all time. Everything we do is with you in mind, and we hope to be bringing you these collections for many years to come.

To all of the above, again, many thanks!

CONTENTS

INTRODUCTION

Thank you for buying this seventh edition of articles and features from our magazine, *Trek*. We are sure that you will enjoy this collection just as much as you did the previous six.

As ever, the articles and features included in this volume reflect the continuing health and growth of Star Trek fandom, as well as the increasing interest shown by the general public in all areas of science, space exploration, and even science fiction. The continuing success of the space shuttle program (and the ever more evident benefits of that program) is beginning to convince the average person of the feasibility and value of space exploration. As a side effect of this, interest in Star Trek continues to increase as well. The third movie will be playing in theaters as you read this; the fourth is already in the planning stages.

Again, we feel we have a fine assortment of articles included in this volume; each, we believe, reflects an important and interesting aspect of Star Trek. For example, articles range from an examination of the music in *Wrath of Khan* to a look at how Star Trek is presented in West Germany to a scholarly but loving look at everyone's favorite furballs, the Tribbles. We think you'll find these—and all the other articles and features included in this collection—extremely readable, informative, and educational, and downright fun!

If you enjoy the articles in this collection and would like to see more, we invite you to turn to the full-page ad elsewhere in this book for more information about how you can order and subscribe to *Trek*. (And, please, if you have borrowed a copy of this volume from a library, copy the information in the ad, and leave the ad intact in the book for others to use. Thanks!)

And if you have been stirred to write an article or two yourself, please send it along to us. We would be most happy to see it, as we are always on the lookout for fresh and exciting new contributions. You may be encouraged to know that *all* of the contributors featured in this volume sent us material after buying and reading one of our earlier collections. If you feel your skills are not up to writing a *Trek* article but you have a good idea for one, please let us know about it. If we like it, we'll assign it to one of our regular contributors and give you credit when it's published. We are especially interested in seeing material from artists, as we are continuing to expand our efforts in the art area.

We *want* to hear from you in any event. Our lines of communication are always open. We welcome (and heed!) your suggestions, comments and ideas . . . you readers are our bosses. Although we cannot give you the addresses of Star Trek actors or forward mail to them, or help anyone get a professional Star Trek novel published, we *do* want your comments on *Trek* and Star Trek in general. It is only through your letters that we know if our efforts, and those of our contributors, have been successful.

If you'd like to send an article or piece of art, obtain information about back issues, or just write to us, our address is:

TREK
2405 Dewberry
Pasadena, TX 77502

Again, many thanks, and we hope you will enjoy *The Best of Trek #7*!

WALTER IRWIN

G.B. LOVE

JAMES HORNER—
WHO'S HE?

by Eleanor LaBerge

Those of you who remember Eleanor LaBerge's article in Best of Trek #5 *discussing the music of the series and* Star Trek: The Motion Picture *will be equally pleased by this follow-up examining the music of* Star Trek II: The Wrath of Khan. *As in the earlier article, you will find that Eleanor discovers facets in the music which take it far beyond the realm of "just background." We, along with Eleanor, would like to take this opportunity to thank composer James Horner for graciously consenting to be interviewed by Eleanor for this article.*

The day *Star Trek II: The Wrath of Khan* opened in a theater near us there was a drenching Pacific Northwest rain blown in by a vigorous westerly wind. It did not have a dampening effect on the enthusiastic crowd in line for tickets. Once inside the lobby, we were in the roped-off guaranteed-seats section, tolerably warm, but with another two hours to wait.

"Why are we doing this?" my ten-year-old muttered.

"Because your mother is out of her mind," my husband answered.

I ignored them because I was intent upon reading the print on a poster fifty feet away from us. Deciphering the credits under the faces of Kirk, Spock, and Khan was difficult, but I finally made out "Music by James Horner."

"James Horner!" I said aloud. "Who's he?"

Months later when I mentioned this incident to Mr. Horner he laughed and said, "Yes, that's a familiar reaction."

James Horner is not unknown in the industry. His music to *Battle Beyond the Stars* is far superior to the film. He is responsible for the theme of the television production *A Piano for Mrs. Cimino* and the motion pictures *Wolfen, Deadly Blessings,* and

The Hand. He acknowledges that he is in love with the challenge of composing for films and is determined to continue in this genre for some time to come.

Jerry Goldsmith, who composed the music for *Star Trek: The Motion Picture*, is twice Horner's age and has a hundred film scores to his credit. In *Wrath of Khan* a relative "beginner" demonstrates remarkable skill in composing the symphonic score which returned to popularity so dynamically with the success of *Star Wars*.

Audiences are accustomed to music that complements another art form for communication. We are familiar with music to the ballet and orchestrations describing literary pieces such as *Peer Gynt* or *Romeo and Juliet*. On the news we are likely to hear music as fitting as a Bach fugue while Mt. St. Helens is erupting or backgrounds as blatantly inappropriate as Tchaikovsky's *1812 Overture* while an All-American Glutton bites into a slice of pizza. The organ or piano accompaniment was so essential to the silent movie that for major films a book of specifically cued pieces was included to guide the local theater's musician. And we have, of course, experienced the constant dubbed-in music of the early talkies and films of the '40s and '50s.

The score of a modern motion picture may contain similar descriptive music, but it is complicated by the fact that for today's sophisticated moviegoer it must unify many other aspects of a production. While it may be something beautiful just by itself, the film soundtrack must be in complete harmony with the theme, the director's plan, the overall mood, and the dramatic interpretation of the actors. There is another crucial factor, and it is not easy to predict: the chemistry between the final soundtrack and the emotional reaction of the viewer.

James Horner set the seafaring mood director Nicholas Meyer intended for *Wrath of Khan*. As the introduction moved the audience among the stars, the viewer could become a part of the great spaceship's voyage through the universe. Segments of chording have an almost religious effect reminiscent of César Franck, and the sensitive listener to this prelude would immediately recognize melancholic overtones. Horner wished to set the stage "moodwise," as he termed it, in keeping with what was going to happen in the film. The dark side of *Wrath of Khan* was suggested—a contrast to the exhilarating, military opening of *Star Trek: The Motion Picture*. An audience receptive to what the composer was saying in tonal language could sense the undercurrent of pathos before any dramatic scene was presented. The listener also perceives something inherent in Horner's style.

He says he has difficulty in writing complete "up" music and is always aware that joy has another side.

Horner felt disturbed by what he called the "massive" feeling of *STTMP*. He felt that Star Trek lost an important personal quality on the wide screen. It was the intent of *Wrath of Khan's* producer and director to restore the feeling of intimacy; to bring back the viewer's feeling that he really knew the *Enterprise* and its crew. Horner's idea of beginning with the Alexander Courage fanfare that meant Star Trek for fifteen years helped to bring back the best memories of the series. He was also aware that Harve Bennett and Nicholas Meyer wanted to "take no chances." A conservative score was in keeping with their opinion that *Star Trek: The Motion Picture* may have lost audiences for future productions. Everyone associated with the new production was dedicated to restoring the potential of the series, and music was to be no exception.

Whether or not Horner's soundtrack satisfied the critical emotional response for the audience is a more difficult question. Many viewers were initially disappointed in the score. There were comparisons to the stirring music of *STTMP*. We know that Jerry Goldsmith's Star Trek composition gained a nomination for an Academy Award while Horner's did not. Horner's contribution was ignored in the 1983 Oscar award night, and it was Goldsmith's *Enterprise* theme that the orchestra played as William Shatner was introduced.

Not only was Goldsmith well known in the industry, in *STTMP* he had a vehicle for long segments of descriptive music that were absolutely solo. His score had no interference from sound effects, action, or dialogue. These compositions, excellent as they were, did not possess the complexity of Horner's interwoven themes and use of musical symbolism throughout *Wrath of Khan*. Unfortunately for the quality of *Wrath of Khan's* soundtrack, Horner's best and most exciting work is lost under the barrage of sound effects necessary for the action, and under the dialogue equally necessary for characterization and plot. Only two times aside from the introduction and credits is the music of this new Star Trek film emphasized: at the brief departure scene of the *Enterprise* on training mission, and in the Genesis theme. We are well into the film before we hear a musical sequence other than the opening one.

Horner's ability to convey the essence of character is clear in the first composition after the opening. The setting is the interior of the *Botany Bay* cargo carrier. This first Khan segment is not one most listeners would chose to hear for pleasure any more than they would have replayed the cloud entity music from *STTMP* for pure enjoyment. In *Wrath of Khan*, the *Botany Bay* sequence (entitled "Khan's Pets" on the recording) is not meant to stand by itself. It is background. Like the voice in an opera, Khan's dialogue is another instrument and the ear is appropriately tuned to his solo voice rather than to the accompaniment. The music is effectively understated. We hear steady rhythm like a heartbeat in the string bass. Without the words and actions one might visualize a predator circling its kill, powerful muscles taut and controlled, movements precise as it measures its prey. Khan says of the past, ". . . on Earth two hundred years ago I was a prince!" The muted trumpets (a technique not original to Horner) introduce the discord in his mind. At this point Khan's fury and frustration are concealed beneath deliberately cautious words and movements. We learn that he is sinister through the music as much as from his behavior.

We move from the horror of Khan's control over Chekov and Terrell to the shuttlecraft en route to the *Enterprise*. There is an ethereal quality in the music as the craft docks. The melodic line interweaves with the Alexander Courage theme and ends almost as soon as it begins. After the welcoming ceremony and Saavik's brief conversation with Captain Spock, we are on the bridge and the ship is ready to depart.

Now the composer must deal with the well-known and expected relationship between Kirk and the *Enterprise*. While James Horner says he did not do any special research into the music of the original series, or for that matter even want to be influenced by it, he had seen some of the reruns and was aware of important factors. He was not apprehensive about suddenly being part of the Star Trek myth nor hesitant about writing for a legend. One of the things he wanted to do for the second motion picture was create a theme which represented the fondness Kirk had for his ship—a "love affair," as Horner termed it. Goldsmith had already given fans an *Enterprise* theme of great beauty. Perhaps this made Horner's task more difficult and also subtly discouraged the fans' emotional involvement with his new Star Trek score.

There is another problem with the two *Enterprise* themes. The more youthful James Kirk of *Star Trek: The Motion Picture* had a different relationship with the ship. In *STTMP* he was returning to possess the *Enterprise* with all the joy of a lover long separated from his loved one. "They gave her back to me, Scotty." There is a contrasting mood in *Wrath of Khan*. Kirk keeps himself a stranger to the *Enterprise*, hiding behind his "appointed tasks," and as McCoy bluntly says is "flying a damned computer" although he wants to be "hopping galaxies." The separation that promotion has effected is a long-established fact. If audiences feel that the love theme Horner gave them is less personal and romantic, it may be because the perception of Kirk and the ship are changed. Horner's *Enterprise* theme speaks of love and longing, but instead of the expression of pure joy we saw in the travel pod in *STTMP*, we now see Kirk look at the *Enterprise* with reluctance, even sadness. "I hate inspections," he says.

Another one of Horner's goals was to write a score that possessed a great deal of energy. We hear the result of this purpose as the *Enterprise* leaves its moorings. The music contains the power of the great starship's propulsion; the feeling of the trainees' youthful enthusiasm; and the thrill of going "out there" that Kirk is struggling to subordinate.

Woven in and out of the *Enterprise* melody are strains that represent the Vulcan. We can appreciate the beautiful Spock composition only in the recorded version of Horner's soundtrack, as it was covered by dialogue both times it was used in the film. Even if we know it is there and listen carefully, we can barely discern the haunting notes, which are dubbed first after Kirk interrupts Spock at meditation, and then again during the death scene. In both instances it is almost impossible to hear. While we might have a subliminal feeling about the background melody, there is no way the beauty of this minute-and-ten-second tone poem could be appreciated in the film. Anyone who forms an opinion of Horner's *Wrath of Khan* on the sole basis of having seen the motion picture cannot give him a fair judgment. This may be the result of the director's style as well as the dubbing. Fans welcomed the fast pace of *Wrath of Khan*, but in this particular case a pause in the action might have added a dimension to characterization. It could have been an opportunity to explore the Vulcan mind in the deep repose of meditation, a closer look at the fans' beloved alien. During such reflection a portion of Horner's theme could have been dubbed giving his composition the feature spot it deserved. It may have been an interesting interpretation of a practice deeply personal to the character of Spock in Star Trek lore.

As we listen to the Spock theme in the recording we hear a high acoustical sound—Horner does not use electronic devices. The high-register melody is joined first by a flute and is followed by a harp in an arpeggio repeated five times. The main melodic line in apposition continues throughout. If there is a song of the stars from deep space as the Kolihari Desert's little Bushman tells us there is, this might well be it.

Horner wanted to describe Spock in a way that was both conventional and unconventional. Not only did he feel that this character had not been given a theme in *STTMP*, he wanted to make Spock "a little more human." He does this in the Spock segment in a way that is consistent with everything we know about the Vulcan/human. The presence of the warm earth tones of harp and flute complement the alien melodic line, resulting in a dual feeling. It is as if the Vulcan and human were present simultaneously in Spock—not in opposition even though the instruments are in counterpoint. There is a unity here; a peaceful quality. It is consistent with the older and wiser Vulcan whom we see from the first moments of *Wrath of Khan*.

The composer set out to give Spock what he called a tremendous warmth. Aware of the character's importance throughout Star Trek and especially in *Wrath of Khan*, Horner wanted to be able to weave the Vulcan theme in and out of subsequent action music. Its strange melody will lead into the more passionate music of Genesis later on.

Horner's skill in combining many separate musical elements in a tonal conflict is vividly demonstrated in the first battle sequence, "Surprise Attack." As the *Enterprise* crew sees *Reliant*, we hear the striking theme of Khan's pursuit. It is far more intense than the hunter clarion call of the Klingons in *STTMP*. It is suitable accompaniment to Khan's arrogance and fanatical desire for revenge. The wildness of strings and the challenging klacker sounds contrast rudely with the *Enterprise* themes seeking dominance. In the film we cannot hear any of the five-minute segment beyond the introduction when *Reliant* is sighted. After the attack, as Uhura announces that the commander of *Reliant* is demanding surrender, we hear the last of the composition. There is obviously, enough excitement in the battle action and in the shock of seeing the *Enterprise* rendered virtually helpless to sustain the scene with no scoring at all. There was probably little need for the music at that point, overshadowed as it was. Once again for those who formed an impression of James Horner's score on the basis of the film alone, the composer is the loser.

There is appropriate silence as the bridge is cleared and we hear the beginning of "Kirk's Explosive Reply." Here the subdued score can be heard, and it contributes to the buildup of suspense. The percussion ticks away Kirk's brief truce with Khan, its syncopated beat a perfect expression of a race against time. French horns, winds, and strings alternate in the *Enterprise* theme leading to the confrontation and victory, which again repeats the Khan instrumentation. It ends in silence as Scotty's shocking appearance shows the audience how costly the battle was. Listening to the 'Surprise Attack'' followed by ''Kirk's Explosive Reply'' on the recorded version is the only way to bring this music alive and appreciate the complexity of Horner's descriptive interpretation.

The next significant musical background complements Kirk's reaction to the Genesis Cave. It is a brief but lyrical preview of a theme that we will hear developed from this point on. If this had been *Star Trek: The Motion Picture* we might have lingered longer and seen more, but *Wrath of Khan* moves swiftly back to the *Enterprise* with no time allowed for meditation. The final conflict begins.

The returning party runs down the ship's corridors with Kirk and Spock once again showing us their famous comradery. Simultaneously we hear a variation of the Genesis theme with the French horn and piccolo octaves apart but in perfect unity of melodic line. One might reflect that here was an interesting symbol of the unity between the human and the Vulcan who ''is and always shall be'' Kirk's friend. All the differences in their personalities seem to complement each other just as these two instruments form a musical partnership on contrasting levels. However meaningful the interpretation may have seemed, Mr. Horner commented that that was more literal than he would usually be! But he did speak of the segment's extreme complexity from this point to the end of the death scene. The composer now has the themes of Khan, Spock Genesis, and *Enterprise* to interweave. It is an accomplishment that lasts for fourteen and a half minutes.

Those responsible for the dubbing sent no thrills down our spines as the *Enterprise* destroyed *Reliant* in the Mutara sequence. What could have been a triumphant crescendo faded into the background with all the energy of a three-toed sloth. The symbolism here was understandable. After all, the battle was not yet won, but the crew and the audience did not know this and were at a peak of elation. Most fans were relieved that the rumors of Spock's demise in battle were apparently not true. The contrast between that ''high'' and the irony of the actual situation would have been more effective if we had been given those chills and thrills. At this particular point Mr. Horner's score could have accomplished this, but instead of reaching a crescendo it limped off into space, triple pianissimo, as crippled as *Reliant*.

We are given no time in the film to analyze this lack of·

musical climax. Spock detects the "odd pattern" which we already know is the Genesis Device on a buildup to irreversible detonation. *Now* the suspense begins again with battle music rising in intensity while Spock tries to put the warp drive back on line. We hear the last efforts of Khan, music appropriate to the Ahab-like quest to destroy that which he perceives as evil before the *Enterprise* regains escape velocity and streaks across the quadrant. The accompaniment to the Genesis Wave's incredible power begins. Special effects alone could not have given audiences such a feeling of awe. The double meaning of Spock's sacrificial act makes this music of death and transfiguration extraordinarily moving in its richness of meaning.

Star Trek fans should appreciate Horner's careful, analytical construction of the score at this point. Horner recalled the scene in which Kirk turned around and saw Spock's chair empty. He was particularly moved by Shatner's performance and wanted to add to Kirk's moment of realization. He intended the musical effect to be something very passionate. To accomplish this he used the Genesis theme visually intercut with Kirk's running down the hall. Spock's theme played in a very high register while the violins were rising—soaring out of range in the same way Spock was to be out of Kirk's reach. Horner set out to create emotion, the scene of the two friends' depth of caring, and he succeeded. He realized that this farewell was almost equal in the fans' perception to the final end of the *Enterprise* itself. His attention to their moments' symbolic significance inspired him to write Spock's theme at the end of the rising cadence *so that there was no chord of resolution*. According to Horner, Nicholas Meyer did not quite support what the composer was trying to do and wanted the chord to resolve. Later when the whole scene and music was dubbed in, both were in agreement.

The empty feeling that the audience had in the beginning of the death scene was profound, and did not need a musical technique. Still, the feeling of incompleteness exists on many levels. There is also an intuition we are given through the music: There is no ending here. Spock will remain not only in memory but in his friend's acceptance of the sacrifice that enables him to be young again. In actual fact, there was no definite ending, no certain outcome, at the time Horner had to complete this sequence. He felt that whatever music he wrote—whether it was to be the music of final and irrevocable death for Spock or, as Horner phrases it, the Obi Wan Kenobi resurrection syndrome, the score had to meet the requirements of both possibilities.

Horner was not responsible for the "Amazing Grace" adaptation idea for the funeral sequence. In fact, he was emphatically opposed to it but acquiesced partly because Harve Bennett wanted the melody and also because there were shots of Scotty playing the bagpipes photographed with other characters. For that reason it seemed everyone was "stuck" with the pipes. The composer reflects that there was something warmly human about the idea, but the end result with the orchestrated version was something of a *non sequitur*. Inappropriate to the preceding score as the sequence was, Horner redeemed it by incorporating Spock's theme at the end as the scene fades into Kirk's quarters. We have a fitting comment musically that Kirk's thoughts were of Spock.

After the reconciliation between Kirk and his son, we are back on the *Enterprise* bridge—the traditional place for the last scene of a Star Trek adventure. This time there is something more. We begin a journey visually and musically to the new world. There is life here—lush vegetation, a gentle wind, and the carrier that brought Spock's body to the surface. It has not been burned by its entry into the planet's atmosphere. The score is one of hope and life, the beautiful melodic line equally lovely in orchestration.

In the music accompanying the credits we revamp the *Enterprise* and Genesis themes. Battle and conflict are left behind and we hear only that which remained afterward. Those who felt disappointed in *Wrath of Khan's* music may have filed out of the theater before this concluding composition. It has excitement and all the impact of the energy Horner gave to this Star Trek project.

The symphonic score is an epic-proportioned tool augmenting a film. Like Nicholas Meyer, a director may want to emphasize character rather than grandeur, but by the very nature of its vast setting, space fiction demands accompaniment equal to the power of imagination which makes a leap of faith: That which is now fiction will one day be truth. The concept of Star Trek is on a grand scale even if it needed to be brought back to greater viewer intimacy. James Horner says he has been asked to write the score for *Star Trek III*. As of the date of our interview (March 1983), there was no definite agreement and no working script. Fans who have given the score of *Wrath of Khan* a fair hearing apart from the inadequacies of dubbing should have no problems with a follow-up Horner score. But the challenge to the composer is clear. In whatever motion pictures he does in the next few years, his scores must reflect growth and maturity. He has excellent role models in Jerry Goldsmith and John Williams, both of whom are remarkable for each new film's freshness of approach. Versatility with a minimum of repetition must be striven for in this field. *MacArthur* and *STTMP* are both "militaristic" scores, but they are as different from each other as the Goldsmith *Waltons* theme is different from them. John Williams's *Star Wars*, *Close Encounters*, *Superman*, *Poltergeist*, and *E.T.* are also prime examples of the importance of innovative approaches from the same composer.

A listener might note that James Horner's intervals of melodic line as well as techniques of instrumentation have more similarities than differences. This is particularly obvious in a comparison of *Battle Beyond the Stars* and *Wrath of Khan*. Yet the sensitivity and beauty of Horner's Star Trek composition interests this "critic" to the point of eagerly awaiting his interpretation of *Star Trek III*.

"Life from lifelessness" is a theme well worth a composer's best efforts. James Horner possesses the talent essential to the task, and could use the phenomenon of Star Trek as one means to further his career. Like the characters in the framework of Gene Roddenberry's Star Trek concept, he must continue to probe inner space. In harmony with the best of Star Trek, he may be inspired by its affirmation of infinite possibilities in the infinite diversity of creativity.

For myself and many fans, I welcome this opportunity to express gratitude to James Horner for what he has already contributed to Star Trek, and to wish him well in future challenges to his career. I sincerely hope that he will prove himself not only in technical competence but in versatility and originality.

STAR TREK JOKES—

by Valerie Parv

The Star Trek fan's humor is well developed and well known, at least in fannish circles. Fandom is a fertile breeding ground for parodies, puns and double entendres, cartoons, and, yes, jokes. Strange to say, we'd never run a bunch of jokes until we received a raft of them from Australian Valerie Parv. So absolutely loony were they that we had to have more. We assigned local fan Jeff Thorpe to gather up some of the sillier and more hilarious ones making the rounds in this area. Here are both batches—enjoy!

Spock, Spock.
Who's there?
Nova.
Nova who?
Nova good bar in this spaceport?

The Kzinti had captured a Medusan, but since Medusans are energy beings, they had trouble deciding how to eat him. The Kzinti captain had the last word. He said they should use lots of sugar, because, "everyone knows a spoonful of sugar helps the Medusan go down."

What do you call it when two science officers are having an argument?
Science friction.

A young man was applying to join Starfleet.
"Where were you born?" asked the recruiting officer.
"Earth, sir."
"What part?"
"All of me, sir."

21

Arex and Christine Chapel were visiting a zoo on Earth. At the lion's cage, the beast opened its mouth and gave a mighty roar. Startled, Arex said he was getting out of there.

"I'll meet you back on board later," said Christine. "I want to see the rest of the movie."

What does a Romulan frog use for camouflage?
A croaking device.

There was a young doc named McCoy
Who cloned himself, more to enjoy
The girls aboard ship
But he made a bad slip
They all wanted the *real* McCoy

Show me Uhura reciting verse at warpspeed . . . and I'll show you poetry in motion.

Sulu: "I've just discovered that Ilia's sister is a redhead."
Chekov: "But I thought Deltans don't have any hair."
Sulu: "She doesn't. She just has a red head."

Dr. M'Benga was experimenting with cloning alien species. His first experiment was a disaster; the result was ugly and obscene. He decided to get rid of it by jettisoning it out of a hatch. Unfortunately, Captain Kirk saw him do it, and now M'Benga is facing a charge of making an obscene clone fall.

After a particularly grueling mission, Captain Kirk complained that he was seeing spots before his eyes.
"Have you seen Dr. McCoy?" asked Spock.
"No," replied Kirk. "Only spots."

If Mr. Spock has pointed ears, what does Mr. Scott have?
Engineers.

Show me a man who is a good loser . . . and I'll show you a junior officer who is playing 3-D chess with his captain.

It seems the Klingons had a diabolical plan to wrap all the Federation starships in silver paper.
Luckily, the plan was foiled.

Spock, Spock.
Who's there?
Epsilon.
Epsilon who?
Epsilon way to Tipperary . . .

Did you hear about the Federation weapons expert?
He never forgets a phaser.

Mr. Spock: "Give me an example of orbital decay."
Chekov: "Er . . . an astronaut with bad teeth?"

Harry Mudd was arrested and charged with fraud for selling
maps to the Fountain of Youth. When computer records were
checked, it was discovered he had been arrested for the same
offense in 1716, 1986, 2005, and Stardate 25.8.

Uhura: "Everyone on this ship thinks I'm crazy because I like
pastrami on rye."
McCoy: "That doesn't mean you're crazy. I like pastrami on
rye, too."
Uhura: "Great! You must come and see my collection!"

Where does a ten-foot Mugato sleep?
Anywhere he wants to.

What do you call a ten-foot Mugato?
Sir.

When the Melkotians beamed Kirk, Spock, Chekov, and McCoy
down to the recreation of the OK Corral, none of the officers
knew how to use the old-style six-guns. You see, they came
from a time when no man had guns before.

Spock, Spock.
Who's there?
Horta.
Horta who?
Horta do something about these jokes.

Mr. Spock: "What is the formula for *pi*?"
Chekov: "Er . . . apple or blueberry, sir?"

Then there was the time Janice Rand complained that someone had cut a peephole into her cabin door.

Captain Kirk promised to look into it.

When the *Enterprise* crew beamed down to the Guardian of Forever, Dr. McCoy refused to go through.

"You're all the same," he grumbled. "In one era and out the other."

What is the Kzinti's favorite food?
Baked beings on toast.

Why was Star Trek so successful?
It had good Genes.

A visiting admiral approached Chekov's station on the *Enterprise*. Thinking he would test the young officer, he asked, "What would you do if the weapons officer suddenly got his head blown off?"

"Nothing, sir."

"Why nothing?"

"Because I'm the weapons officer, sir."

Uhura was working at her console when she suddenly straightened up. "I think there's a sick crewmember on Deck 9," she said. As no message had been received, Kirk was baffled, but sent McCoy to check it out. Sure enough, the doctor reported that a crewmember had, indeed, collapsed where Uhura had predicted.

Impressed, Kirk turned to her. "You must be psychic, Uhura. How did you know that crewman was ill?"

Uhura smiled. "I had my ailing frequencies open, sir."

Spock, Spock.
Who's there?
Sackett.
Sackett who?
Sackett to me, Sackett to me . . .

What is Sargon's favorite song?
"Everybody Needs Some Body Sometime."

Notice aboard the *ENTERPRISE*!
Rule 1. The captain is always right.
Rule 2. If the captain is wrong, refer to rule 1.

Sarek and Amanda were dating
Amanda was patiently waiting
For signs of romance
Soft words, a slow dance
What she got was an efficiency rating

Sulu discovered Kevin Riley standing below a gigantic golden statue of a young woman. Riley reported that the eyes were made of diamonds. "How do you know?" asked Sulu.

"I climbed some stairs inside," said Kevin, "For the girl is hollow and I have touched her eyes."

Spock, Spock.
Who's there?
Plasma.
Plasma who?
Plasma the salt, please.

What would you have if all the Star Trek fans in Switzerland got together?
The Geneva Convention.

McCoy: "I've borrowed Mr. Scott's bagpipes."
Kirk: "But you can't play them."
McCoy: "While I've got them, neither can he!"

Noticing medals on Balok's chest, Kirk asked, "Did you win those in combat?"
"Oh, no," said Balok. "I don't believe in military service."
"Did you shrink from battle?" asked Kirk.
"No," shrugged Balok. "I've always been this size."

What did Dr. McCoy say when he saw his first Communist?
"He's red, Jim."

Why couldn't Kirk close his operations manual?
There was a Wolf in the Fold.

What do McCoy and McDonald's have in common?
Feinbergers.

Mr. Spock: "A syzygy is three heavenly bodies lined up in a row.
Give me an example."
Sulu: "Mudd's Women!"

Lieutenant Kyle: "Dr. McCoy, I sleep all day, stay awake all night. I'm hot all the time and can't stop dancing. And I see rings before my eyes! What's wrong with me?"

McCoy: "Sounds like Saturn Day Night Fever."

What did McCoy say to Kirk in "The Empath"?

"This is another Vian mess you've gotten us into."

When writing up Miramanee's people for the medical journals, Dr. McCoy discovered that the animal skins the wives slept on seemed to affect the number of children they gave birth to. For example, Medicine Chief Salish had three wives: the oldest, who slept on a bearskin, another, who slept on a leopard skin, and the youngest, who slept on a hippopotamus skin. The two older women each gave birth to baby boys. When the youngest wife became pregnant, Salish predicted she would have two sons. When twin boys were born, McCoy was astonished.

"How did you know?" he asked Salish.

"Simple," answered the Medicine Chief. "The sons of the squaw on the hippopotamus are equal to the sons of the squaws on the other two hides."

MORE STAR TREK JOKES

by Jeff Thorpe

Overheard in a corridor:
Crewman: "I've got a brother at Starfleet Science Academy."
Crewwoman: "What's he studying?"
Crewman: "Nothin'. They're studying him."

Do you know what they call a Klingon with half a brain?
Gifted!

Do you know what they call a Klingon with no brain at all?
Normal.

Dr. McCoy was impressed by the professional manner of new *Enterprise* psychiatrist Dr. Zhrink. After a long shift, an amazed McCoy asked him, "How can you stay so fresh and cool after eight hours of listening to such terrible problems?"
Dr. Zhrink shrugged. "Who listens?"

McCoy was giving one of his periodic lectures to Captain Kirk. "Jim, I recommend you give up drinking, cut out poker, stop staying up late, and, especially, quit running around with women.
That would be best for you."
"Frankly, Bones," grinned Kirk, "I don't deserve the best. What's second best?"

Mr. Spock was helping Engineer Scott fix the transporter. "Grab that blue wire," said Scotty. Spock did so. "Feel anything?" Scotty asked.
Spock shook his head no.
"Well then," said Scotty, "Don't touch the other one or you'll drop dead."

What is the longest four years of a Klingon's life?
Third grade.

The new ensign reported to sickbay for her physical. When she stripped, Dr. McCoy nodded approvingly. "You look nice and trim."

"Thanks," she answered. "I weigh one hundred pounds stripped for gym."

McCoy shook his head. "That guy has all the luck!"

Captain Kirk: "Since all of you crewmembers performed so inefficiently today, there'll be no liberty at Starbase Seven."

Voice: "Give me liberty or give me death!"

Kirk: "Who said that?"

Voice: "Patrick Henry."

McCoy: "Should we have a friendly game of cards?"

Kirk: "No, let's play poker."

How do you get a one-armed Klingon out of a tree?
Wave to him.

"Dr. McCoy," said Sulu, "Every night I have the same dream—four beautiful women break into my cabin and try to seduce me."

"So what do you do?" asked McCoy.

"I push them away."

"Well, what do you want me to do?"

"Please, Doc," pleaded Sulu, "break both my arms!"

Harry Mudd was on trial for one of his many crimes.

"Do you mean to tell me," said the judge indignantly, "that you murdered an old lady for only three credits?"

Harry shrugged. "You know how it is, your honor. Three credits here, three credits there . . . it all adds up."

Why can't Klingon kids play in sandboxes?
Cats keep trying to cover them up.

During his first expedition to Denebia 7, Dr. McCoy came staggering into camp one evening. His uniform was in tatters, he was covered with bruises and scratches, and he was still shaking with fright and excitement.

A fellow officer leaped up and cried, "Leonard! What happened to you?"

McCoy slumped into a chair and gasped, "A Denebian slime devil chased me!"

"Slime devils look scary," said his friend, "But they can't hurt you."

"They can," groaned McCoy as he reached for a drink, "if they make you jump off a fifty-foot cliff!"

How did T'Pring's parents react when they learned she was not marrying Spock?
They were Stonned.

Harry Mudd was on trial again.

"Harry," said the judge, "You're accused of throwing your wife, Stella, out of the window. This is a most serious crime."

"But your honor," cried Harry, "be lenient. You've met my wife."

"Yes," answered the judge with a shudder, "and I don't blame you for what you did. But don't you understand she could have *landed* on somebody?"

What are eyeglasses called on Vulcan?
Spocktacles.

Mary Sue: "I just got engaged to Kevin!"
Mary Jane: "Oh, really?"
Mary Sue: "No, Riley."

What kind of noise is made by Vulcan popguns?
T'Pau.

Why did the Klingon cross the road?
To conquer the other side.

Kirk: "I had a date with a two-headed Venusian girl last night."
McCoy: "Have any luck?"
Kirk: "Well . . . yes and no."

Scotty and Sulu had been at the K-7 saloon for three hours when suddenly in walked a strange alien being. He was eight feet tall, weighed less than a hundred pounds, and had orange skin, purple hair, and six yellow eyes. To top it all off, he was wearing a red-and-blue-striped suit. Scotty stared at him for a long while and finally rose and staggered over to the being.

"Pardon me for askin', friend, bu' wha' do ye look like when Ah'm sober?"

The next day, the bartender was just opening up the place when a pink elephant and a rhinoceros came strolling in. The bartender shook his head. "Sorry, boys, Scotty hasn't come in yet."

What's black and white and red all over?
A Cheron with a sunburn.

New crewwoman: "Where do I eat?"
Uhura: "You mess with the officers."
New crewwoman: "I figured that, but where do I eat?"

McCoy: "Do you serve crabs here?"
Mess officer: "We serve anybody. Sit down."

A young crewman, wanting leave, went to Captain Kirk's quarters and told a sad story about his sick wife, who was longing to see him.

Kirk shook his head angrily. "I just talked to your wife via subspace radio, Johnson, and not only is she not sick, she said whenever you get leave all you do is get drunk, mistreat her, and run around with other women. Request denied."

The forlorn crewman saluted and turned to go. At the door he paused and turned back to Kirk. "Captain," he said with a rueful grin, "I thought I was pretty good, but you're a better bluffer than I am. I ain't even got no wife!"

Uhura was having a rough time getting friendly with the shy young ensign. Finally, she asked, "Would you like to see where I was operated on for appendicitis?"
"Gosh, no!" he said, "I hate hospitals!"

Kirk was chatting with a newly commissioned ensign when a crewman approached and asked to speak to him.
"Go ahead, son," Kirk said.
"It's kind of confidential, captain. I'd rather not say it in front of the ensign."
"Well," said Kirk, "spell it then."

Dr. McCoy finished his examination of Scotty and shook his head. "Scotty, I can't find any reason for your stomach pains. Frankly, I think it's due to drinking."

"In that case, Leonard," said Scotty, "I'll come back when you're sober."

During his first visit to Neural, Kirk's new friend Tyree told him he'd have to pass a manhood ritual. "First you have to drink a gallon of wicki-wacki juice, then make love to a Kanatu witch woman, then wrestle a Mugato. Then we will consider you a man of our tribe."

Kirk gulped, then downed the entire gallon of wicki-wacki juice. A little woozily, he headed out into the night.

Several hours later, he came back. His uniform was torn to shreds, he was cut and bruised in a dozen places, and he was almost exhausted. "Okay," he gasped, "now where's this witch woman I'm supposed to wrestle?"

ANSWER YOUR BEEPER, YOU DREAMER!

by Jacqueline Gilkey

We receive many articles which try to express the inner turmoil that being a Star Trek fan can sometimes cause. Friends, family, and co-workers don't always understand or appreciate our hobby or our devotion to it, so it is understandable if once in a while we tend to start talking to ourselves . . . or, once in a great while, to Kirk, Spock, and various others of the Enterprise *crew. The following—ah—discourse is among the best we've ever seen in describing that mental mixture of frustration, rhapsody, and plain old wishful thinking that makes up a Star Trek fan.*

Why are you smiling? Look, just because your beeper goes off, it doesn't mean the *Enterprise* is trying to contact you. Come on, now! You're in the real world, remember? A respiratory therapist!

Why is it that every time I walk down the hallway at work, I think I'm walking the corridors of the Starship *Enterprise*? Huh? Every time I write in a patient's chart, my mind is off pretending that I am a young medical officer in Dr. McCoy's Sickbay. What's happening to me?

Since we're on the subject of work, should you dare to torment your coworkers with one more, "Ahead, warp factor three!" as you go off to do your breathing treatments, well, you're sure to drive them to the point of avoiding you. So, dreamer, go into the workroom where it says "Mr. Spock is on the ventilator" (suffering from radiation poisoning, no less!) and erase it. And, dammit, take off that stupid "Beam me up" button you constantly wear. How many people have asked you what it means? Then you're disappointed because they don't share your enthusiasm. It really surprises you when a few of them tell you that they've never even *heard* of Star Trek!

But no. That's hardly the case with you. You spend so much time thinking about Star Trek that your personality continually reflects serious obsessive components. You're even beginning to show signs of delusions of grandeur. Ha! Imagine believing that you are talented enough to write the script for *Star Trek IV*! I see trouble brewing down the road for you.

Actually, if you'd take the time to notice, people at work are beginning to get sick and tired of your constant attack upon the typewriter. Give them a break, won't you? Haven't you noticed that even your own typewriter at home has had enough of this silliness? Your fingers are rebelling against you. Look at them! They're hardly able to stand yet another pounding from that overworked manual typewriter. The poor pathetic thing should break down for good.

I guess that once I get home from work today I could force myself to go outside for a walk. Perhaps I might call up my scuba-diving friends or . . . I might even get back on my motorcycle and go for a ride. But gee . . . what's the use? Sitting on Max, the wind whistling through my helmet, just does not satisfy me anymore. It feels so, well . . . unstable. Hmm . . . maybe it's me who's the unstable one. I just can't get my mind off of Star Trek!

Look girl, tonight when you go home, I demand you immediately take down that poster of Spock. And really, that *Enterprise* poster? It's just that, only a poster! How can you stare at that thing and honestly believe it could ever get off the ground?

Grow up! Get rid of those *Enterprise* crew pictures which intervene between you and the living-room wall. Reminds me of something you'd see in the post office. The infamous Starship Seven strike again. Especially the one with the nickname. What is it? . . . "Bones"! The reason for your blind devotion to him escapes me. After all, you have a more accessible male friend. Have you forgotten him? Aren't you a wee bit cognizant of his existence? If so, I suggest you diversify your energies in pursuit of a relationship more tangible than those conjured up by the sight of a picture or those described by a book!

You know, you're beginning to sound a little like Mr. Spock. Which reminds me. I need to steer clear of bookstores for a while. Why, however in the world could I have asked that overwrought salesgirl about ordering some Star Trek books? That look on her face! She was angry with me! All she had to do was spend twenty minutes of her time searching through the microfilms. I remember how happy she looked while telling me that all the books I had requested were out of print. Except one. "*I Am Not Spock*," she said. She sure as hell wasn't!

I can see that any further discussion attempting to dissuade you from continuing with this Star Trek thing would be worthless, but hear me out! As you attend the next Star Trek convention, remember exactly how ludicrous you must appear to the nonbelievers as you stroll through the convention center in your black pants, boots, and blue shirt. Let me be the one to remind you that those few days alone are the only time when public display of such a shirt, with its gold braid on the sleeves and the insignia whose meaning is known only to a privileged few, is looked upon with equivocal interest. Then, after it's all over, take note of how your stomach growls because you've gone and spent all of your hard-earned money to buy Star Trek memorabilia, and now there's nothing left with which to buy groceries to stock an empty refrigerator!

Still, knowing you as I do, I imagine you'll just pass it all off as the price paid for being given the opportunity to participate in such an exhilarating event. That would be just like you. You've been so . . . irresponsible lately!

Now answer your beeper, you dreamer!

"Answer your beeper, you dreamer," says Ben, gently nudging my arm.

Detached, I rise. A familiar hand moves to the phone. The fingers punch out the numbers 2-1-3-5. There is a ringing in my ears, and then a voice that says:

"Hello, intensive care. May I help you?"

"Hi," a distant voice answers back. "This is sickbay . . . er, respiratory therapy!"

Ben's mouth drops open. His is beginning to fear for my sanity. My unseeing eyes fall upon him.

"Ben to space cadet," he says.

Oh, Ben, I think. If only those puppy-dog eyes of yours were blue mirror images of this planet of ours, why, I could be staring at Dr. McCoy.

"What's up, Jax?"

"Ventilator changes in ICU."

Ben points to the blackboard. "On Mr. Spock, I presume?"

"Very funny, Ben!" He knows better than to mess with me when I am attempting to unite the real world.

"Come on," I say, dragging him out of the workroom toward intensive care.

Halfway down the hallway, a resident passes us muttering, "Beam me up?"

Ben whips out his beeper-communicator and attempts to flip up the invisible grid. With synchronous precision, the little black box beeps back at him.

"Ben to *Enterprise*," he says. "Two to beam up, Mr. Scott."

Stopping dead in his tracks, the resident veers around to evaluate our behavior. He fears for our sanity. Ben and I manage to conjure up our most pathetic expressions in an attempt to excuse our eccentricity. Disgruntled and impatient, the resident turns from us and walks quickly away. Ben and I enjoy a fit of hysterics.

"Boy," says Ben, "I hope that wasn't a psych resident!"

"Who cares?" I respond, laughing. Then off we go toward the intensive care unit, the look of disbelief on the resident's face pleasantly stored away in our memory banks.

"You'll get me hooked yet!" Ben tempts.

To Ben and me, intensive care appears to be a cavern of imminent disaster. Beeping, humming, and unsettled tension fill the air. A nurse barks at a half-dazed patient lying in one of the beds.

"Take a deep breath!" (Mr. Spock?)

The patient writhes in pain.

Ben and I walk to the purring ventilator and make the appropriate changes.

"Gases in an hour!" the nurse shouts after us.

Over at bed three, the situation looks grim. We peer at the medical scanner.

"Heart rate, two hundred ten. Blood pressure, eighty over thirty-two. Respiratory rate, forty-five." reports Ben. A dwindling cardiac output causes the patient to gurgle like a baby.

"Gee, if this keeps up much longer, we'll have a code on our hands," I reply. "Someone had better call Dr. McCoy!"

As the tension level within the intensive care unit continues to rise, Ben and I decide it's time to retreat back to the safety of our own department--before all hell breaks loose!

Later that evening, after the code, we sit in the lounge. For weeks now, Ben has been witness to my zealous attempts at story writing. He stares at me in amazement as I scribble on a piece of paper. Curiosity overcomes him and he asks, "What in the world are you writing?"

Biting on the tip of my pen, I look up.

"Ben," I begin, "what would you say if someone said to you, 'Is that the reason?' "

"The reason for what?"

He's confused. I know what I mean—why doesn't he? I explain it to him.

I trace back through the thoughts and feelings of the characters in my story. Ben becomes intensely absorbed; he makes a gesture showing he comprehends their motivations.

"So, Ben," I ask again, "what would be your reply if someone said to you, 'Is that the reason?' "

Ben paces the floor reflectively. Instead of the profound response I expected, all I get is, "Well, what do you think?"

Honestly, Ben, what kind of an answer is that?

The next shift arrives for duty and report begins. Anyone unfamiliar with the bizarre vernacular might think the ongoing conversation of extraterrestrial origin. IPPB, PEEP, ABG, and IMV dot the conversation. Someone points to the blackboard and asks, "What about Spock?"

Questioning fascination fills the faces of the next shift.

"Vital signs stable," I begin seriously. "Heart rate, two hundred forty-two. Blood pressure, eighty over forty. Respiratory rate, sixty-one. Give him a few cc's of Benjisidrine, and he should be extubated by this time tomorrow."

"That's stable?" someone observes sagely.

Ben winks at me. "It is if you're a Vulcan!"

I leap into the front seat of my car. Engaging aft thrusters one quarter impulse power, I cautiously proceed through the maze commonly known as the parking garage. Once outside its confines, I advance into warp drive.

"Out there. Thataway!"

The tape player in my car enthusiastically devours the cassette with the score of *Star Trek: The Motion Picture*. Harmoniously intertwining melodies tear my heart apart with an insatiable yearning for my own chance at interstellar travel. I am . . . inspired!

"Home, the final frontier.
These are the voyages of the Street Vehicle *Valiant*.
Its thirty-five-minute mission,

To explore strange new road surfaces.
To seek out and discover new potholes and unclearly defined
   detour routes.
To boldly go where no car has gone before!"
(Rattle, hesitate, SWISH!)

   I continue listening to the *STTMP* soundtrack with devotion.
Suddenly, as if from nowhere, my scanners detect a Thunderbird
of Prey.
   "Damn those Romulans! First the cloaking device, and now
this!"
   The vessel bears down on me, provoking attack.
   "Deflector shields up!" cries my mind. "Standby photon
torpedos!"
   "Shields up, sir. Torpedos ready for fire on signal."
   "FIRE!"
   HOOOOONNNNNKKKK!!!!
   Inevitably, the Bird of Prey draws in closer.
   "Photon torpedos ineffective, sir!" I choke out, noticing that
my heart has repositioned itself at the back of my throat. I
envision *Valiant*'s demise.
   "Evasive starboard!" I scream, taking over the conn. Swerv-
ing to the right, I punch the gas pedal to the floor. Valiant
dances nimbly away from the Thunderbird.
   "You did it!" congratulates my mind.
   "I did nothing! Except almost get myself killed!"

   To my relief, the remaining twenty minutes of my journey
home prove uneventful. I finally reach my destination. Why, if a
man's home is his castle, then surely a girl's apartment is . . .
   "Really a mess."
   Partially written scraps of paper lie all over the floor. I begin
to gather them up. In the process I spill a bottle of correction
fluid left open on the coffee table. Tossing the papers aside, I sit
and begin to type.
   The ribbon in my typewriter has become frayed with use. It
revolts against another impulsive creative session. I stop to hunt
for my Merriam-Webster dictionary, *Roget's Thesaurus*, and
Stewart Bronfeld's *Writing for Film and Television*. I remember
quite distinctly placing them in one corner of the living room or
on the kitchen table or . . . somewhere? Passing by the record
player, I notice *Inside Star Trek* still spinning there from the
night before.
   "Hey! Where are my rubber Spock ears?"

I search frantically for them, tripping over the stack of *Trek* magazines also lying haphazardly askew on the floor.

"What's this? My phaser!"

My senses detect a strange life form. I spin around to face the alien. Crouched down, with both hands gripped tightly onto the butt of the phaser, I await its approach.

"There it is!"

Covered with fine fur, it is approximately twenty-six centimeters in height, excluding the long bristling tail with flicks from side to side. Back arched, the creature stands on four erect legs. I catch a glimpse of razor-sharp fangs as the furred life form ever so slightly opens its oral cavity.

"Preowit!"

Unable as I am to understand this foreign tongue, I engage the universal translator. The creature assumes an even more aggressive position. Pointed ears press close to its head. I set my phaser on stun. Again the creature speaks.

"Preowit!!"

The translator interprets "preowit" into "You have neglected me!"

I reply, "My cause is just."

Without further warning, the alien creature leaps at me, hissing and growling, surgically sharp needles protruding from its footpads. With the phaser still locked on target, I drop to the ground to avoid contact.

"Where in the blazes is *Enterprise*?"

Like Dr. McCoy, I too am not fond of the idea of having my molecular structure scattered throughout the vacuum of space, but at this point I am desperate. For what seems like an eternity the creature and I wait, each pondering the other's next move.

Enterprise finally comes into view, but she is not functioning under her own power. Her destination is controlled by the alien. Highly intelligent, it is capable of determining how best to inflict intense suffering upon my sensitive form. The starship is flung headlong into the wall; it explodes into four separate pieces. My phaser tumbles from my hand as I struggle to avenge *Enterprise*. The furred creature, possessing great agility, slips gracefully away from my enraged grasp.

Snapped back into reality, I walk to the fragmented starship. Gathering her pieces into my arms, I carry them gently to the coffee table. A tear rolls down my face. With stoic courage I recall her once majestic form, then human emotion overcomes me and I begin to cry. I think of *The Wrath of Khan*.

"Lock phasers on target."

"Locking phasers."

"Phaser bank one, fire! Evasive action!" (Oh, too late.)

"Begging the admiral's pardon, sir, but don't you think we should have raised the shields?"

Enterprise doesn't look much like the pride of the fleet anymore. Sacrilegiously, my mind envisions me playing Frisbee with her primary hull.

"Look sharp, mister!" I say out loud.

Regaining my composure, I begin making repairs on her. She *will* fly the skies of my living room again!

The telephone rings. From under the sofa peers a frightened Marvlin Marie, her eyes as large and black as the twin moons of Asteroidus. Before it can reverberate through my senses again, the telephone is swatted on a journey toward the floor.

"Me—ouch!" says my feline sidekick as she scampers toward the kitchen.

The call seems . . . unimportant to me. I no longer seem to be able to respond to something someone says about this or that, or the inevitable:

"Maybe we can get together for lunch sometime?"

"Maybe . . ." I manage weakly as my mind begins to wander. "Gee," I think, "What if this were a call from Starfleet Headquarters? Now that would be important!"

I stand before the admiral.

"Mr. Gilkey, it has been my observation that you have chosen to isolate yourself from the others around you. On what premise is this behavior based?"

"Sir, I regret the alternative life-style I have taken up is due to an obsession of unusual nature."

"Oh?"

"Yes sir. It occurred during my last assignment when I was transported to the Earth colony Omaha, Nebraska, for the Love of Trek convention."

"Go on."

"As I'm sure you'll recall, sir, the purpose of the assignment was to make contact with 'the Star Trek fan.' "

"And what were your observations, Mr. Gilkey?"

"I found them an intelligent, vibrant people, and quite loyal in their own right, sir!"

"Explain."

"At one time this particular life form could be found in great abundance at these briefings—er—conventions. And their numbers spanned the continent! Yet, sir, there were times when this species seemed on the verge of discontinuity."

"And why is that?"

"I don't know. But observing them elicited my own diligent belief in their cause."

"Which is, Mr. Gilkey?"

"Why, to promote the concepts of unity, peace, and brotherhood, as it is propagandized by the Star Trek philosophy."

"And how many Earth inhabitants profess to pursue this Prime Directive?"

"Unknown, sir! Outside of these . . . conventions, it is difficult to ascertain their loyalties. It is positive that some of them are quite conspicuous in their outright devotion to the cause, but, for the most part, sir, they are subdued. Example: I have offered numerous communiqués to those of the group with . . . status. I have received no reply."

"And what are your intentions at this time, Mr. Gilkey?"

"I wait. It's only a matter of time before the Great Bird of the Galaxy—"

"Great Bird of the Galaxy! Surely you are not attempting to credit this devotion to the Prime Directive to Romulan intervention?"

"No, sir, I . . ."

"Jax? Did you hear me?" says the person on the other end of the phone line. I make my apologies and concentrate on the real conversation at hand.

"So call me sometime, okay? I was really beginning to think that you had fallen off the face of the Earth!"

"Beamed up . . ." I respond dreamily.

"What?"

"Oh, nothing."

Anxious to return to my work, I bid the proper farewells and hang up. Walking to the record player, I replace *Inside Star Trek* with *Star Trek Bloopers*. I sit and listen once, just for fun.

Scotty says, "We'll havta do thot again."

Okay, I'm easy enough to get along with. The blooper record spins around again. It sounds a bit scratchy. Well, I guess the needle *is* long overdue for replacement, but, gee, I haven't bought anything lately. Except of course those Star Trek pins, patches, posters, fan magazines, paperback books, comics, dolls, games, puzzles, records, video discs, viewfinder, and . . . A doleful expression emerges upon my face in lament of the now broken *Enterprise* model.

"You're not going to buy anything?" Dad asked incredulously of me one day when we were down at the New Jersey shore. I sensed the beginning of yet another of those "You should save your money as you might need some of it someday" lectures coming on.

"Nope!" I replied, trying to avoid an argument. I just had to add, however, "Not unless it's something Star Trek!"

Dad laughed. "You've got to stop living in the future."

"Doctor McCoy, will you please beam down with the medicine?"

What? Did I hear McCoy's name mentioned?

I perk up, listen closer. "Bones" forgets where to exit the bridge. Maybe *he* needs some medicine? No, I decide McCoy just needs to be beamed directly into the center of my living room. Well, I guess that wouldn't be wise. This place is really a mess, and besides, there's nothing in the refrigerator. Certainly he wouldn't be interested in moldy bagels. But then again, he might just want to analyze my home-grown version of penicillin. Hmmm?

On the blooper record, De Kelley is laughing. I smile and gaze fondly at his picture hanging on the wall. The wheels in my mind begin to turn again. The blooper record strikes at the core of my motivation as I hear:

"Fifty-five apples, one."

Bill, De, and Leonard run through their lines.

Suddenly I'm standing with Gene on the set of *Star Trek IV*. The production is evolving before my proud eyes. Yes, the human adventure continues with the introduction of this new character, so vital to Leonard McCoy's existence. . . .

FADE IN

EXTERIOR SPACE—*Enterprise* zooming by on starry field

KIRK'S VOICE

Captain's Log Stardate 8301.20. . . .

The doors of the elevator (turbolift) swish open. I enter, presenting myself as company to one of Abington Memorial Hospital's most prominent physicians. He smiles at me, noticing the "Beam Me Up" button I proudly wear.

"Beam me up, heh?" he asks.

"Yeah . . ." I reply in defensive readiness. "I love it!"

"Aye lass, me too!" he responds in mimicry of Montgomery Scott. "Just gae me thae word and I'll blast thaem damned Klingons ri' ow o' thae sky. . . ."

Come on now. For the sake of a dreamer's sanity, please . . . "Beam me up, Mr. Scott!!!"

A LINGUISTIC ANALYSIS
OF VULCAN

by Katherine D. Wolterink

We occasionally receive articles purporting to be "Vulcan dictionaries" or "glossaries"; we've even had one very strange submission which took each Vulcan phrase and word and attempted to integrate them into the Tarot, Old High Germanic, and something called "anti-Jungianism." Most of these articles on the Vulcan language are a collection of the writer's favorite gibberish, usually dressed up with a liberal sprinkling of K's and sp's. As any kind of reliable guides to the meaning of Vulcan, they are worthless. This article by Katherine Wolterink, however, follows the strictly confining rules of phonetics and thereby gives us a look at Vulcan which we have never had before.

Aren't you just a little bit curious about Mr. Spock's native language, Vulcan? What does it sound like? Does it have a grammar? Would it be hard to learn? I've been musing about these questions, and others like them, for a long time. Finally, my curiosity got the better of me and I decided to look for some answers. I found a total of 103 words in Vulcan, which occur in three of the original televised episodes, "Amok Time" (14), "Journey to Babel" (3), and "The Savage Curtain" (1); in one of the animated episodes, "Yesteryear" (15); and in the two full-length movies, *Star Trek: The Motion Picture* (56) and *Star Trek II: The Wrath of Khan* (14). I limited the sample to words spoken by live actors portraying native Vulcans. Using the International Phonetic Alphabet, I made a phonetic transcription of the words, phrases, and dialogue I discovered. A phonetic transcription is a written record of the distinctive sounds of a particular language, in this case Vulcan. It identifies the differences between sounds which result in differences in meaning, and helps us to understand the sound patterns of the language. It describes not how a language is written or spelled but how it sounds.

As soon as I had made the phonetic transcription, it became clear that the sound structure of the language spoken by Mr. Spock and Lieutenant Saavik in *Wrath of Khan* is very different from that of the rest of the samples. I put that material aside temporarily, and focused my attention on the remaining eighty-nine words. Eighty-nine words is not a very large sample, but—as far as I have been able to discover—it is all the spoken Vulcan that exists. In spite of the meager amount of material, I think I can describe some of the general characteristics of Vulcan and draw some tentative conclusions.

Once you have a phonetic transcription, what kind of things can you use it to find out? Most accurately, things about patterns of sound: what vowel and consonant sounds occur in the language as compared, for example, to English; what consonant sounds occur at the beginning, in the middle, and at the end of words; what kinds of consonant clusters occur; what particular vowel sounds are dominant.

Vulcan uses all of the vowel sounds that occur in English except the /u/ sound which we hear in the word "f*u*ll." This includes the three dipthongs: /aɪ/, the vowel sound in "t*i*me"; /au/, the vowel sound in "h*ow*"; and /ɪ/, the vowel sound in "t*oy*." I also found one instance of the dipthong /iɛ/, which does not occur in English.

Sixty-nine percent of these words are dominated by either front vowel sounds (like the vowel sounds in the words "h*ea*t," "f*a*te," and "h*a*t") or back vowel sounds (like those in the words "*a*re," "b*oa*t," and "s*o*me"). Fifty of the eighty-nine words, or 57 percent contain exclusively front or back vowel sounds. The result is that Vulcan has a very consistent vowel sound quality, and is characterized by strong, pure vowel sounds. This may account, in part, for the fact that Vulcan so often sounds like Latin spoken with a German accent.

All the consonant sounds which occur in English are present in Vulcan, except /θ/, the *th* sound in the word "*th*in"; and /ð/, the *th* sound in "*th*en". However, there are no Vulcan words beginning with the consonant sounds /g/, /m/, /n/, /tʃ/ (the *ch* sound in the word "*ch*ild"), /dʒ/ (the *j* sound in "*j*ust"), /w/ or /y/. Interestingly enough, the /k/ sound occurs at the end of words only if they begin with the consonant sound /s/, like Spock's name.

It is more difficult to draw conclusions about the grammatical structure of a language, because it depends on word content and function—that is, on accurate translation. Even here, however, it is possible to learn something. All of the Vulcan which is introduced in the three original television episodes and in the animated episode occurs in the form of isolated words, which are immediately translated or clearly explained by the character using them, usually Mr. Spock. In these four episodes, all but three of the words are nouns—thirty in all. Twelve of the nouns are names of people, some of whom, like Spock, are very famous. T'Pau, Sarek, and T'Pring all come to mind.

You will have noticed, no doubt, that the names of all Vulcan men begin with the consonant sound /s/, and that the names of all the women follow the /tp/ initial consonant sound pattern. Lieutenant Saavik's name is the obvious exception, since it follows the masculine pattern, although she herself points out that it is not a proper Vulcan name.

In *Star Trek: The Motion Picture*, the translation of the Vulcan phrases which occur in the *Kolinahr* ritual is given in the form of English subtitles. This form of translation, while it gives you the general idea, makes analysis challenging—to say the least. This is because analysis of grammatical structures depends heavily on accurate translation of specific words. All I can provide here are tentative observations. In the sample of eighty-nine Vulcan words, sixteen are verbs, fourteen of which occur in *STTMP*. On the basis of this evidence, it appears that Vulcan employs at least three verb tenses: present, present perfect, and future. It also uses the command or imperative form of present-tense verbs, for example in such expressions as T'Pau's emphatic *"Kroykah!"* which abruptly halted proceedings during the *Koon-ut-Kalif-fee* ritual in "Amok Time."

Vulcan also seems to use both of the articles "the" and "a." There are three forms of the word "the": /ti/, /to/ and /ɛl/. The article "a" occurs only once and is represented by the vowel sound /a/, which we hear in the word "some", In terms of other kinds of words, Vulcan appears to use possessive forms or cases, prepositions, adverbs, and most of the other grammatical paraphernalia we are familiar with in English. However, on the basis of such scanty evidence, it is impossible to draw any conclusions about these aspects of language structure.

Now, what about the language that Spock and Lieutenant Saavik are speaking, in their private conversation, just after Admiral Kirk arrives on the *Enterprise* in *Wrath of Khan*? Vulcan society is very formal. The culture is steeped in ritual, and almost all of the spoken Vulcan we have any record of is either about or a part of particular rituals: *pon farr* and *Koon-ut-Kalif-fee*, the *Kolinahr*, and the *Khas-wan*—the rite of passage for young Vulcan males. Spock's mother remarks about his pet *sehlat* and Spock's remark to Nurse Chapel about *plomik* soup are notable exceptions. What passes between Spock and Saavik is the only spoken record we have of personal, private conversation between Vulcans. At first, when I discovered the radical differences between their conversation and the rest of the sample, I thought perhaps these were due to dialect. Since this is not a ritual occasion, perhaps they are speaking colloquial, everyday Vulcan. However, the differences in the patterns of sound and the structure of the languages are too great. On the basis of sound linguistic evidence, I have come to the conclusion that Spock and Saavik are not speaking Vulcan.

So, if not Vulcan, what? I believe the only logical conclusion is that they are speaking Romulan. If you have only seen the movie *Star Trek II: The Wrath of Khan*, you will not be aware of the fact that Lieutenant Saavik is half Romulan. You will learn that she is if you read Vonda McIntyre's excellent novelization of the screenplay. It explains a lot. The language spoken on Hellguard, where Saavik spent her first ten years, was Romulan. She speaks fluent Earth Standard (English), a language which, according to the Romulan commander in "The *Enterprise* Incident," is extremely difficult for Romulans to master. Although Saavik has repudiated everything Romulan associated with her past, and aspires to become thoroughly Vulcan, she may not have had time—yet—to become fluent in Earth Standard and Vulcan, both complex languages. It is hardly surprising that Spock should speak fluent Romulan. Finally, I see no reason to introduce speculation about yet a third, completely unknown language. The simplest explanation which is congruent with all the facts is usually the correct one.

If eighty-nine words in Vulcan is a meager sample, fourteen in Romulan is pitiful. Most of what I have been able to deduce about Romulan has to do with the ways in which it differs from Vulcan.

Like Vulcan, Romulan does not appear to use the /u/ vowel sound which occurs in English. In addition, however, it seems to lack the high-mid front vowels /e/ (the vowel sound in "f*a*te") and /a/ (the sound in "s*o*me"); and the central vowels /æ/ (as in "*a*t") and /ʔ/ (the accented "schwa" in the word "b*u*t"). None of the three diphthongs which occur in English is present, but there is one instance of the diphthong /iI/, which does not appear in English. The vowel sound /o/, as in "b*o*at," is always accented. Fifty percent of the sample words end with /a/, as in "far," or /o/ vowel sounds. In addition, ten of the fourteen words are dominated by back vowels: the open, round, full vowel sounds which occur in English in words like "noon," "flow," "law," and "are." This is one of the reasons Spock sounds, in this conversation, rather as if he is talking with a mouth full of marbles.

Romulan, like Vulcan, appears to lack the /θ/ and /ð/ consonant sounds which we use in English. While the voiceless stop /p/ occurs in Romulan, the voiced stop /d/ does not. Similarly, the voiceless fricatives /k/, /s/, and /ʃ/ (the "sh" sound in "shine") occur—and it is reasonable to assume that /tʃ/ (the *ch* consonant sound in the word "child") does—but the voiced fricative sounds /g/, /z/, /ʒ/ (as in "leisure"), and /dʒ/ (the sound of the *j* iin the word "*j*ust") appear to be missing in Romulan.

In addition to the /k/ consonant sound in Romulan, there is an aspirated /k/ sound, rather like the *k* sound in English at the beginning of the word "*Kh*an." It occurs in the beginning of the word /kʰ'omi/, which seems to mean "human." Here it is followed by the vowel sound /o/. It also occurs in the middle of the word /akʰ'lami/, where it is followed by a consonant sound: /l/. /akʰ'lami/ may mean something like "one is." The aspirated /k/ sound occurs twice in Vulcan. Both times it is at the end of the word "Spock," spoken by the high priestess during the *Kolinahr* ritual. However, she also says his name with the unaspirated /k/ sound twice, and I take the /kʰ'/ to be an aberration, rather than evidence of a regular occurrence of the aspirated /k/ consonant sound in Vulcan. Incidentally, Vulcans frequently pronounce Spock's name as if it were the word "spoke," in English. This most often seems to occur in stress situations, or when a speaker is delivering a rebuke.

Finally, Romulan has a number of words which begin with consonants that never occur in word initial position in Vulcan. In the conversation between Spock and Saavik, five of the fourteen words begin with the consonant sound /w/, and one begins with the sound /y/. The frequent occurrence of these vowellike consonant sounds at the beginnings of words contributes to the distinctive sound pattern of spoken Romulan.

Three phonetic characteristics contribute significantly to the consonant pattern of Romulan. Ten of the fourteen words begin with vowel sounds or vowellike consonants. In addition, 71 percent of the sample is dominated by back vowel sounds. This preponderance of vowels, combined with the dominance of sibilant consonants (the /k/, /s/, /ʃ/ sounds dominate because there are no voiced fricatives), accounts in large part for the open, liquid quality of spoken Romulan.

Given a word sample of fourteen items and a translation based on English subtitles, it is almost impossible to say anything about the grammatical structure of the language. I can make only one speculative observation. Both Vulcan and Romulan seem to indicate changes in verb tense or form by changes in the ends of words, just as many Earth languages do. The Vulcan world for "was" in the phrase "our race was saved" is /orsi/. The word for "were" in the phrase "animal passions were cast out" is /orti/. As you can see, /si/ changes to /ti/. Similarly, in Romulan /iʃɛn/ seems to mean "he is + a negative," while /iʃmɛni/ seems to mean "he is + an intensifier". The /ɛn/ changes to /mɛni/.

It is reasonable to assume that a Vulcan would not find it terribly difficult to learn to speak Romulan, were he so inclined, since all of the vowel and consonant sounds which occur in Romulan are present in Vulcan, except the aspirated /k/ sound. It is not clear that the reverse is true. I suspect that it would be somewhat difficult for a Romulan to master spoken Vulcan, since he would be required to produce a number of vowel and consonant sounds, in particular the voiced fricative consonant, which occur in Vulcan but not in Romulan.

There is also the question of the relationship of language to culture, and to social attitudes and values. Given the dichotomy between the social attitudes of Vulcans and Romulans, and the general hostility of Romulans, it seem likely that their differences would create an obstacle to learning. This, it seems to me, may be the crux of the issue. The purpose of language is communication. In the episode "Metamorphosis," Captain Kirk explains to Zefram Cochrane that the universal translator is based on the theory that certain concepts are common to all intelligent life and have correspondences in all languages. He is not entirely talking through his hat. The work of the renowned Noam Chomsky, in transformational grammar, is based on the theory of universal grammar and the existence of deep structures common to all languages. If this is so—if there are universal concepts and structures common to all languages—and if we are able to put aside our ancient animosities, perhaps there is hope that not only the Vulcans and the Romulans but even we, who speak the languages of Earth, may be able to come to an understanding. If it depends on this, on our ability to surrender our prejudices and hostility, the world of Star Trek suggests that we will succeed.

Note: I am indebted to the following texts for theoretical background for this article: Noam Chomsky, *Language and Mind* (1968), and Peter Ladeford, *A Course in Phonetics* (1975).

STAR TREK LIVES
IN GERMANY

by Charlotte Davis

*Charlotte Davis has been living in West Germany for many years
and is intimately acquainted with Star Trek fans and fandom
there. As it is in many foreign nations, Star Trek is shown on
German television with overdubbed translation. The results, as
you will see in this article, are somewhat surprising.*

As most American Star Trek fans know via correspondence or
newsletter, Trek fandom does exist in Germany. It is, however,
thinly distributed throughout the country and mainly concentrated in those areas where contact with Americans, and thus
weekly access to the original versions of the programs, is possible.
You can find no such profusion of Star Trek clubs over here as
you can in the United States; in all, we have three larger clubs
with a subscribing membership, newsletters, and a nucleus of
two or more members who organize it all. The best-known clubs
and those with the largest number of members are:

> *Guardian of Forever* in Bochum (about fifty members)
> *Star Trek Central* in Augsburg (about thirty members)
> *Star Fleet Command* in Berlin (about sixty members)

Most German fans belong to one or more German clubs as
well as to at least one English or American club and in addition
(although this may be typical of all fans everywhere) have an
extensive network of penfriends virtually all over the Trekker
world.

Ever since coming out of the woodwork, German fandom has
had to struggle against overwhelming odds. For instance, any
news about the actors, films, or new developments is unavailable
in Germany itself, the only sources of information being English

or American newspapers and magazines. Science fiction prozines have to be ordered from outside the country, as the science fiction market is virtually nonexistent; the genre of SF films and literature does not command the same success in Germany as it does in the Anglo-American world. As a result, fans are kept busy translating information to include in newsletters so that all can share it.

The oft-remarked dearth of fan fiction in Germany is directly connected with the lack of information on, and exposure to, Star Trek; it is impossible to write about something one does not see much of. English and American zines appear so slick and over-whelmingly superior to German fandom's attempts that most fans relinquish any idea of writing and prefer to receive, not transmit, thoughts, ideas, and the love of Trek via original fiction.

Very little exposure? Permit me to specify. Star Trek was shown in Germany for the first time during the period from 1972 to 1974, with numerous time shifts due to programming changes. In all, only thirty-nine of the original seventy-nine episodes were broadcast; distribute that thirty-nine over a two-year period and it becomes evident how comparatively seldom the series was actually shown. In spite of the fans' letter campaigns, a long dry spell followed. It was not until 1978-9 that some of the thirty-nine previously shown episodes were rerun at biweekly intervals. Again, they were often canceled at the last moment. A few more episodes were rerun in 1980, but it was not until this year that Star Trek returned to the screen regularly—in eighteen episodes, accompanied by television magazine articles which were more or less derisive of fans, Star Trek, and conventions.

These irregularities were partly overcome by means of video-tapes bought in England—an expedient not open to all fans because of cost, as the tapes sell at nearly double the U.S. market price.

The second reason for the surprisingly slight response Star Trek has had in Germany is the alterations which are made in the episodes themselves. Faulty translations, cuts, and changes in plot were made before German fans even got to see a single episode.

The quality of the script translations and loyalty to plot are frequently deplorable. The characters must, of necessity, coincide with their original versions, but the true changes began with the choice of German speakers redubbing the American actors' voices. The diversity of accents and intonations (so important for giving the crew believability and characterizing each person as to

origin and even personality) is as good as absent; except for
Chekov, all speak exactly alike. An effort is not even made to
introduce varying German local accents, which would at least
attempt to parallel the variants of spoken English as shown in the
original series. The German voices are relatively well selected,
roughly paralleling those of the originals—except the one chosen
for Spock. It is definitely incongruous with the Vulcan's character;
a voice higher in pitch than "Kirk's," highly emotional, convey-
ing no hint of the Vulcan's stern control and discipline in speech.

In one case I observed, the film itself was tampered with. In
the original version of "City on the Edge of Forever," Joan
Collins portrays Edith Keeler, but in the German version, her
face is matted out and the face of a German actress superimposed.
Blatant errors in lighting and an easily distinguished "outline
effect" made the change all too obvious even to a person who
had never seen the original.

Dialogue translation is very freely effected; colloquialisms are
placed into the dialogue at random. For example, we at times are
treated to Captain Kirk joking in German whereas his English
statement is perfectly serious. (In "That Which Survives," before entering the caves housing the dead colony's computer
system, Kirk says, "Well, boys, Dad say 'let's follow our
noses.' ") The same is done to other plots, subsequently trans-
forming them into something little better than an amusing children's
program.

Nor are character names left unaltered; and not because they
would have embarrassing or humorous connotations in German.
Some of the most obvious and senseless are:

Lady Amanda	*Lady Emily*
Ambassador Sarek	*Ambassador Starek*
Edith Keeler	*Edith Sonnenschein (Sunshine)*

At times a character is made to appear ludicrous, such as
Kahless the Unforgettable, who is described as "a mass mur-
derer who specialized in killing and inheriting from wealthy
widows." This is indeed an unforgettable change and hair-
raising for anyone who knows the original!

Also often detrimental to the German versions are cuts made to
fit the episodes into a forty- or forty-five-minute time slot; sometimes scenes necessary for understanding an episode are omitted.

I have been asked to analyze two episodes and compare the
American original with the translated and cut version shown on
German television. As I have seen most of the original episodes
but once, I must examine the two I am most familiar with:
"Amok Time" and "Charlie X." "Charlie X" gives us an

example of relative respect for the episode's integrity; examples of severe changes can be seen in "Amok Time".

Example A: "Charlie X" The German version of "Charlie X" is relatively close to the American original. There are only a few cuts, and only one is very extensive. (We are not shown the Recreation Room scene, including Uhura's songs, the card game, and Charlie's demonstration of sleight-of-hand.) However, the story is not distorted and, as I was able to observe while viewing with a non-Trekker German family I am acquainted with, the emotional impact remains the same.

Example B: "Amok Time" I need not give a synopsis of the American original, as it is familiar to all fans. I will add translations of parts of the German dialogue as well as descriptions of the action to illustrate changes. I myself challenge the reader to find any sense in the alterations inflicted.

The teaser remains as an uncut, word-for-word translation of the original, and as such is very effective in creating interest. Later, however, McCoy describes Spock's condition to Kirk in the same terms as he does in the original, but concludes with: "I have a new, previously untested drug. If you don't get him to Vulcan, I will have to use it on him or he will die." This and Spock's own urgent request for R&R on Vulcan prompt Kirk to change course.

Admiral Komack then gives orders to divert from Vulcan to Altair, which Kirk obeys, giving Spock roughly the same consolation as in the original. We next see Kirk in his cabin, thinking over the situation, then deciding to ask Chekov just how much time the *Enterprise* would lose by dropping Spock off on Vulcan. The following scenes (Kirk learning of Spock's unauthorized order to redivert to Vulcan, and Spock's subsequent visit to sickbay) remain unaltered. The exam over, McCoy tells Kirk of Spock's condition according to the values revealed by the examination, and says Spock knows what is wrong, whereupon Kirk goes to Spock's quarters to find out the details. This scene, which is important to the Kirk/Spock relationship, is cut right after "It is a thing no offworlder may know!" and resumes with Kirk's question "And you can be cured on Vulcan?" Spock's answer to this is: "Yes, they know how to treat my condition." Kirk leaves, determined to ask for permission to divert.

As in the original, Kirk's request is refused, and this is where the German version really begins to diverge from the original: Kirk *does not* go against Admiral Komack's orders. McCoy once more confronts Kirk with Spock's imminent death, and concludes,

"This gives me no other choice but to use that medication. We know as good as nothing about the effects, but it will give him at least a chance. May I proceed?" Kirk replies, "Yes, Bones, we have no other choice."

Again, there is another cut; the scene between Nurse Chapel and Spock is cut right after she passes her hand in front of his eyes to see if he is asleep. The brief conversation with Vulcan Space Central is omitted. The viewer is immediately confronted by the viewscreen image of T'Pring. The exchange of greetings between her and Spock is extremely informal compared to the original version:

T'Pring: "Spock, I am here."

Spock: "T'Pring, what are *you* doing here?"

T'Pring: "Why are you surprised, Spock? You have never really been away from Vulcan, and you have never really left me. I am waiting for you."

Uhura then asks, "To whom are you speaking, Mr. Spock?" Spock answers, "To T'Pring. She is my wife."

We are not shown the turbolift scene in which Spock asks Kirk and McCoy to be his witnesses at the ceremony. Instead, we are taken directly from the bridge to *Koon-ut-Kalif-fee*. The following scenes, however, from the beamdown to the end of the combat, have been translated without any changes, nor are any cuts evident. After the battle is over and McCoy asks Spock for his orders, there is another minor change in dialogue: Spock answers, "I will follow you in some minutes. I must speak with T'Pring first."

Their brief conversation is mostly unchanged, except for the insertion of T'Pring's statement "So you set me free," just before Spock comments that he sees no logic in preferring Stonn over him. Another change comes at the end of T'Pring's explanation of why she chose Captain Kirk as her champion. Instead of "I would have your name and your property and Stonn would still be there," she is made to say, ". . . and Stonn considered the possibility of having me as his wife a source of greatest joy." Thus her explanation and motives are very effectively diffused, and she seems a nicer, less calculating person.

The sickbay scene is left unchanged, except that we get a different explanation for Kirk's being alive! McCoy says that he had no other choice but to give Spock the untested drug. It saved his life but gave him hallucinations, which must have been quite harrowing to judge by his reactions. In other words, the entire episode on Vulcan was a dream! One of the most famous of all

Star Trek episodes is thus callously and childishly relegated to cliché status.

A final insult is added by eliminating McCoy's quip about Spock's emotional reaction and substituting "Well, I did have the last word this time!" as Kirk and Spock depart sickbay.

Even when episodes (such as "Charlie X") are only minimally damaged, the shoddy translations do quite a bit of damage. For example, Captain Kirk begins his man-to-man conversation with Charlie by saying, "Well, let's get going and paint the Easter eggs!" Charlie's startled reaction—"Easter eggs?"—has Kirk explaining, "Well, what I mean is, just relax and tell me what happened in the corridor." A weak attempt at consistency is made right after the *Antares* has blown up: "All the eggs we are getting out of the food processing unit have been painted." Kirk turns to Charlie, who turns away to leave the bridge choking down laughter.

Such additions and/or deletions and attempts at humor can be seen in virtually every German-language episode of Star Trek and often manage to warp, obscure, or even totally destroy the message or meaning of an episode, making German Star Trek little better than run-of-the-mill space opera. This practice, together with the infrequency of screenings, has made it difficult for German fandom to come into being, much less even marginally parallel American or English fandom for initiative or persistence.

It would have been interesting to do a comprehensive analysis of all the translated episodes and look for common factors, but the two examples given will suffice to present German Star Trek at its worst and best. The problems inherent in adapting, translation, and trimming episodes for foreign audiences are legion, but one would think that Star Trek, with its universal message of peace and hope and its future setting, would—with care and respect for the original versions—adapt more easily than most. One can only hope that German audiences may one day see all of the episodes presented in a fashion that will enable them to enjoy and learn from Star Trek as much as we have.

As a little bonus, you can have fun guessing which episodes of Star Trek match up to these titles I have literally translated from German into English:

"The Haunted Castle in Space"
"Space Fever"
"Throughout the History of Mankind"
"What Is That Humming?"
"Planet of the Immortals"
"The Dangerous Planet Girls"

IN SEARCH OF
STAR TREK FICTION

by Barbara Devereaux

Readers have been asking us for years to run an article examining the Star Trek novels. To be honest, we couldn't get anyone to write the article because it was just too much work. Too, the Bantam Star Trek books were generally considered to be not worth such an examination. A few months ago, however, Barbara Devereaux wrote to inquire if we'd be interested in such an article. Would we! Not only did Barbara reread all the novels and write the article, she went to the trouble of contacting the editors at Pocket Books to learn some of the background of the novels and to keep this article as up-to-date as possible. We think you're really going to appreciate her efforts.

There is something about Star Trek that inspires creativity. A lot of it. After watching the original episodes thirty or forty times and seeing the films umpteen times, there is still an insatiable desire for more. A surprising number of people have decided to solve the problem of acute Trekaddiction by taking pen in hand or plunking themselves in front of a typewriter and creating their own unique versions of Star Trek. A number of professional writers, as well as fans, have tried their hands at Star Trek fiction, but to all of you out there still busily writing away, rest assured the ultimate Star Trek novel has yet to be written.

Ann Crispin, however, has made a pretty good stab at it. *Yesterday's Son* (Pocket Books, 1983) is a novel that will give every Trekker a warm glow. Crispin continues the story of "All Our Yesterdays" by Jean Lisette Aroeste by coming up with the logical suggestion that Spock fathered a son by Zarabeth. Spock discovers his son's existence and, accompanied by Kirk and McCoy, goes 5,000 years into the past of Sarpedion via the Guardian of Forever to rescue the boy. Unable to arrive precisely when they wish, Spock and his friends find the son, Zar, a young man in his twenties. Zarabeth, killed in a fall, has been dead several years. The rescue, however, is not the important part of the story.

Most of the novel revolves around the relationship between Spock and Zar, and Spock's difficulties in accepting Zar as his son. The characterizations are handled with warmth and sensitivity and the plot is enlivened with Romulans lurking nearby who are on the verge of discovering the secret of the Guardian of Forever. The novel ends with a twist that is sad but utterly appropriate. Perhaps the highest praise that one can give to *Yesterday's Son* is to say that it has a feel of inevitability to it. It seems so obvious a sequel that it's amazing that someone didn't do it years ago, and it requires a gifted writer to create that kind of ''obvious'' story.

Black Fire (Pocket Books, 1982) has the distinction of being one of the few Star Trek novels in which the characters *really* sound like themselves. One can practically hear the voices of Messrs. Shatner, Nimoy, and Kelley. It's like coming home.

As Theodore Sturgeon comments in his introduction, the book literally opens with a bang when there is an explosion on the bridge of the *Enterprise*. Then Cooper does something that has often been discussed, but never attempted. The crew is evacuated to the lower sections of the ship and the saucer section is detached. Amazing!

Convinced the explosion is the work of a saboteur, Spock and Scotty jump ship to go after the bad guys, who turn out to be ''Tomariians.'' They are imprisoned on the Tomariians' planet along with a Romulan commander named Julina and assorted Klingons. Julina promptly falls in love with Spock, as does the Tomariian commander, Ilsa. The distinctive qualities of their love makes for interesting reading. A back injury, sustained in the explosion on the *Enterprise*, renders Spock helpless and dependent on Julina and Ilsa. Cooper skillfully avoids the hurt/comfort syndrome characteristic of so much fan fiction (see Rebecca Hoffman's ''Alternate Universes in Star Trek Fan Fiction,'' *Best of Trek #4*) by pointing out in a chapter entitled ''The Pet'' that Ilsa's ''care'' is, in fact, manipulation of the worst sort. Ilsa obviously enjoys Spock's helplessness, and the reader is repelled by the idea.

Spock twice attempts suicide in order to force Scott to escape back to the *Enterprise* without him. Needless to say, both attempts fail. Spock is rescued by Scott the first time, and after the second attempt, McCoy and Kirk arrive in the nick of time to save him. Cooper never becomes saccharin or overly emotional during the rescues, but rather reflects a strong, certain grasp of the characters and their reactions.

When Spock and Scott are returned to the *Enterprise* they are both court-martialed for being AWOL with a stolen shuttle. Spock gets a stiffer sentence, as he contacted the Romulans to warn them about the Tomariians. Scott is demoted and transferred off the *Enterprise*, and Spock is sentenced to a Federation prison. The prison is depressingly like those in our time—so much for twenty-third-century prison reform. Spock and a Romulan cellmate escape from the prison and seek refuge with, of all things, a band of space pirates. Cooper provides us with a truly memorable scene of Spock attending a pirates' banquet, where he fits about as well as a Tribble at a conference of Klingons. Then Spock and his Romulan friend, Desus, wind up serving the Romulan Empire and Spock becomes a Romulan subcommander.

At this point, of course, the ever-alert Star Trek reader smells a rat—and figures out the plot about twenty pages before Kirk does. It's embarrassing to be smarter than a starship captain, and the transparency of the plot is a weakness in the novel. However, the problem may have occurred because Cooper was forced to rewrite and completely revise the second half of the novel.

M. S. Murdock's *Web of the Romulans* (Pocket Books, 1983) gives us an inside look at Romulan society, which turns out to be more neo-Roman than alien. Although the Romulans are appealing and believable, the main characters are not as well drawn as is the world around them; we also learn nothing new about our heroes. By way of a subplot in *Web of the Romulans*, the *Enterprise* develops a serious problem in its central computer. Unfortunately, the reader is deprived of the surprise and enjoyment that comes in discovering exactly what the problem is because a publicity blurb blasts it all over the back cover.

The Long Trek of Marshak and Culbreath

The number of Star Trek novels written by Sandra Marshak and Myrna Culbreath places them in a class by themselves.

Except for James Blish's *Spock Must Die!* a period of almost seven years passed without the introduction of any new Star Trek fiction until the 1976 publication of Marshak and Culbreath's *Star Trek: The New Voyages* from Bantam Books. With a foreword by Gene Roddenberry and introductions by the cast, the book contains eight short stories (as well as a "Sonnet from the Vulcan") written by fans. Like all the Star Trek works published by Bantam, *New Voyages* is now out of print, but it is worth prowling through the dusty recesses of secondhand-book stores to find a copy, if only for the very remarkable "The Enchanted Pool" by Marcia Ericson, wherein Spock makes the acquaintance of a wood nymph.

Star Trek: The New Voyages was followed, logically enough, by *The New Voyages 2*, also edited by Marshak and Culbreath. Published in 1978, this volume contains six short stories, including one coauthored by Nichelle Nichols, and several works that defy description.

Marshak and Culbreath contributed one short story to the volume, "The Procrustean Petard," in which Kirk and most of the other crewmembers, excluding Spock, undergo sex changes via machines left by a long-dead, evil civilization. The same thing happens to a shipload of Klingons, who take the change rather badly. Feminists are likely to be unhappy with the story's premise that a woman is incapable of commanding a starship; on the other hand, it is entertaining to watch Kirk struggle with problems that most women solve every day without thinking about them, i.e., contending with unfriendly machines or with too friendly strangers in a bar. Fortunately, Kirk figures out a way to undo the process, although (again in a move that will incur the wrath of feminists) a female crewmember decides to remain a man to improve her career opportunities. While a man, her lover, decides to stay a woman, the female-into-male crewmember pays a penalty for her choice: an extra chromosome which makes her act irrationally. Hmmm.

The Price of the Phoenix, Marshak and Culbreath's first full-length novel, was published in 1977 and starts out with a dynamite idea.

The villain, Omne, has invented a gadget that will create life. It will create an exact duplicate of a person, complete with memories, emotions, ideas, and personality. The duplicate will be a real person, not an android or alien disguised as a human. Omne then proceeds to murder Kirk and offers Spock a duplicate Kirk—for a price. The ransom for the duplicate Kirk is the Federation, which Spock supposedly has the power to deliver into Omne's hands. Spock agrees to the deal, figuring he'll retrieve Kirk II and then figure out a way to double-cross Omne. But hold on! Now the story gets complicated, because it turns out the original Kirk isn't really dead. Spock and the Romulan commander from "The Enterprise Incident" spend the rest of the novel trying to rescue Kirks I and II.

There are a number of problems with *Phoenix*, one of which is its violence, which occasionally shades into sadism. In one scene, evil Omne beats Kirk I savagely and then, having failed to "break his spirit," binds up his wounds with some magic healing stuff that comes packaged in an aerosol can. (A *spray can* in the twenty-third century?) Omne seems to derive equal pleasure from beating our hero to a pulp and then caring for him. Later, there is a fight to the death between Omne-and Spock and it's Spock's turn to be beaten to a pulp. Even so, he manages to kill Omne, and Kirk I gets to save Spock with the magic spray can. Both scenes reflect the hurt/comfort syndrome of fan literature, and, perhaps, are a reflection of the influence of fan literature on Marshak and Culbreath's early work.

Another problem with *Phoenix* is in the sexual orientation of the characters. Kirk, for instance, spends his time trying to prove he's a real macho man by refusing to cry when Omne beats him up. This type of thing is more typical of seventh-graders' playground rituals than of mature starship captains and villains. It would be nice to think that Kirk is confident enough of his own worth that he doesn't feel he has to prove anything—to himself or others.

Phoenix never does delve into any of the intriguing problems that the power to create life would cause; however, these problems double in size in the sequel, *The Fate of the Phoenix* (Bantam Books, 1979). *Fate* resurrects evil Omne, who is still intent on making life miserable for Kirks I and II, if not for the entire galaxy. Kirk II has fallen in love with the Romulan commander, who was never really in love with Spock, despite what you saw in "The Enterprise Incident." With McCoy's surgical assistance, Kirk becomes a passable Romulan and goes off with the commander to conquer the Empire, leaving Kirk I in his original role on the *Enterprise*. Marshak and Culbreath follow what seems to be a trend in science fiction and portray the Romulan commander as a rough, tough lady who can outfight most men. Regrettably, liberation seems to be equated with the ability and willingness to kill. The commander seems intent on humiliating Kirk, and Kirk's willingness to put up with these nasty episodes is supposedly proof of his love for the Romulan.

Sex as conquest is another theme that runs through *Fate* (as well as all four of Marshak and Culbreath's novels). This is particularly disturbing given Star Trek's early commitment to equality of the sexes. Conquest is just that, no matter which sex is the victor.

The plot of *Fate of the Phoenix* becomes hopelessly confused

when a second Omne appears on the scene and starts to masquer-
ade as Spock. Thus, neither Kirks I or II nor even the reader
knows if we are dealing with Spock or Omne II. As Marshak and
Culbreath point out, the one bedrock certainty in the universe for
Kirk is knowing that he can trust Spock. When Kirk is put in a
position of wondering if Spock is Spock, the bottom of the
universe falls out. The effect is just as disconcerting for the
reader.

Omne II is so evil that Omne I mellows out a bit and helps
Spock (the real one), and both Kirks fight him off. Fortunately,
Omne and Kirk II disappear through a vortex in space that won't
open again for fifty-four years (53.725, to be exact), so the
reader won't have to worry about a rescue attempt until the year
2033. Like *Price of the Phoenix, Fate of the Phoenix* never
adequately resolves the conflicts inherent in the power to create
life.

In 1982, Marshak and Culbreath took a stylistic leap and
published *The Prometheus Design*. One may (and will) argue
that there are a number of flaws in the characterizations in
Design, but the feel of the book is extraordinary. The writers
have managed to achieve a truly alien (if not necessarily Vulcan)
atmosphere and the book even comes with a Vulcan glossary (for
those of you whose Vulcan is a little rusty).

The novel was published between *Star Trek: The Motion
Picture* and *Star Trek II: The Wrath of Khan* when Trekkers
everywhere were dealing with the terrible problem of the effect
of V'Ger on Spock. Was the effect permanent or had Spock,
indeed, become more human? Marshak and Culbreath attempted
to solve the problem by having Spock flip back into his pre-
V'Ger state. The problem with this solution is that it's just not
logical. Cruelty is never logical, and it is doubtful that Spock
could maintain his pre-V'Ger stance for any long period of time.
It is more likely that if Spock couldn't resolve his Vulcan/human
conflicts, he would retreat to Vulcan rather than inflict his pain
on his friends.

Savaj (neat name!), a Vulcan commander, appears on the
Enterprise and relieves Kirk of command because Kirk is being
influenced by aliens. Savaj places Spock in command of the
Enterprise, since Vulcans are less susceptible to the alien influence.

Much of the story then revolves around Mr. Kirk's inability to
accept the fact that Captain Spock is running the show. The
characterizations here are somewhat askew as Kirk begins to act
like a rebellious five-year-old and Spock like a short-tempered
parent. At one point, when Kirk's impertinence has tried Spock's

patience once too often, Spock literally sends Kirk to his room until he is ready to apologize and behave himself. When Kirk disobeys Spock's orders, he is summoned to Spock's quarters to face up to Vulcan-style punishment and is quaking in his regulation boots at the prospect of facing an angered Captain Spock. One of the more endearing things about Kirk is that there is very little in the galaxy that frightens him, and he would certainly never be afraid of Spock. The parent/child roles for Spock and Kirk just don't ring true.

Spock slips further out of character when he assumes a "Vulcan command mode" wherein he demands instant obedience from crewmembers and starts to act like Super-Vulcan, literally able to leap tall buildings (in this case walls) in a single bound. Spock as Super-Vulcan comes perilously close to becoming precisely what Leonard Nimoy has fought for years to avoid—a very unbelievable cartoonlike character.

In one scene, however, in which Spock is assisting an injured McCoy, he reverts back to being the wise, compassionate Vulcan we all know and love. In doing so, he helped McCoy and the reader deal with some of the thorny philosophical questions that the novel raises. Good Star Trek always offers the reader or viewer ideas that are simple, but vital enough to move mountains. *The Prometheus Design* is full of thought-provoking ideas on everything from experimentation on animals to love and violence in the universe.

There is one other flaw in *Prometheus Design* that the authors picked up from the original television series. It seems that the aliens are interfering in the natural evolutionary development of planets, and our heroes can tell this at a glance by consulting their handy copies of the "Richter Scale of Cultural Development." Cultural, scientific, and technological development can no more be predicted than can evolution, which is, by definition, unpredictable.

Triangle (one is horribly tempted to call it "The Pythagorean Design"), published in 1983, actually involves *two* triangles.

The first is a result of the authors' picking up on an idea mentioned in Gene Roddenberry's novelization of *Star Trek: The Motion Picture*. In his "introduction" to Roddenberry's book, Kirk mentions that he is a believer in old-style humanity as opposed to a new species that is evolving on Earth, the *new humans*, who, because their individual consciousnesses are submerged into a group consciousness, are more intelligent and adaptable than "old-style" humans.

In *Triangle*, the new humans are vying for power with another collective consciousness, the Totality. Both groups are trying to recruit Kirk, knowing that if Kirk joins them, others will follow. Thus, the three points of the triangle are the new humans (or Oneness), the Totality, and Kirk (ably assisted, as usual, by the two points of his personal triangle, Spock and McCoy).

Assuming for a moment that the new humans are a more highly evolved life form (and the question is open to dispute), the story immediately begins to unravel, because it depends on Kirk's *choosing* to join the new humans. Evolution is not a matter of choice.

The second triangle is of a more old-fashioned, eternal variety. Kirk and Spock fall in love with the same woman. The lady in question is a Federation Free Agent named Sola Thane and, in terms of personality, seems to be a cross between the Romulan commander and Han Solo; however, she dresses in a copper-colored jumpsuit and has an energy coil that reminds one of Wonder Woman. Kirk, who has always had a secret desire to be a Free Agent, feels that he's met his match in this lady. Spock takes one look at her and immediately suffers an acute attack of *pon farr*.

Spock is still bothered by the unfinished business of "Amok Time," and is too far from Vulcan to reach the safety of his home planet. The only alternative is to take a mate; however, he refuses to take the woman Kirk loves, and he believes the human female crewmembers are all too fragile to cope with Vulcan passions. The fact that Spock's mother is human and did (and, presumably, does) quite well in coping with Vulcan passions is conveniently overlooked. Marshak and Culbreath also overlook the fact that the *pon farr* involves a telepathic link as well as sexual attraction. It is questionable whether Spock could be attracted to a woman with whom he had not shared the mind meld.

As in the other Marshak and Culbreath novels, sexual relations in *Triangle* are portrayed in terms of conquest and surrender with disturbing overtones of violence. Spock's motivation in refusing Sola's advances are right on target, however, in that Spock believes he was responsible for denying Kirk his love for Edith Keeler and Spock cannot again hurt Kirk by denying him the woman he loves. Spock thinks that Kirk has lost so many friends and loves that, this once, he should win. Sola persuades Spock that losing his first officer and closest friend would be equally devastating for Kirk.

Kirk's reaction to the Spock/Sola liaison is equally on target. Although he is in love with Sola, he is glad that Spock has finally fallen in love and takes a wicked delight in teasing Spock about the torrid love affair. Sola is no help at all, since she loves both Kirk and Spock and can't make up her mind.

As with *The Promethean Design*, *Triangle* conveys an extraordinary *feel* of the alien, although this novel is more an alien time than a place. We do, indeed, feel that we have been transported to the twenty third century. The problem is that the characters, Spock and Kirk in particular, seem to lose a great deal of themselves in the process. With the exception of a few scenes, the characters all sound alike.

The three-way conflict in *Triangle* is never resolved, as Sola ends up taking off with Soljenov of the Totality. It seems a little unfair to build up the kind of tension that *Triangle* does and then wimp out at the end by failing to resolve the conflict. The novel is ready-made for a sequel in which the Free Agent returns and is forced to make a decision. The conflict between the new humans and the Totality also remains unresolved; however, that is less disturbing, as the two groups seem nothing more than two sides of the same unappealing coin.

There is one other nagging and somewhat embarrassing point that should be mentioned about the Marshak-Culbreath novels. In all four novels, our heroes invariably manage to lose their clothes. Well, most of them anyway. Actually, it's just Spock and Kirk who keep appearing in the—uh—altogether. Apparently, the naked McCoy holds little interest for the writers (sorry about that, Bones). Most of the time, the story doesn't even justify Kirk's and Spock's being out of uniform, much less out of clothes.

Vonda's Vision

The quality of Vonda McIntyre's two Star Trek novels comes as no surprise to those readers who are familiar with her earlier, non—Star Trek novels such as *Dreamsnake*. With the exception of the death-of-Spock scene in the *Wrath of Khan* novelization, McIntyre's *The Entropy Effect* (Pocket Books, 1981) contains the single most powerful scene thus far presented in a Star Trek novel. About halfway through the book, Jim Kirk is killed on the bridge of the *Enterprise*. Murdered. Just like that. The scene is devastating in its suddenness and in its terrible violence. There is no glamorization of violence here. The shooting is piercingly real, filled with details of blood splattered on control panels and the crew in disarray. For those who lived through the Kennedy assassinations and the murders of Martin Luther King and John

Lennon, it is all hauntingly familiar. It seems that in the twenty third century everything changes and nothing changes.

The reaction of the crew, and, in particular, of Spock and McCoy, is perfect. Spock manages some first aid, but quickly realizes that the captain's condition is hopeless. While McCoy is frantically working over him, Spock initiates a mind meld to ease some of Kirk's pain and fear. In a flash of understanding, Kirk knows he is dying and realizes that Spock, who refuses to break the meld, will die with him. Kirk wrenches himself away from the meld and—almost—dies in Spock's arms.

Spock's reaction to Kirk's death is, of course, logical. There is none of the murderous rage that gripped the Spock of the Marshak-Culbreath novels. Rather, there is, predictably, quiet, courageous acceptance. Spock does exactly what Kirk asks him to do: He takes care of the ship. McCoy manages to stabilize Kirk's vital signs and, with the help of elaborate machinery, is keeping Kirk alive and ignoring the fact that his brain is dead. Spock helps McCoy face the truth and supports McCoy (literally) as McCoy removes the machinery and allows Kirk to die. It is only as a gentle aside that McIntyre mentions that after all has been attended to on the *Enterprise*, Spock plans to turn the ship over to a new commander and then transfer as a science officer to another starship. Spock knows, without questioning the reasons, that he will never serve on the *Enterprise* without Kirk.

Spock is forced to go back into time to prevent Kirk's death and, more important, to repair the damage that has been done to history through the tampering with time by a physicist who has solved the problem of temporal physics. At this point, the book becomes Spock's novel as he goes back farther and farther in time, each attempt failing by seconds. Spock is forced to live Kirk's death over and over, and the reader is drawn into the terrifying consequences of a small mistake magnified through history like a stone sending ripples through a pond. By the time the last ripples reach the shore, they have become waves that threaten to engulf the entire galaxy.

McIntyre provides a romantic interest for Kirk in the person of a fighter commander, Hunter, who is also the mother of a small child and part of a family-community. Yes, there is a life outside of Starfleet! She has asked Kirk to join the family several times, and each time Kirk has refused because of his own fears of emotional commitment. McIntyre provides some new insights into Kirk's emotional reserve and his fears of trusting too much of his emotional life to anyone.

While Spock is transporting through time, McCoy assumes

command of the *Enterprise*. McCoy is obviously not cut out to be a starship commander, and his fumbling attempts at command provide some comic relief. Equally comic is poor Scotty, who, as usual, is stuck down in the engine room and complains that no one ever tells him what's going on. He starts to suspect that Spock and McCoy are responsible for Kirk's murder and is torn between his loyalty to them and his fierce sense of justice.

McIntyre's treatment of minor characters is also skillful and sensitive. Sulu, who has an understandable crush on Hunter, is really in love with a security chief, Mandala Flynn. The development of both the Kirk/Hunter and Sulu/Flynn relationships is handled gently and delicately. Although there is some conflict in each relationship (enough to make them interesting), neither relationship is marred by overtones of violence. Enough background is provided about both Hunter and Flynn to make them appealing and vulnerable.

There are several alien crew members introduced in *Entropy Effect*, and they too are both believable and appealing. When one of the security guards, Jenniver Aristeides, blames herself for Kirk's and Flynn's deaths and threatens suicide, Spock is able to communicate with her from the perspective of a fellow alien who, like Aristeides, is a product of genetic engineering. McIntyre invents several planets and cultures in great detail so that the reader may savor this scene and the depths of Spock's compassion and tolerance.

McIntrye's novelization of *Wrath of Khan* does justice to the film (which is saying a lot!). She has taken Jack Sowards' screenplay, a work of gentle genius, and turned it into a first-rate novel. Better yet, she has filled in a number of the points that were left on the cutting-room floor when the film was edited. Observant Trekkers immediately guessed, for instance, that Saavik wasn't a *real* Vulcan. For one thing, she didn't look like a Vulcan, and for another thing, she swore ("Damn") upon discovering the *Kobayashi Maru* in the Romulan Neutral Zone. Swearing is emotional, illogical, and undignified. As every Trekker knows, a real Vulcan would never swear. But when McIntyre reveals that Saavik is half Romulan, it explains everything. Romulans are capable of anything, even (gasp!) swearing. Of course, we are never told what Klingon cruisers are doing around the Neutral Zone in defiance of the Organian Peace Treaty, but you can't have everything.

McIntyre also explains why Chekov didn't just transport up to the *Enterprise* upon meeting Khan. That explanation comes as a great relief to the thousands of viewers in theaters across the country who were thumping their neighbors on the back while screaming, "Your communicator, Chekov! Beam up! Beam up!" Talk about frustrating.

There are any number of other details in *Wrath of Khan* that help satisfy the Trek reader's Vulcanlike need for consistency. We are presented with a new generation of Starfleet cruisers, the galaxy-class ships. After fifteen years, it's not surprising that Starfleet would come out with a new model. Moreover, McIntyre follows up on even minor characters with tender, loving detail. We know that Kyle is on the *Reliant* and that Hunter (from *Entropy Effect*) has been given command of one of the new cruisers. The regular crew are all present and accounted for as well. Oddly, the only character who receives too little attention is Carol Marcus. We know she is a brilliant scientist, a gutsy lady, and a good mother to David, but we never really understand why Kirk loves her. Kirk's flirtation with Saavik is certainly understandable, as Saavik manages a wonderful combination of intelligence, innocence, and vulnerability (not to mention a gamine beauty), but we never do get to know Carol Marcus. Perhaps in the sequel.

One other point that both the novel and film slide over is the question of Kirk's guilt in the entire affair. It is true that he never bothered to check on the progress of the people he left on Alpha Ceti. There is more than a little irony in the fact that Kirk and the *Enterprise* crew paid so dearly for Kirk's neglect.

The scene in which Chekov and Terrell are tortured with the Ceti eels is written with chilling realism. It is remarkable that someone as obviously sensitive and compassionate as Vonda McIntyre can be so brutally graphic when dealing with violent scenes—but perhaps it is precisely her gentleness that makes her so honest about violence. The same realism permeates Spock's death scene; McIntyre adds details (like the machinery becoming slippery with Spock's blood) that make the reader wince with pain. Spock's deep sense of peace and purpose serves as a perfect counterpoint to the pain. There is never the slightest hint of sensationalism in McIntyre's rendering of these scenes. There is just truth.

Roddenberry Does It Again

As one might expect from a book hatched by the Great Bird of the Galaxy, the characterizations in the novelization of *Star Trek: The Motion Picture* (Pocket Books, 1979) are well-nigh perfect. As Van James pointed out in his review (*Best of Trek*

#3), the novel explains much more about Kirk's painful three years at Fleet Headquarters and of his need to resume command than does the film. It is regrettable that Vice Admiral Ciani is killed off so early in the novel, however. She is an intriguing blend of qualities, and anyone who can earn the title of "Nogura's staff whore" deserves to live through the novel—and maybe reappear in future novels.

In terms of believability, *verisimilitude*, the novel does a commendable job of providing a great deal of scientific description that is both detailed and accurate. For instance, a wormhole is in fact a possibility in hyperspace, although thus far most theories have suggested that it would be microscopic in size. Nevertheless, it *could* happen.

In the novel, much is made of Spock's telepathic awareness not only of V'Ger, but of Kirk. Thus Spock's conflict is strengthened in that he is torn between his attraction to V'Ger, which represents the logical, Vulcan way, and the reality of his link with humans in general and Kirk in particular. It is difficult to understand why Spock would hope to find his answers in a being which is basically malevolent. By their fruits ye shall know them, Mr. Spock. Admittedly, V'Ger's "evil" is largely a result of ignorance (see Joyce Tullock's "Approaching Evil," *Best of Trek #5*), but nevertheless, it is evil.

Spock's resolution of his conflict is implied in his response to Scott's offer to take him back to Vulcan. "Unnecessary, Mr. Scott. My task on Vulcan is completed." That impression is reinforced by his comment to McCoy (in the book, and not in the film) that anger, jealousy, etc. are *misuses* of emotion. The ABC "expanded" edition of *Star Trek: The Motion Picture* provides even more data on Spock's transformation as it includes a scene wherein Spock weeps for V'Ger and its painful search for meaning that is so like his own.

A Trek Trio

We have three more Pocket Books novels to consider. Hang in there as Pocket Books' writers seek out new life (forms) and new civilizations, explore strange new worlds of fiction, and boldly— well, you know the rest of it.

In *The Abode of Life* by Lee Correy (Pocket Books, 1982), the *Enterprise* gets caught in an "extreme gravitational anomaly" and is thrown 300 parsecs (give or take a few parsecs) to an unexplored region of the galaxy. There the crew discovers a single, unstable star and one planet called Mercan. The planet is in such a remote sector of the galaxy that no other stars or planets are visible; as far as the Mercans know, they are alone in space. Are they surprised when the *Enterprise* parks at their front door!

Kirk's problem is that he must obtain the Mercans' help to repair the warp engines and do so in a way that does as little damage to the Prime Directive as possible. His job is made more difficult by the fact that the planet is on the verge of civil war between a conservative group, the Guardians, and a more progressive group, the Technics. The Guardians are a quasi-religious group who stay in power through their ability to predict the periodic disturbances caused by the unstable sun. They also control all the transporter devices (that's right, transporter devices) that are the sole means of travel on the planet. To add a little spice to the story, all Mercans are armed with old but very lethal revolvers and are ready to shoot first and ask questions later.

Spock has an easier problem to contend with—he calms down the unstable sun by zapping it with a couple of photon torpedos. McCoy spends his time patching up bullet holes and worrying about the sun's going nova.

One of the weaknesses of the novel is Correy's explanation of the Mercans' advanced technology. Spock speculates that the planet may have been "seeded" with humans (or humanlike beings as had many other planets encountered by the *Enterprise*. This theory (technically called "panspermia") was popular in the 1960s and used a number of times in the original series. However, it has been thoroughly discredited in today's scientific community. If Spock mentioned it in the 1980s, he might be laughed off the bridge. Also, the theory can become an easy way of explaining the presence of humans in far-off reaches of the galaxy instead of inventing new and believable alien societies.

Another problem arises when Kirk gets himself enmeshed in a Prime Directive tangle. That's not surprising, since application of the Prime Directive has always been more than a little confused and inconsistent (see Steven Satterfield's "Star Trek: Concept Erosion," *Best of Trek #5*). In "The Omega Glory," Kirk reminds Captain Tracey that they cannot interfere with the evolution of a planet's society even if it means their own deaths or the deaths of their entire crews. In "The Apple," the Prime Directive means noninterference with viable societies, and apparently the definition of "viable" is a matter of the captain's discretion. Eventually, costumes were necessary when visiting aliens, as any contact with humans would contaminate the developing society ("A Private Little War"). Obviously, this strategy works only for human or humanlike societies.

There are any number of important questions concerning the Prime Directive that remain unsolved. After all, not only contact with aliens could affect the evolution of a society—even *thinking* that alien life is possible could affect a society. (How many of you feel that your lives have been affected by "knowing" Spock?) Does the ban on contact with alien societies undermine the *Enterprise*'s mission of seeking out new life forms and new civilizations? Is it right (or even logical) to deny a people knowledge of the galaxy around them? Is such "protection" simply a reverse kind of elitism? Perhaps the Directive should merely prohibit "forcible" interference with the development of a society. When does morality necessitate interfering with a developing culture? Can the Federation tolerate a society that condones slavery? Infanticide? Nuclear war? And, finally, if contact (on whatever level) is forbidden, how does a planet join the Federation?

No wonder Kirk is confused.

In *The Abode of Life*, Kirk makes it clear that he'll do whatever is necessary to ensure the survival of his ship. Some of his strategies are a bit unnerving. In one scene, in an effort to convince the Mercans that the *Enterprise* is for real, Kirk uses two beams of "white light" to boil the ocean. Honest. "It didn't last long—only two seconds—but it was enough to boil a square kilometer of ocean and leave a rising cloud of stream." Too bad for the fish.

With the exception of the space seeding and the lack of ecological concern, the scientific detail in *The Abode of Life* is well done. However, the novel is more for those readers who prefer the "science" part of science fiction. Readers who are interested in character development will be disappointed, as we learn nothing new about the characters.

After Kirk, in a brilliant display of diplomatic maneuvering, has brought peace to the planet and repaired the warp engines, there is a final log entry that will make sensitive Star Trek readers wince with pain. If there is one thing readers like in Star Trek novels, it is consistency. The error in the log entry is tiny, but nonetheless disconcerting. "Spock is basically a very violent man who keeps his emotions under tight control and who doesn't like to fight . . . except during *pon farr*, when I personally know that Spock can be very violent indeed." The *pon farr* is a secret! No one outside of Vulcans, except for Kirk and McCoy and a few select humans (like Amanda), knows about it. So what's Kirk doing talking about it in a regular log entry?

The Covenant of the Crown by Howard Weinstein (Pocket Books, 1981) is less a work of science fiction than an adventure set in outer space. King Stevvin of the planet Shad has been in exile eighteen years, ever since young Lieutenant Kirk helped the king and his wife and young daughter to flee when the planet was on the brink of falling to rebel forces. Kirk is now assigned to return the ailing king (the queen died earlier) and his now grown daughter, Kailyn, to Shad. However, the king knows he will not survive the trip and asks Kirk to help his daughter gain her crown and assume her rightful place as Queen of Shad. The crown has many of the properties of the sword Excalibur of Arthurian legend, although Spock insists the story is more like Bible stories of ancient Earth than Arthurian legend—hence the title of the novel.

The rest of the book revolves around Spock and McCoy and their efforts to help Kailyn win her crown. Kirk stays in the background and on the *Enterprise*, where he discovers that one of the king's servants is a Klingon spy. The unusual combination of Spock and McCoy is made particularly enjoyable by the fact that Weinstein's characterizations are virtually flawless. McCoy falls in love with Kailyn and must eventually admit that the difference in their ages is an insurmountable barrier to their love. Weinstein handles the relationship with warmth and sensitivity. Kirk and Spock are both very patient with McCoy, although Spock is somewhat embarrassed when McCoy turns to him for advice. Chapel thinks that McCoy is making a perfect fool of himself and says so.

Like *The Promethean Design*, *Covenant* was written between *Star Trek: The Motion Picture* and *Wrath of Khan*. Weinstein opted for precisely the opposite of Marshak and Culbreath's handling of the great Spock dilemma. He made Spock more human. The most notable instance of Spock's newfound sense of comfort with his own humanity is his response to the princess when she gives him a big hug. He is mildly amused that she is so gentle with him because she obviously believes that all Vulcans will disintegrate at the slightest touch. Weinstein's handling of the new Spock is perfect. Spock is the same logical, slightly straitlaced Vulcan we all know and love, but he has matured into the Spock of *Wrath of Khan*.

Howard Weinstein's second Star Trek novel will bring back a scoundrel we all know and love, Harry Mudd. This time around, Weinstein will focus on Scotty and give him some of the well-deserved attention that has been up to now lacking in most Star Trek fiction.

Robert E. Vardeman's *The Klingon Gambit* (Pocket Books, 1981) is fun. Following in the noble tradition of "The Trouble with Tribbles," it is high comedy from start to finish. The *Enterprise* turns into a parody of itself when the crew comes under a strange, alien influence. Chapel gets into a fistfight with a scientist over Spock. Spock veers crazily from Super-Vulcan to cowering human. McCoy rebels against all machines and starts sewing up wounds with a needle and thread. Yech, how primitive! Scotty and an amazing sidekick named Heather try to develop the universe's most efficient warp engines and start pilfering parts from all over the ship. Klingons are getting nastier and Andorians are getting crankier and, to top it all off, Kirk can't seem to make decisions.

The only disappointing part of the book is when Kirk discovers exactly what is turning his ship into a loony bin. And if anyone out there can figure out what the title has to do with the story, please write immediately and enlighten all of us.

Vardeman's second Star Trek novel, *Mutiny on the Enterprise*, was published in October 1983.

If you saw *Star Trek II: Biographies* sitting on a bookstore shelf, you would assume it was another publicity thing with interviews with the cast. Well, you would be wrong. William Rotsler's book is a series of sketches of the *characters*. Presumably, the material was all stolen from Starfleet archives. The best part of the book is its bibliography, which includes such titles as "Kahless the Unmerciful" by Asimov Coleman, *The Tribble Manual* by Gerald Davis, "What to Do with a Pregnant Tribble" by Gerald Friedman, and *Xenobiology* by Dr. Leonard McCoy. All of these titles will be available at your local bookstore—in about three hundred years.

Bantam Star Trek

Gordon Eklund's two novels, *The Starless World* and *Devil World*, are remarkably similar. In *The Starless World* (Bantam, 1978), the *Enterprise* is being held captive inside a Dyson sphere. A Dyson sphere is essentially a hollow planet with a sun inside. In this case, the sun is a god. A shipload of Klingons are also being held captive, and they don't like it either. One of the females from the sphere, a cute little white-furred alien named Ola, falls in love with Kirk and eventually helps everyone escape.

In *Devil World*, rather than face a merciless sun god, Kirk and company face the natives of the planet, Heartland, who are exactly like the devils of Christian mythology. In *The Starless*

World, Uhura is kidnapped by servants of the sun god—Kirk rescues her. In *Devil World*, Crewman Doyle is lost to the bad guys. Ola, in *The Starless World*, buys Kirk's freedom with her life. In *Devil World*, Gilla Dupree, an artist with whom Kirk is in love, buys his freedom with her life. There is a nice moral to each story, but the author cops out on it because of his determination to provide his readers with a happy ending. The sun god releases Ola. Gilla Dupree was dying anyway from some dread disease. In essence, the author deprives his characters of their heroic gestures.

In many ways, *The Galactic Whirlpool* by David Gerrold is the best of the Bantam collection. Gerrold has a passion for explaining the *why* of everything, and although the plot is not exactly new, each move, each decision, each bit of equipment is described exactly and precisely. The book is also filled with Gerrold's unique brand of humor. Only the inventor (discoverer?) of Tribbles could bring us the amazing story of Emperor MacMurray. This gem is certainly destined to be a Star Trek classic.

Joe Haldeman contributed two novels to the Bantam series, *Planet of Judgment* and *World Without End*. In *Planet of Judgment*, our heroes are part of an experiment being conducted by an interesting group of beings called Arivne. The experiments take the form of dream sequences that reveal a great deal about each character. Kirk, for instance, dreams that he is captain on a nineteenth-century clipper ship. In the end, the experiment is called off because Spock does the unpredictable, if not the illogical, thing and sacrifices his life for Kirk's. In Star Trek novels, love always confuses the heck out of the bad guys.

World Without End is another story about people inside a spaceship headed toward disaster. The people inside, of course, think their spaceship is the world. Haldeman was getting a little Trekked out on this one. Most writers have a strong need to create their own worlds and own characters, and there is a limit to how long they can wander through Gene Roddenberry's. For Joe Haldeman, the limit was one book. A contract with Bantam forced him to write *World Without End*. That may explain why the doomed spaceship is controlled by a giant artichoke called a Father Machine. Fortunately, Spock saves the day by initiating a mind meld with the artichoke and convinces it to release the captive *Enterprise*. The Klingons in the story aren't quite so lucky—the Father Machine likes to *eat* Klingons. *World Without End* is, no doubt, Haldeman's last Star Trek novel. (However, with the debut of *The Forever War* onstage in Chicago, he has found new worlds to explore.)

Perry's Planet by Jack C. Haldeman II (yes, they're related) is similar in its plot to "Spock's Brain." Wayne Perry, who is three hundred years old, is interfaced with a computer that he built and that is running his planet. However, he's getting a little tired and (naturally) picks Spock to help the computer along. The story is complicated by the fact that Perry had invented a virus that makes people incapable of violence. Haldeman neglects the fact that there is a difference between passivity and peacefulness. Vulcans, after all, have been at peace for a thousand years, but they are by no means passive.

Trek to Madworld is another Trek comedy. With a slightly off-the-wall introduction by David Gerrold, the novel introduces us to a gnome named Enowil who is really a crazy Organian. And Stephen Goldin, the author, is a koala. *You* figure it out. Mr. Goldin's wife is not Mrs. Goldin, but Kathleen Sky, the author of *Vulcan!*

Spock Must Die! is, of course, by James Blish, a gifted writer who won a Hugo award for his novel *A Case of Conscience*. *Spock Must Die!* is not his best book, but is entertaining Star Trek and, at the time of its release from Bantam in 1970, was enthusiastically welcomed by Star Trek fans, who had been clamoring for *more*.

In a plot that is similar to that of "The Enemy Within," Spock is duplicated by a transporter accident and the novel concentrates on the efforts of Kirk and crew to discover which is the real Spock and which is his evil twin. The scientific detail is well-thought-out, and it is fun to read Star Trek with a British accent. However, the characterizations are not as well developed as they could have been; the duplicate Spock's "evil" thought processes are never explored in any depth, nor is Kirk's reaction to seeing his best friend split in two.

The Star Trek novels, be they published by Bantam or Pocket Books, be they original or adaptations, be they by seasoned professionals or first-timers, all have one thing in common: They are the products of the continuing love and devotion that Star Trek fans have felt for the series and its characters for many years. As long as such devotion continues, there will always be someone writing new Star Trek.

STAR TREK: A
PHILOSOPHICAL VIEW

by Michael Constantino

There is a long, involved story behind this article. About two years ago, Michael Constantino sent us a copy of his thesis, "Star Trek: A Philosophical and Theological Analysis and Personal Reflection," which he had completed as a requirement for his B.A. in Liberal Arts and Philosophy. We enjoyed it so much that we wanted to publish it as an article. It was, however, much too long, so Michael gave us permission to trim it down. Once we had done so, we discovered that it was still a bit too technical for the average reader. Mike's thoughts on Star Trek and what it means were so interesting, however, that we refused to give up. Again, the article was compressed and subtly rewritten. Finally it reached the form you see here—an effective mixture of scholarly thought and entertaining prose. We hope you enjoy reading it as much as we enjoyed bringing it to you.

As every fan knows, the cancellation of Star Trek after the 1968–9 season marked the beginning of the series' greatest popularity; for once in syndication, Star Trek reached a base which was far broader and deeper than that of the initial three-year run. In conjunction with this worldwide syndication came the emergence of Star Trek conventions, fan clubs, merchandising paraphernalia, the animated series, original and adaptation paperbacks, etc., culminating in the release of *Star Trek: The Motion Picture* and *Star Trek II: The Wrath of Khan.*

Why did Star Trek become so popular and why has it remained so popular? One explanation is that the show is highly popular among young people; its imaginative, original adventuresomeness, coupled with its scientific accuracy, makes for a superb literary drama. Gene Roddenberry always insisted that literature was literature, be it called science fiction, Shakespeare, or Cowboys and Indians—the trick is to make the audience believe "I am there." If nothing else, Star Trek makes you believe that its universe, if not real, is at the very least extremely possible. The futuristic technology in Star Trek is so plausible that many viewers have been inspired to try to implement comparable advances in real life. This plausibility, or believability factor, is such a vital element of the series that enormous amounts of time and energy were invested in it during the filming of the episodes. Every effort was made to convince the viewer that "he is there."

Besides the appeal of its literary aspects and scientific "believability," Star Trek also has an intellectual and emotive dimension that, in part, helps to explain its popularity. Intellectually, Gene Roddenberry uses the medium of television to discuss such pertinent issues as war, sex, human rights, economics, politics, sociology, religion, technology, and the evolution of man and universe. Emotively, there is an atmosphere of *esprit de corps* that exists among both the production team and cast of the show and the fans themselves.

Star Trek also has a psychological appeal. Several episodes have been used as effective therapeutic teaching devices for the emotionally disturbed. For the emotionally stable, Star Trek provides a context (and, in Mr. Spock, an example) within which the "alien" in us all can feel at home. Star Trek helps each of us to come to terms with the rejected parts of ourselves and with the world around us.

Another reason for Star Trek's popularity is that it projects basic insights into the mystery that is man, cosmos, and God. Through its use of metaphor and symbolic imagery, Star Trek provides insightful glimpses into the nature of reality.

One of the basic images in Star Trek is that of man as a free, self-determining entity. In various ways, a number of episodes vehemently protest any restrictions to man's freedom, be they internal or external in nature.

Several episodes, for instance, depict the *Enterprise* encountering societies which are stagnant and paradisiac in nature. In both "Return of the Archons" and "This Side of Paradise," Kirk and his crew, despite the tranquillity, peace, and absence of evils, feel that something is missing. Star Trek tells us again and again that paradiselike societies are stagnant and unchanging, certainly not meant for man, who will wither and die within them. Such a society can be had only at the expense of man's freedom and creative growth; and this price, according to Star Trek, is not worth paying.

Star Trek also frequently demonstrates man's hatred of captivity. In several episodes landing-party members are held captive by aliens. As might be expected, the awesome dynamism of Captain Kirk's powerful spirit will have none of it. He points out that it is in the nature of man to be free; without freedom, without obstacles to overcome, man will weaken and die.

This same view is presented by Christopher Pike and his crew in "The Menagerie." The mind-reading Keepers are astounded to discover that the *Enterprise* crewmembers, despite a benevolent and extremely pleasurable captivity, prefer death to a lack of freedom.

Opposing forces often cause constraints of exterior freedom in Star Trek. These external powers can be considered to be either living, nonliving, or situational. The first group can further be subdivided into humanoid and nonhumanoid. The former is best exemplified by the Klingon and Romulan empires, both fiercely set against the ideology of the *Enterprise*. In order to counteract the repressive attacks of the Klingons and Romulans, the *Enterprise* steals an advanced tactical military device ("The Enterprise Incident"), resists a probing of interstellar defenses ("Balance of Terror"), and repels Klingon interference in the development of a primitive culture ("A Private Little War").

Humanoid life forms that threaten to suppress or destroy man's independence include alien life forms from another galaxy ("Operation: Annihilate," "Catspaw," "By Any Other Name"); bizarre organisms that literally feed on human fear ("Wolf in the Fold"), hatred ("Day of the Dove"), and salt ("The Man Trap"); or deadly viruses ("The Naked Time," "Miri," "The Deadly Years").

Another exterior, hostile power, nonorganic in nature, consists of computers or computerlike devices ("The Changeling," "The Ultimate Computer," *Star Trek: The Motion Picture*); androids ("That Which Survives," "What Are Little Girls Made Of?," "I, Mudd"); and a devastating mechanical planet destroyer ("The Doomsday Machine"). These repressive nonorganic entities—generically classified as technology—reveal a very important Trek notion, namely that technology exists for man and not man for technology. Spock tells Kirk that computers make excellent and efficient servants, but adds that he has no desire to serve under one.

Technology, in other words, exists for the express purpose of promoting man's freedom. Any other reason is a gross aberration and ultimately results in the dehumanization of man. Star Trek does not tell us that technology is evil—attempts to reject technology and return to a more primitive form of existence are just as dehumanizing and foredoomed (e.g. "The Way to Eden")—but that technology is neutral in design, capable of either promoting or negating man's freedom. It is up to man to decide which of these it will be.

In addition to these organic and nonorganic external forces that threaten man's self-determination, Star Trek also presents an assorted array of situations that do the same. The best example occurs in episodes in which the *Enterprise* finds itself transported back into time ("City on the Edge of Forever," "Tomorrow Is Yesterday," "Assignment: Earth"), or into a parallel universe ("Mirror, Mirror," "The Tholian Web," "The Alternative Factor"). Unless these menacing situations can be surmounted by the return of the *Enterprise* crewmembers to their own time or universe, captivity or destruction will result.

The interior impediments to man's creation of self can also be subdivided into three classes: dark forces inherent to his being, a desire to be God, and attempts to exorcise an aspect of his humanity.

Concerning the first, various Star Trek episodes note that the dark, instinctual drives of humankind must be creatively and constructively sublimated lest they become a threat to freedom or continued existence. Kirk, Spock, McCoy, and others have stated that man "has inherent, violent tendencies"; is "a killer first, a builder second"; is "one of the new predator species, a species that preys even on itself"; has a "primitive self" that he keeps buried and dare not expose; and is cursed with having "a primitive and savage civilization, having "an innate Beast that will consume him," and being "inherently self-intolerant" and "essentially irrational." The dynamic energy and insatiable appetites of these instinctual drives are a constant threat to destroy man. Witness Star Trek's constant allusions to war: the Eugenics, nuclear, and bacterial wars of the late twentieth century and the genocidal war of the twenty-first; wars that had destroyed comparable civilizations on Cheron and Omega IV. We are "present" during the 1969 crisis in Earth history in which a nuclear war was averted only through the intervention of an agent of a superior alien race ("Assignment: Earth").

Despite the potency of man's instincts, in every instance Star Trek makes the point that he does not have to be a slave to them. As Kirk tells us, it is a simple decision—we are not going to kill today. Moreover, Star Trek also tells us that these forces, for all their destructive power, must not be eradicated, for they are an integral part of man's being. They must instead be transformed from impersonal, unknown forces into personal, known ones, thus enabling man to creatively displace them into constructive channels.

Nowhere in Star Trek is this more dramatically demonstrated than in "The Enemy Within." Because of the transporter malfunction, Kirk is transformed into two selves. One is his primal nature, free from all repression, discipline, and moral restraint, seeking only to fulfill its voracious appetites. It is the "dark, brutish aspect of human nature which every mortal carries within him from birth to the grave." The other self is Kirk's "lamb," his personality void of his primal nature—meek, mild, submissive. The former, for obvious reasons, is not fit to command. But neither is the latter, for Kirk's lamb, without his "wolf," is racked by doubt and indecision, his thoughts disjunct and disorganized. Kirk's task is that of integrating both aspects of his personality into a unified self—as must every human. As Dr. McCoy explains, "We need both parts. Compassion is reconciliation between them." Kirk is eventually restored to normal, but not before he has symbolically repaired the rift within himself by accepting the existence of the "wolf" and acknowledging it as a necessary part of his soul.

Another episode which strikingly demonstrates the necessity of bringing to light and rechanneling the dark urging of one's interior nature is "And the Children Shall Lead." In this story, a personification of pure evil—Gorgon—unleashes the Beast (or irrational fears) that lies buried within the depths of each person's psyche. These fears, if not suppressed or brought to consciousness, have the potential to destroy an individual. As Gorgon remarks, "In each of our enemies is the Beast which will consume him." The beast unleashed in Kirk, for example, is his fear of losing command of the *Enterprise*, a vessel with which he has established an intimate symbiotic relationship. With the help of Spock and with his own heroic strength of spirit, Kirk manages to overcome his fear and regain control of himself and of his ship. Once again he becomes the strong, resourceful commander that the crew looks to for guidance and strength.

A third instance of this confrontation with one's dark forces— Kirk is again the example—is in "Obsession." This episode depicts Kirk grappling with a guilt complex arising from an event that had occurred twelve years earlier only to be rekindled in the present story. The audience is placed inside Kirk's head, experiencing the pain of guilt and self-intolerance that threatens to devour him. "Hate of the self," quotes Spock, "always undeserved, will ultimately crush you." Eventually, Kirk's rationality, with the aid of Spock, McCoy, and the subsequent series of events, overcomes his obsessive guilt complex and he becomes his usual integrated self.

Other interior compulsions with which various individuals in Star Trek have had to contend include prejudice ("Let That Be Your Last Battlefield," "Balance of Terror"); jealousy ("Is There in Truth No Beauty?"); hatred ("Day of the Dove"); and self-doubt (*Star Trek: The Motion Picture*). In each of these cases, the inner compulsion—whether prejudice, jealousy, hatred, or self-doubt—must be brought to awareness and actively encountered. Only then will an individual have a chance of integrating these diverse drives into a unified self. The key in all of these examples is to transfer the energy of the dark interior powers—primal instincts, irrational fears, self-intolerance, or potentially destructive emotions—into creative, liberating channels.

The second instance in Star Trek in which interior obstacles hamper man's self-determination is an inordinate desire to be God. Two episodes dramatically demonstrate this. In "Return to Tomorrow," the *Enterprise* crew encounters the last three remaining members of a race destroyed by an unknown cataclysm; the essence of their minds—pure energy—trapped in translucent globes. Kirk, with his typically human pride, communicates with Sargon, leader of the survivors, about the catastrophe that they had loosed upon themselves: "Then perhaps your intelligence was deficient, Sargon. . . . We found the wisdom not to destroy ourselves."

Sargon replies, ". . . there comes to all races an ultimate crisis which you have yet to face. . . . The mind of man becomes so powerful he forgets he is man. He confuses himself with God."

This dream of becoming a godlike master race was the Arretians undoing. The temptations and responsibilities of that awesome power were simply too great for any individual or culture to bear.

In "Where No Man Has Gone Before," the *Enterprise* passes through the barrier at the edge of the galaxy, and the forces in it affect two crewmembers, Gary Mitchell and Dr. Elizabeth Dehner. Mitchell immediately (Dehner more slowly) begins to exhibit mental powers, the development of which is so great that within a month, speculates Spock, he will have as much in common with the *Enterprise* crewmembers as they have with white mice. At one point Mitchell says, "If I keep on growing, I'll be able to do things a god can do." And later, he tells Dehner, "You'll enjoy playing God." Unfortunately, Mitchell's wisdom didn't increase along with his psychic powers; he jokes about compassion and his soon-to-be-realized ability to squash Kirk like an insect. By gaining such powers, Mitchell has lost his "lamb," his capacity for compassion, and Kirk is eventually forced to destroy him. Thus Star Trek demonstrates that attainment of powers beyond the scope of one's wisdom and compassion enslave and destroy man, rather than liberate him, much less elevate him to "godhood."

This notion that "uncontrolled power turns even saints into savages" is a theme in many other episodes. It arises whenever the *Enterprise* crew encounter a life form that is superior or one that is inferior. An example of the former occurs in "Who Mourns for Adonais?" In this narrative Kirk and his people encounter the Greek god Apollo—literally. According to this episode, the Greek gods actually existed as quasi-gods who had the extraordinary ability to discharge, like an eel, an enormous amount of energy through their bodies. Now Apollo once again demands to be considered a god by the crew. In return for their love, loyalty, and worship, he will give them a "life as simple and pleasureful as it was those thousands of years ago on our beautiful Earth so far away." Apollo, however, despite his countless years of experience, lacks the wisdom to realize that mankind has outgrown him and is no longer able to supply that for which he so ravenously hungers. Hence he struggles to force the *Enterprise* crew to submit, eventually becoming a slave, then a victim, of his own awesome power. His power is eventually destroyed and he joins his fellow gods in their "home to the stars on the wind."

An example of Kirk and his people encountering a less-developed life form occurs in "Patterns of Force." A Federation cultural observer, John Gill, violates the Prime Directive and institutes a government based on Nazism over the internally fragmented society of planet Ekos. Gill believed that a Nazi state (he believed it was the most efficient state Earth ever knew) could accomplish efficiency without sadism. At first it worked beautifully, uniting the planet and speeding up evolution by several generations, but soon one of Gill's underlings staged a *coup d' état* and established a regime as brutal as Earth's Nazi state.

When Spock wonders how Gill, a brilliant and logical man, could make such a terrible mistake, Kirk answers that Gill failed to learn from history; that any man who holds that much power, even with the best of intentions, can't resist the urge to play God.

Consequently, Star Trek is telling us that man's will for power, his innate tendency toward self-aggrandizement, must be creatively channeled into appropriate outlets or evil will surely result. He must avoid his perpetual temptations to play God and lord it over his fellow human beings, allurements that only serve to enslave if not destroy him. Instead man must become ever more liberated, learning to actively and wisely actuate the full height, depth and breadth of his humanity.

Attempts to exorcise this humanity, the third internal obstruction to man's self-determination, is also subtly, yet forcibly, conveyed by Star Trek. The most visible example of this is seen in Mr. Spock. Audiences identify with Spock's ongoing internal battle: with the sense of pride that he experiences in being a Vulcan and in the logicality that is an integral part of his heritage; with the division and alienation that he encounters in having to live with his human half in an alien world of humans; with his attempts to suppress and even exterminate this emotive inheritance; and with the pain he feels in those instances when his emotions burst through.

Our sense of affinity with Mr. Spock—a symbol of man's efforts to control his instinctual yearnings—is further enhanced by the complete calm control that Spock constantly exudes. Since the majority of individuals experience the antithesis of this in their lives, the Vulcan way of life has a certain appeal. Perhaps logic is a solution to man's destructive tendencies. Perhaps the human race would be farther ahead if it were to suppress, if not eliminate, its emotional ancestry.

The full implication of this position is made manifest in *Star Trek: The Motion Picture*. At the beginning of this adventure we find Mr. Spock on Vulcan attempting to exorcise, through the ancient discipline of *Kolinahr*, his burdensome human half. During the final, most crucial part of the ritual, Spock feels his mind probed by the immeasurably powerful consciousness of V'Ger. Immediately, Spock perceives the threat that V'Ger poses to Earth. Consequently, his mind is bombarded with a torrential flood of emotions: fear that the Earth is in great danger, love for his human compatriots, and shame for having experienced these emotions. For during the arduous months of *Kolinahr*, Spock's emotions have not been slowly negated; instead they have merely hidden themselves, only to arise at a more opportune time. All is not lost, however, for in his brief contact with V'Ger, Spock detects an omniscient, incessant pattern of pure, unadulterated logic. Perhaps this is where his answer is to be found. Hence

Spock rejoins the *Enterprise*, deducing that a direct confrontation with V'Ger will be the final solution to his problem.

During the course of Spock's stay on the *Enterprise*, his initially cold aloofness and distaste at being around humans is slowly dispelled by the warm comradery of the other crew members. Eventually, the *Enterprise* encounters V'Ger and the final truth to Mr. Spock's difficulty is revealed.

In a violently disruptive mind meld with V'Ger, Spock learns that V'Ger is unable to feel, that it is a "barren" mind. It feels no joy, pain, or challenge; it has "less wisdom than a child."

Now the full implication of Spock's revelation can be seen: Any attempt on the part of man to eradicate the emotive aspect of his personality is doomed to failure. Such an endeavor is an aberration of one's humanity. As Leonard Nimoy said, "Lack of emotion is pathological; restraint is civilized. . . . Feelings and emotions can never and must never be replaced. We must never do away with man's humanity." For even if a person were to rid himself of his emotions, and then learn (as did V'Ger) all that is learnable, he nevertheless would be forced to say, "Is this all that I am? Is there not more?"

Such an endeavor, therefore, would not liberate man. Instead, it would condemn him to a never-ending battle with his own nature. Kirk realizes the hopelessness of such a task; he tells Spock, "Why fight so hard to be part of only one world? Why not fight instead to be the best of both?" Man, in other words, being an intellectual and emotional being, must judiciously cultivate both complementary aspects of his personality. Only in such a way will he open himself up to realize the freedom that is innately his and attain the fullness of his humanity.

Star Trek also uncovers another way in which man attempts to eradicate an essential aspect of his character. It is his efforts to advance his intellectual or spiritual faculties at the expense of his physical body. Even though Star Trek hypothesized that the most advanced life forms in the galaxy are pure thought or energy—the Organians, Triskelions, and Arretians are illustrative examples—the series also tells us that there is an inexpressible delight and joy in having a human body. Witness the Arretians' intense gaiety, despite their unimaginable evolutionary development, at temporarily entering the bodies of Kirk, Spock, and Anne Mulhall. It is the physical sensations that thrill them—breathing, the pumping of blood, touch. Such, Star Trek tells us, is the immeasurable joy of mankind's bodily gift—and the incalculable loss when the body is absent.

Similarly, the discovery of the body's heightened sensuality by highly sophisticated androids ("Requiem for Methuselah," "What Are Little Girls Made Of?"), by primitive cultures ("The Apple"), by aliens inhabiting human bodies ("Catspaw," "By Any Other Name"), and by Mr. Spock (*Star Trek: The Motion Picture*) also testifies to this notion. There is initially confusion as the newfound sensations evoke an ambiguous array of emotions. Soon, however, the confusion is accepted and the individual begins to enthusiastically embrace the unfathomable wealth of sensations and passions.

The danger of the cultivation of the intellect at the expense of the body is also revealed in several Star Trek episodes. Both "The Menagerie" and "The Gamesters of Triskelion" highlight this point. "Menagerie" deals with the inhabitants of Talos V, who, driven underground by a catastrophic war, concentrated solely on developing their mental powers. They discovered too late, however, that such powers were "a trap"; to their dismay, the Talosians found that dreams had become more important than reality, and they had given up creativity. In "Gamesters," the disembodied minds are continually bored, and turn to "gambling" on their gladiatorlike captives as their sole diversion. Kirk tells them, "A body is no good without a brain. But you've found that a brain isn't worth much without a body."

Once more the denial of an integral aspect of man's being—whether it be his emotions, his body, or his freedom—is forcibly demonstrated by Star Trek to be an aberration of who and what he is. It offers the enticing lure of a pseudo-life void of the hurts and heartaches caused by the emotions, or the pseudo-life of a disembodied intellect or paradisiacal existence. However, these powerful inducements are, in actuality, deadly traps. They shackle, enslave and destroy man, robbing him of his precious freedom.

Star Trek repeatedly tells us that man, to be whole, cannot deny any part of his self. His mind and body, his emotions and his intellect are all part of what makes him a man. Star Trek, in sharp contrast to the theory of dualism (the division of mind and body; the mind considered the primary aspect of man, the body merely tolerated), frequently emphasizes, even venerates, the bodily dimension of man's being. Thus, the mind and body together is seen as a wonderful organism that reflects the grandeur of the cosmos. There is a bipolar relationship between body and mind. Star Trek explicitly states this notion in Kirk's aforementioned statement to the Triskelions that a body isn't much good without a brain, but a brain isn't much good without a body. Kirk also remarks in "Spock's Brain" that "the body and the brain comprise a being." Moreover, the novelization of *Star*

Trek: The Motion Picture contains references to the sexual intercourse of the more sexually mature Deltan race, an experience that is not delegated solely to the physical but one in which mind and body are completely and intimately shared.

Mr. Spock's Vulcan heritage also supplies an insight into the unitary composition of man. Witness the intimate connection between mind and body which is displayed by Spock as he uses his mind to control intense bodily pain, to heal himself of severe internal injuries, and to go without food and sleep for weeks. Furthermore, there is his unique ability to perform the Vulcan mind meld, wherein two minds literally become one, each person sharing fully in the consciousness of the other. Its execution can be wholly accomplished only through the physical contact of the two parties.

Dr. McCoy likewise demonstrates this interconnectedness of mind and body in his holistic approach to medicine. For McCoy, both the body and the mind contain protective and rejuvenative mechanisms whose functions are inseparably bound, serving to complement and supplement one another.

There is also seen in Star Trek evidence of a bipolar relationship between man's intelligence and emotions as personified in the figures of Dr. McCoy, Mr. Spock, and Captain Kirk.

Dr. McCoy represents the emotive aspect of man. From his compassionate, sentimental handling of his patients to his wildly irrational outbursts, Dr. McCoy reveals the full gamut of man's affective tendencies.

Mr. Spock is the antithesis of McCoy in that he is a symbol of all that is rational in man: the keen precision of the intellect; the coolness and control of character; the stoic indifference to life's fascinating array of fluctuating events; the pristine logic with which problems are dealt.

As might be expected, these two opposing poles often come into conflict with one another, striking head-on with a resounding clash. (Nowhere is this more dramatically displayed than in the scene in "Bread and Circuses" in which Spock will not let McCoy thank him for saving his life.) Despite the apparent antagonism of these two poles, man cannot exist apart from either of them. The unappealing ramification of eradicating man's emotive aspect is the barrenness of V'Ger; the exorcism of man's intellectual dimension would be equally grave; man would be forced into an animallike existence completely at the mercy of his insatiable instinctual drives, much like the "evil Kirk" of "The Enemy Within."

Hence these two poles of emotion and intellect never exist

apart from one another but can only reciprocally coexist in the individual. This idea is personified in the figure of Captain Kirk, who combines the best of the two worlds—the Spockian rationality and the McCoyan emotionalism. The result is that he is able to transcend the limitations of each of his components and achieve a higher dimension of being, a notion supported by his role as captain of the *Enterprise*. Kirk himself offers an insight into this process of integration in "The Tholian Web" when, in a "posthumous" message, he advises Spock to not only temper his judgment with intuitive insight, but to seek and heed the advice of McCoy.

Kirk's emotive aspect manifests itself in a variety of ways: the vibrant radiance of his spirited personality, his passionate love of life, the intense loyalty and devotion he extends to each crewmember, the exuberance with which he approaches his captaincy, and the intimate symbiotic relationship he has acquired with his vessel.

The intellectual bent of Kirk is revealed primarily in his awareness of the weighty duties and responsibilities that being a starship captain entails, in the detachment he strives to bring to taking a decisive course of action, and in the adroitness with which he points out the logical fallacies in the programming of sophisticated computers such as Landru, M-5, and Nomad.

The key task for Captain Kirk, then, is to ensure a harmonious balance between the two aspects of his being so that he doesn't lapse into an undue emotional state such as guilt ("Obsession"), vengeance ("The Conscience of the King"), or personal ambition (*Star Trek: The Motion Picture*); or into the sterile intellectualism of the logical and harsh "commander." A slippage into either extreme, emotionalism or intellectualism, hinders the efficiency with which Kirk meets the duties and responsibilities of his captaincy. Thus Kirk's intellect must serve to temper the dynamic energy of his emotions, creatively channeling them into decisive, forceful action, while his passions vitalize an otherwise barren intellect.

Man, Star Trek therefore tells us, is like a magnet: He exists as a structural tension held together by a polarity of his parts. Just as a magnet cannot exist apart from either of its poles so, too, man cannot exist apart from either part of his nature.

This identity-in-difference or integrated diversity of man's composition is symbolized by the Vulcan philosophy of IDIC—the greatest joy of creation is in the infinite ways that infinitely diverse things can join together to create meaning and beauty. So too, Star Trek tells us, can the dual natures of man cojoin in an infinite variety of ways to create the beauty and meaning of an individual person.

We now turn to Star Trek's response to the question posed by philosopher John Donne, "If I must someday die, what can I do to satisfy my desire to live?" The reply to this fundamental question, according to Donne, establishes the flavoring of a given civilization. The Star Trek response to this question is that of exploration and discovery. That is, if man must someday die, he satisfies his desire to live by first exploring the height, depth, and breadth of both the cosmos and his own personality. This theme of exploration is revealed in the prologue that heads each episode of Star Trek. This is precisely what the *Enterprise* does. With space as its final outward frontier it explores strange new worlds: worlds that approximate Earth-Mars conditions or worlds that are barren wastelands; worlds that are virtual gardens of Eden or worlds that only appear to be such; worlds whose sun is about to supernova or worlds whose birth was in the not too distant past. The list is endless. And on these planets new life and new civilizations are encountered; organic-nonorganic; humanoid-nonhumanoid; hostile-benign; representing the entire evolutionary ladder. Moreover, the *Enterprise* goes where no man has gone before, traveling beyond the edge of the galaxy, back into time or into parallel universes.

In addition to this outward exploration there is a corresponding inward one, an investigation that depicts the richness and fullness of man's long, arduous development—past, present, future. He is seen in the innocence and naiveness of his childhood ("The Apple," "The Paradise Syndrome"); in the inner fragmentation and destructiveness of his adolescent years—a time period corresponding to our present day and age ("Assignment: Earth," "A Taste of Armageddon," "Space Seed"); in the growing maturity of his young adulthood—typified by the twenty-third century in which the Star Trek epic takes place; and in the wisdom of old age, where it is speculated man will be at the height of his evolutionary development, existing as pure thought or energy ("Return to Tomorrow," "Errand of Mercy").

During the course of this evolution, man is seen at his best— and worst. He is portrayed as a brutal, sadistic beast full of lies, hate, and prejudice, capable of deadly destruction and selfannihilation; and, yet, he is also a kind, merciful being capable of feats of great compassion and benevolence. He is able to accomplish great intellectual achievements, yet reveals the full range of human emotions. He has the ability to revert to his animalistic heritage or to become fully human and, hence, fully divine. The point is that Star Trek explores the full dimension of both man's other and inner world, of space, the final frontier, and the diversity of his own infinite potentialities.

It is these fundamental human themes that are implicitly unveiled in the Star Trek mythos—man's self-determination, his unity of being, and his response to the question of death are reflected in all our lives. Star Trek is communication of a legacy, a legacy of faith, hope, and love in and for man, in and for the cosmos with which he is so inseparably intertwined. As Stephen Whitfield said in "The Making of Star Trek":

"Whither Star Trek? It doesn't really matter. We have its legacy . . . all we have to do is use it."

THREE

by Diane Webster

When Diane Webster submitted three short articles in one batch, we quite enjoyed all of them, but regretfully decided to reject all of them because they were too short for our needs. Then G.B. had one of his brainstorms: Why not publish all three as one article under one banner? Why not indeed?

On Understanding Non-Trekkers

You are in the middle of one of your very favorite Star Trek books and a friend of yours asks what you're reading. "Star Trek," you reply. "Star what?" your friend asks.

The little scenario above has happened to me many times. It can happen at any time or any place, and not just with books, either. It can happen with T-shirts or anything else that deals with Star Trek.

We Trekkers aren't quite as isolated as we used to be; there are more of us than ever before. But there still is a fraction of the population that truly does not know what Star Trek is. I've spent the past couple of years trying to tell such people about the most important concepts of Star Trek, hoping that they would see what an important idea Star Trek is. But that, of course, did not work. Lately, just repeating my original statement of "Star Trek" while smiling rather indulgently at the blank look on their faces is all I do. Every once in a while, though, I get the surprise of my life when the person I just said that to asks, "Oh, you mean with Captain Kirk and Mr. Spock? I like that show myself." A pleasant surprise to be sure, but a surprise nevertheless.

In order to understand non-Trekkers you must first put yourself in their place—not an easy task, to be sure, but one must try. First, think of a television show that you do not like, or have never been interested in enough to even try watching. Why don't you care for that particular show? Perhaps it has a main theme that you do not like, or you consider it stupid and nonstimulating or nonentertaining. As many reasons as you can think of for not watching a particular television show, there is probably someone out there thinking of the same reasons not to watch Star Trek. Well, that's fine, but what about people who make statements about Star Trek that just aren't true?

These people are much harder to explain, but I shall do my best. First of all, there are people who say that there is only one storyline to Star Trek. This probably came closest to being true during the third season, but despite the third season's flops, even it had some very good episodes—shows that challenged you to accept new concepts and new ideas; and with a little bit of work, even the worst of these third-season shows could be improved. Then there are those who claim that the actors and actresses on Star Trek are not up to par, that they simply can't act. Since we all know how wrong these people are, we can only assume they have never watched the show and are repeating criticism they've read or heard.

We know that critics are among those who are definitely non-Trekkers. Well, most critics don't like most television shows, and nine times out of ten, the shows they do like, none of us would watch on a bet.

So as you can see, a great many of the non-Trekkers that you meet can be explained, if not altogether excused. In my opinion, the best way to deal with the people described in this article is to just smile a lot and remember IDIC!

The Care and Feeding of Your Favorite Trekker

I sometimes think that a care and maintenance manual should come with Trekkers. We are a breed set apart, and I have met very few people that are fans of Star Trek who are average. They have special qualities and interests that make them different from your average human. This sometimes makes our family and friends uncomfortable, as they don't always understand how we can take "just a television show" so seriously.

For instance, we all believe in basic humanity, and because of the IDIC concept we believe in a basic "to each his own" philosophy. We strive to understand, and change for the good as individuals. We believe in friendship as represented in Star Trek: that people can be friends, no matter what their race or religion or sex or even interests. Of course, having a common ground, such as work or school, helps, but it is not always necessary.

I have found being the only Trekker in a one-Trekker household difficult at times. Even my very tolerant family doesn't always understand my "obsession," as they call it. If you too live in a one-Trekker household, or if your friends and co-workers don't understand your love for the Star Trek family, here are some procedures which you should instruct the non-Trekkers in your household to follow in case of an emergency:

Star Trek, being a syndicated show, isn't always available in all parts of the country at all times. (If it were not for the miracle of cable television, I wouldn't be able to watch it myself.) Therefore, after long periods of not being able to view this favorite show, the Trekker you are concerned about may suffer from withdrawal symptoms. The symptoms vary from person to person, but overall involve periods of irritability, frantic switching of channels (caused by trying to find something "good" to watch), staring glassy-eyed at a blank television screen, and a tendency to discuss nothing but any and all aspects of Star Trek. When the person you are concerned about reaches this final stage, it is absolutely essential that you get some form of Star Trek into her immediately, if for no other reason than your own sanity (if you are not a fan of Star Trek). If you can find a channel someplace that is playing Star Trek, get her to it; if not, put a paperback or any other ST-related material into her hand and make her look at it.

Be encouraged, however, by the fact that most Star Trek fans recognize the beginning symptoms of withdrawal and make an effort to cure themselves before it gets this bad. But be careful not to get caught with your guard down, as some Trekkers in withdrawal may become violent.

Christine Chapel's Early Life

Christine Chapel was the second child born to Christopher and Ann Chapel, who lived in the Delta region within Federation territory. Christopher was a diplomat with the Starfleet Diplomatic Corps; Ann was a research scientist in Starfleet. Most of their professional lives had been spent based somewhere within the Delta system, and over the years, they had urged many of their relatives to move to the system and join them. The Chapels were a close-knit family; the more of them that were gathered in one place, the better they liked it.

Christine's only sibling, a sister, Adrianna, had been born

thirteen years before. Adrianna was somewhat of a disappointment to her parents. Despite the fact that in her own way she was quite pretty, and very intelligent, especially in science and mathematics, she was a loner and seemingly emotionless. Her fellow students, erroneously considering her to be stuck-up and resenting the fact that she usually finished first in any competition or test, gave her the nickname "Number One." This so distressed Adrianna that she became even more reclusive and unresponsive. The arrival of Christine about this time, and the attention their parents gave the new baby, made things even worse. This display of emotional problems naturally very nearly broke Ann's and Christopher's hearts; to have their child become distant and cold was almost unbearable.

Being reasonable people, however, they gave her what love and affection they could and hoped that she would grow out of it. Feeling that in Christine they had been given another chance, the baby soon became the apple of both parents' eyes.

As soon as she could, Adrianna applied for and was granted admission to Starfleet Academy. Although they were sorry to see her leave, Christopher and Ann could then devote their entire energies to raising the "little princess," as Christopher called the now five-year-old Christine.

The following summer, Ann took Christine on a visit to her parents' farm. Enthralled by the farm animals, Christine soon became attached to a small dog which followed her everywhere. One day the dog was stepped on by a horse and badly injured. For the first time Christine's latent medical talents became evident. With only a little help from her grandfather, she nursed the little dog back to health. To everyone's relief, the dog fully recovered; her mother had been worried about Christine's reaction if it hadn't.

As time went by, Christine's natural medical ability became more and more evident. Fearing that she too would develop emotional problems should she not be allowed to follow her natural abilities and instincts, her parents fully supported her, encouraging her to study the scientific subjects needed for a medical profession. As her talents and gifts and interests were wide-reaching, it was soon obvious that Christine would make an excellent doctor or xenobiologist or researcher or do well in any one of a number of professional positions. But Christine came to feel that by becoming a nurse, she could best serve herself and the medical profession, for a good, well-educated nurse was expert in many fields and as valuable as a doctor in many situations.

One of her professors in school was Dr. Roger Korby; he recognized Christine as one of the best and most promising students that he had taught in a long time. Feeling that she would waste her abilities as a regular nurse, he urged her to join his research staff after graduation. She agreed and added the necessary courses in bioresearch to her schedule.

In the weeks following Christine's addition to Korby's staff, her natural ability and technical training quickly won her the respect of Korby and her fellow workers. As months passed, Christine found herself falling in love with Korby. Upset that she was breaking one of the strictest rules of nursing—not to become emotionally involved with superiors or patients—Christine told Korby she wanted to quit. When he forced her to tell him why, he admitted that he was in love with her as well. The question of ethics need not bother them, for he revealed that he was planning to quit his practice and join an exobiology research team leaving for Exo II. Christine begged to go along, but he refused, saying it was too dangerous and that he needed her to help complete his research here. They became engaged, and shortly thereafter Roger left.

Even though Christine sometimes felt that perhaps she and Roger hadn't gotten to know each other well enough before becoming engaged, his letters were warm and reassuring, and she remained content as long as she heard from him regularly. Before long, however, she stopped hearing from him, and soon news came that his expedition had been lost. Determined to search for him, Christine decided the best way to get to deep space was to join Starfleet. Her excellent credentials, and the ever-present shortage of nurses, got her a commission, and after a quick refresher course in space medicine, she was assigned to the *Starstalker*, designed by Montgomery Scott and commanded by James T. Kirk. When the success of the trial runs got Kirk command of the *Hua C'hing*, Christine asked to accompany him, as she felt her chances of getting to Exo II would be better on a starship. Similarly, she followed Kirk to his command of the *Enterprise*. (During the time she served with Kirk, Christine continued her studies and eventually gained several more degrees, including one as a Doctor of Research Sciences.)

It was on the *Enterprise* that Christine's life was to take the most drastic turn of all: She fell in love with the half-Vulcan science officer, Mr. Spock. She fought against her feelings, however—not only did she feel she was being unfaithful to Roger, she knew that there was little hope for any kind of relationship with Spock. Still, she couldn't help being attracted to him, and she was quite unhappy.

When the *Enterprise* discovered Roger Korby alive on Exo II, Christine felt that she could now revive her feelings for Roger and forget Spock—she could quit Starfleet, get married, be happy. But the revelation of the tragic circumstances of Korby's survival shattered Christine's hopes. When the android Korby destroyed himself, Christine finally allowed herself to admit that she was in love with Spock, even though, once again, consummation of her love seemed hopeless. Too, she had, almost without realizing it, built a satisfying career for herself in Starfleet, as well as a satisfying relationship with Dr. Leonard McCoy.

Somewhat to her surprise, Christine Chapel discovered that the *Enterprise* was now her home, and the members of its crew her family. To no one's surprise (except perhaps her own) she decided to stay aboard, where she became one of the most popular and respected members of the "best crew in Starfleet."

INDIANA SKYWALKER MEETS THE SON of STAR TREK

by Kyle Holland

Not everyone liked Star Trek II: The Wrath of Khan. *In fact, a number of our readers expressed extreme dislike for the film, for a wide range of reasons. In the following article, Kyle Holland explains why he didn't care for* Wrath of Khan *as a Star Trek story; he further examines factors underlying the film and its success which he feels do not bode well for the future of Star Trek. Is he right? Judge for yourself.*

Movie reviewers, television reviewers, and Star Trek fans seem to be in general agreement: *The Wrath of Khan* successfully translated Star Trek to the big screen, just as it predecessor, *Star Trek: The Motion Picture,* failed to do so. In conventional terms, *Wrath of Khan* is certainly a better "movie" than *STTMP*. But the spirit of Star Trek has always been to keep ahead of convention (suffering a bit for doing so, if necessary) and to pave the way for new and better standards. If one follows such logic, then *Star Trek: The Motion Picture* was a more authentic contribution to the shaping of Star Trek than was *Wrath of Khan*.

Wrath of Khan has a dramatic structure calculated to please the masses: An insane, bloodthirsty menace of a man has vowed his vengeance upon the good crew, and you may be sure that there will be plenty of torpedos and flying guts before Good triumphs. *STTMP* offered no such dramatic handle to the viewer. If you weren't content to experience the journey toward, near annihilation by, and ultimate reconciliation with V'Ger, you didn't get your money's worth. This is why so many have commented that *STTMP* improves with multiple viewings: You watch it for a second time (or more) only if you are willing to experience it. You are open in a way that few who watch the film for the first time are.

Star Trek: The Motion Picture can best be appreciated by repeated viewings. *Wrath of Khan*, on the other hand, is a shoot-'em-up in the style of *Star Wars* and *Raiders of the Lost Ark*—very thrilling the first time you see it, but not much left for a second viewing. In essence, *Wrath of Khan* is indeed a "movie," relying on suspense, which is exhausted once the action is run through. *STTMP*, on the other hand, is a film novel, revealing new patterns and nuances, new poetry, as it becomes more familiar.

If, as the Star Trek constituency, we claim to cultivate a sense of the future, we *must* recognize *Wrath of Khan* as part of a contemporary phenomenon—the one-time, pay-for-thrills motion-picture show—that cannot last. In future, films will be integrated into home technologies as disks, cassettes, etc. and will be purchased on the basis of their multiple-viewing merits. Under these standards, *STTMP* will easily qualify for inclusion in home libraries; it will, in its way, be a forerunner of future "good movies." This is the Star Trek tradition.

Beyond the sheer commercialism it embodies, the structure of *Wrath of Khan* raises philosophical questions to which we should be sensitive. The format is ironclad: Khan is evil, pure evil, and cannot be redeemed. Now just think back over all seventy-eight television episodes, and even the professional and fan fiction. When did you see a villain like this? An antagonist with whom meaningful communication is impossible, whose viewpoint cannot be comprehended by the *Enterprise* crew (or vice versa), an antagonist who can never be enlightened and with whom there can be no rapprochement, or even a truce? There was no villain like this in the series, but Khan is like this in the movie, because the premise of the plot would collapse if he were not. This is the first Star Trek in which there is a real alien: Khan himself.

The dramatic structure of *Star Trek: The Motion Picture* is purely within the developmental trends established by the series—so much so that many have repudiated it as a rehash of "The Changeling." Decrying the allusiveness of the film is something like giving demerits to Tolstoy or Faulkner because some of their novels depended upon characters or plot lines (or even whole passages) from earlier short stories. The themes of mistaken identities and intentions, evolution in both human and nonhuman spectra, and the longing for identity through confrontation with one's creator are central Star Trek themes, and we should consider them seriously whenever they are offered to us. "The Changeling" was indeed the sketch upon which the "novel"

Star Trek: The Motion Picture was based, and that sums up the relationship between the two.

Many, many people (including Leonard Nimoy) have said that there is more of "the characters" in *Wrath of Khan*. Nimoy's comments clearly were directed toward the *potential* movie in the unedited footage, which did indeed include characteristic exchanges; much of this was ultimately edited out, since as an action film *Wrath of Khan* could not afford to linger over the development of characters who should, ideally, be interchangeable with Luke Skywalker and Indiana Jones. What about the movie to which we now have access? In peculiar ways, real violence was done to the characters. As the old proverb says, you should be wary of wishes, for they may come true. . . . If you want a lot of "the characters" in a movie, you should be prepared for things to happen to them.

On television, when things happened to characters, it usually meant that they were hurt or captured, worried over, then rescued or healed; or they were struck dead, mourned, then revived. Deep emotional experiences were usually caused by aberrant conditions of one sort or another—meaningful enough while they lasted, but you knew that by next episode all traces of trauma would be gone. For all that, the series was not shallow for a very fundamental reason: Each character had a set of built-in and unresolvable conflicts which both animated and limited his or her actions, regardless of plot. These inner dynamics, it must be recognized, were primarily crafted by the actors themselves, with cooperation from Roddenberry and Fontana. One can only admire the stamina of this group in attempting (often without success) to fend off the attacks of bad writing which plagued the series. In the end, they won: After many bizarre diversions, the characters they created stood as vivid, integrated, and consistent.

A movie, even a Star Trek movie, cannot consist of two hours of injuries, rescues, fistfights, resurrections, and counterlogical assaults on arrogant computers; and if you want something to "happen" to the characters, it has to be something that will not wear off in five minutes, and—one hopes—that is consistent with the characterization itself.

Before discussing each film's handling of five pivotal Star Trek "characters"—the Federation, the *Enterprise*, Kirk, Spock, and McCoy—it must be noted that we are not told the chronological relationship between the two films. In real time, there was about a ten-year lapse between the last television episode and *STTMP*, although we are informed that the events of the film take place (almost unbelievably) about two years after the

Enterprise's return from its "five-year-mission." *Wrath of Khan* followed about two years later in real time, and *Star Trek III* is apparently scheduled to follow about two years after that. But (reasons to be discussed) internal evidence suggests that the events of *Wrath of Khan* happen at least five years, perhaps more, after the events of *STTMP*.

The Federation

This was a valid presence in the series. With its Prime Directive and the *Enterprise*'s peaceful mission of exploration (Kirk explained patiently to Garth that he was no longer a combatant, but now an "explorer"), its purposes were clear. But there was not only idealism behind the Federation's nonmilitaristic attitude. We saw many instances in which the amicable reputation of the Federation brought it lucrative trading contracts or access to natural resources (usually at the expense of the aggressive Klingons); in addition, this policy seems to have been the key to political stability. Think of Kirk's lecture to Spock-2 on the longevity of the Empire (several hundred years) compared to that of the Federation (several thousand years).

We recognized the ranks and uniforms (casual togs, unsuitable for combat, certainly), and we knew something of Federation procedures. We knew, too, that they could fight, and fight effectively—but only if and when other alternatives did not exist.

It is not very surprising that in *Star Trek: The Motion Picture* this Federation is headquartered in a very beautiful San Francisco. We get glimpses of its shuttle platforms and logos, and its staff bustling about; we find out that Star Fleet Command is headed by Admiral Nogura, who is apparently a tough guy (in the novelization of *STTMP* he is actually exploitive of Kirk—for the greater good, of course). Basically, we see the Federation going about the business we expect of it, and the physical details are pleasing and familiar.

By the time of *Wrath of Khan*, it appears that the Federation has been overwhelmed and drastically altered by some cataclysm—possibly revolution. The jumpsuits of *STTMP* are replaced by highly militaristic get-ups; if they had high bearskin hats they would look exactly like the guardsmen at Buckingham Palace. You can hear the psychological sabers rattling when they walk. The only aspect of training we glimpse is a simulated battle scenario, and the grimness with which it is taken by both Kirk and Saavik suggests that this is not a peripheral aspect of the curriculum. The assertion that Kirk underwent the same simulation as a cadet is intended to suggest that this is part of Federation tradition. But the actors have wisely suggested that in earlier days *Kobayashi Maru* could hardly have had the same significance: The gleeful mugging of Sulu and McCoy as they "die," together with Kirk's reluctance to admit that he "passed" the test by cheating, assure us that the test is a bigger deal now than when they were young. We also have to swallow the extraordinary attitude of the scientists of Regula I toward the Federation. Carol Marcus, for her own reasons, is merely less than confident that the Federation will not corrupt Genesis into a weapon; the rest of her team are frankly suspicious, and her son openly paranoid. Is this the way the scientists of Memory Alpha felt?

The Enterprise

The transformation of an inanimate (in fact, nonexistent inanimate) object into a living presence was a special achievement of *STTMP*. The long approach of Scott and Kirk to the ship in the shuttle was a crucial step in this transformation, and this sequence may be taken as a study in the creative application of modern special-effects technology: The intent is not to startle, frighten, or thrill the viewer, but to create a reality that did not exist before. The effect is reinforced in the many flank and distance shots of the ship in transport, in jeopardy, in release. The interior of the ship is believable. Clearly, the *Enterprise* has undergone some interior redecoration since its return. Its pale blues are suitable for extended habitation—much more so than the reds and oranges that were part of the old decor. The officer's quarters are efficient but not spartan—very much in the style of the voyaging *Enterprise*, but more moody, comfortable. Indeed, like a living entity (the *very* "living machine" that V'Ger considers it to be), the *Enterprise* has a mood of its own, a patient, contemplative, yet inquiring spirit.

In *Wrath of Khan*, the *Enterprise* has become, for all practical purposes, a battleship. The sickbay is no longer a chamber of wonder and discovery; it is full of bloody boys, many dying. Now the site of ship detail is the torpedo run (in a bit of heavy-handed theme-mongering, we are forced to note that Spock's coffin is actually one of these instruments of death). Kirk's quarters are fitted with oak and antique weapons as befits a man of war; in fact it is merely because of the threat of combat that he has assumed command of the ship. And in its visual representation, the *Enterprise* has no independent existence. It is merely a part of the battle panorama, dodging, shooting and rolling.

Kirk.

We used to know Kirk. He was that prickly individual always trying to overcome his temper, that physical guy trying to become gentle, that fighter trying to become peaceful, an infant trying to become wise. Enlightenment and backsliding were the constants of his experience, since, as he was proud of saying, he was "human." Love and companionship he viewed as necessary to life, but unattainable in their absolute forms; when he and Spock nodded to each other at the end of "The Naked Time," their meaning was clear enough. And finally Kirk was the victim of that peculiar emotional projection whereby the *Enterprise* became the symbol of his own origin and his own destiny.

This Kirk fits very naturally into *Star Trek: The Motion Picture*. Two years behind a desk, a pawn of the Admiralty, has made him childishly ruthless in his determination to "get back" the *Enterprise*; his claim that it is merely the exigencies of the moment which prompt him to assume command fools no one. His return to the *Enterprise* is the first of the "capturing God" coils in the film's complex structure. Slowly he learns to handle the ship and himself. With his old stubbornness he tries to reassume his role as human sounding board to Spock. Above all, we recognize him for his openness to V'Ger and his fearlessness, his confidence in the success of communication and compassion when approaching it.

Shatner's splendid performance in *Wrath of Khan* is the only means of recognizing the erstwhile captain. Somehow, he has again given up the *Enterprise* (Spock tells him bluntly that for him to do other than command the ship is a "waste"—apparently he saw *STTMP*, which is more than can be said for Admiral Kirk). He has no passion for getting her back; he seems to spend a lot of time mooning around his apartment, where he is told by McCoy (who also saw *STTMP*) to get back his command. This Kirk is marvelously blasé and mature. He doesn't stop himself on the verge of temper outbursts, he doesn't muse aloud about how much wiser he is now than he was an hour ago. He doesn't look for and try to cultivate evidences of warmth and communicativeness in Spock, he doesn't have any eyeballing sessions with McCoy. We are told, as if this were a new "fact," that this Kirk is still incomplete, but what is this mysterious something he is missing? Why, a wife and child, of course, who are promptly produced (literally out of thin air), providing him with new (and boring) preoccupations. It is probably because of these new problems that Kirk gives not a moment's consideration to the misfortunes (for which he was indeed partly responsible) that drove the egomaniacal Khan to madness.

Spock

He is, of course, the center of *Star Trek: The Motion Picture*, and those who claim that they can't get enough of "the characters" from the movie should consider this. When McCoy says, only half sarcastically, "Lucky for you we just happen to be going your way," he is speaking for all of us; the search for V'Ger is Spock's own. The visual subtlety and power of the *Enterprise* interiors are, it may be suggested, inspired by Spock and the relationship of the physical journey of the ship to Spock's spiritual journey. The view of Vulcan included early in the film is fully consistent with the series, yet surpasses anything we have seen. And the Vulcan scenes contribute to the integrity of the film as a freestanding entity, establishing Spock's condition at the beginning of his search, and the nature of his calling. The brittle Spock who appears on the *Enterprise* bridge is more complex than any Spock we have met before, yet fully recognizable; he is fresh from a major disappointment, a failure (of the sort only Spock could experience), and this is indeed how he should behave. The discussion with Kirk and McCoy is authentic Star Trek: Spock's unexpressed (but evident) anguish, McCoy's baiting sarcasm, Kirk's willingness (and inability) to understand, his resentment of rebuff, his tenacious loyalty. This scene is right. The same can be said, surprisingly, of the sickbay scene. Think of creating a scene in which Spock is supposed to squeeze Kirk's hand, profess that this "simple feeling" (of what? hand-squeezing? human contact? friendship? love?) is superior to anything else in the whole universe. Suppose you hadn't seen it, you just had to create it, and it had better not be soppy or bizarre, or invite whistles from the audience. It would not be easy—unless you left the execution to the instincts of the creators and actors of Star Trek. And this scene works, against all odds. It is something that happens to Spock; and if you didn't think it showed, you missed the warm, meaningful looks he was giving his friend, the wisdoms he was speaking about V'Ger (himself), the new directness of his speech.

You probably missed them in *Wrath of Khan* too, because they weren't there. The emotional premises of *Wrath of Khan* are not clear. Both Spock and McCoy apparently decided to stay with Starfleet (why?). Only Spock, it seems, is actually attached to the *Enterprise* under normal conditions. Nevertheless it appears that the three are used to spending time together, possibly even seeing each other on a daily basis. Kirk does not take the wry pleasure in the Spock-McCoy debate that he would after a separation—he just considers it annoying and cuts it off. They are three old friends who know each other thoroughly. And this is as it must be, since this movie will not allow a drama to develop among the three, as did *Star Trek: The Motion Picture*. Kirk's drama is to come from the materialization of an old lover and a son. Spock's is to come from a heroic death.

The treatment of Spock in *Wrath of Khan* is so insipid that it is actually insulting to the audience. Those who are not familiar with Star Trek must wonder who the guy with the funny ears is; those who *are* familiar with Star Trek must also wonder who the guy with the funny ears is. Fortunately it is common cultural knowledge that he is half-human, half-Vulcan—you won't find this out in the film. Since we must surmise that he is in daily contact with Kirk, meaningful stares would probably be out of place, but why should Spock act like a cold fish? During the five-year mission, Spock at his Vulcan worst was never like this; in fact, the Spock who got off the *Surak* and fixed the *Enterprise* engines in *STTMP* was considerably more soulful. We can only conclude that the revolution which militarized the Federation has left Spock drained of enthusiasm for life.

No wonder! For the first time, Nimoy has been miscast as Spock. Spock, a scientist whose previous experiences as a commander so often came near to disaster, is now inexplicably commander of the *Enterprise*. Spock, with his respect for authority, has now *become* the authority, as commander and teacher—no duller prospect could loom for the character's creator. The mentor/student, father/daughter relationship with Saavik is not believable: The last we saw of Spock, he was still an emotional child, and said so. In fact, it is part of his destiny to always be an emotional child, but to keep up with Kirk he is supposed to assume the role of "parent." In total, the film allowed Spock exactly one authentic word (as opposed to whole scenes in *Star Trek: The Motion Picture*): On his way to the reactor room, Spock short-circuited McCoy's objections with a nerve pinch and, lowering him, touched his temple for mental contact, saying, "Remember." For about twenty seconds, we see Star Trek: First the nerve pinch (beggars can't be choosers), Nimoy's own creation, then the one-word (and rather effective) allusion to the tag scenes from "Requiem for Methuselah." We are not surprised to discover that even this meager offering was not in the original script.

McCoy

Supporting actors can hardly be inconsistent, and since the doctor is only allowed to support, we recognize him always and everywhere. But as a support, his role fluctuates according to what is happening to Kirk and Spock. In *Star Trek: The Motion Picture*, the man shines. He has left the Federation—that sounds right—and he has been "drafted" back. His objections are all authentic; we don't have to hear the explanations to believe it. His blunt talk to Kirk about his *Enterprise* complex pushes us several steps forward; we couldn't go on the way we were, and this is the first time Kirk's problem has been stated out loud for him. For Spock, the doctor does as much as he ever could—a little effusion, a little sarcasm, a little huffing and puffing, and a lot of waiting. If things are "happening" to Kirk and Spock, as they are in *STTMP*, McCoy must be there.

Only the artificial and ridiculous happens to the two in *Wrath of Khan*; inside them there are no events, and so the doctor is just hanging around. Why is he mucking about with the command crew in the *Kobayashi Maru*? Why is he standing around on the bridge or on the Genesis Planet, hands behind his back? Nothing to do. Nobody to talk to. When the doctor has nothing to say, you know you are far from the heart of Star Trek.

Wrath of Khan is an entertaining movie masquerading as a Star Trek adventure. "Space Seed" was pillaged of the Khan character to create a facade of continuity; the earlier Khan was much more interesting than the devil (no offense to Milton) we are confronted with in the movie. The Star Trek figures, as scripted, are unrecognizable. How did this happen?

One could point to individuals; producers and writers with other than the best integrity of the entire Star Trek phenomenon at heart; a director who, in his novels, has been doing for years to Sherlock Holmes what he is commencing to do to Star Trek; and so on. But these people are only doing what they are supposed to do: make popular movies—and *Wrath of Khan* was a *very* popular movie.

The real problem, perhaps, is that we have not recognized that Star Trek has taken on a bilevel existence, and we must develop bilevel standards of appreciation. Space movies and action movies are the current trend. What smarter move could there be than to make a popular space movie based upon cult heroes who have a broad and enduring constituency? You'll grab the best from both worlds. If, in the process, you maul, distort, and kill those very heroes—so what? The object is to sell tickets. It will never be in the spirit of Star Trek to wish for a closed, esoteric stratum into which popular and commercial values do not enter; on the other hand, let's recognize the cynicism of *Wrath of Khan* for what it is. It is a kind of parallel universe, not our own.

The final argument for this point is the overall visual treatment of the figures in the two films. Remember that in two years they couldn't have changed all that much. In *Star Trek: The Motion Picture*, the pale hues of the ship and the uniforms serve to emphasize the human presence. Faces are as important here as they were in the series. You see people when they speak, you understand more than their words. The camera was interested in the beauty of the individual faces and figures: Kirk standing still as the tinted door of the briefing room drew closed before him; the trim doctor in full beard; Spock telling with childlike intensity of his Vulcan contact with V'Ger. The crew has reached a point of mature beauty to which the camera is open and sensitive, and these images are themselves an advancement of the legend.

Compare this to the brutal lighting schemes of *Wrath of Khan*. The bridge of the *Enterprise* is bathed in an ugly red haze (a cheap and convenient solution to the perennial problems of screen visibility), and everybody on it looks ninety-two and unshaven (women included). The ravages inflicted upon the images of the "heroes" themselves were not, obviously, a major consideration. The same can be said for the uniforms. They have a certain dash. Unfortunately they also make Spock look extra-gangly and Kirk extra-dumpy. Not important. Add to this the terrible chopping of Spock's hair and the conclusion is inevitable: No respect for these characters as characters was operating here. If, in the overall interests of a flashy production, the heroes had to be uglified, so be it.

The Wrath of Khan notwithstanding, the human adventure is still just beginning.

THE TRUTH
ABOUT TRIBBLES

by J. Matthew Kennedy

Everybody loves Tribbles. Who wouldn't? But, like Uhura in that famous episode, if they're going to be dissected, we don't want to know about it. New contributor J. Matthew Kennedy has managed the operation in a way that is entertaining and educational—and guaranteed to be bloodless.

The Tribble, "the sweetest creature known to man," is also a misunderstood one.

Tribbles have appeared in two Star Trek episodes written by David Gerrold: *The Trouble with Tribbles* and the animated episode *More Tribbles, More Troubles*. Although Tribbles appeared in only these two shows, they hold a special place in Star Trek fandom. Yet little effort has gone into trying to understand these small fuzzy creatures.

Perhaps the greatest fallacy most fans commit is to consider the Tribble a simple parasite, living off of the generosity of humans. In truth, the Tribble is a highly developed mammal which evolved in response to the conditions and stresses placed upon it by its native ecology, and it occupies a specific niche in that ecological community. But what sort of role does the Tribble play in the ecology of its homeworld? In what kind of environment did the Tribble evolve?

In neither of the two episodes nor in the related literature were we shown the Tribbles' homeworld or given a description of it. Even without such description, however, it is possible to theorize the Tribble's life cycle by using observed characteristics.

The most concise source of information about Tribbles is David Gerrold's book *The Trouble with Tribbles*. Gerrold states that a Tribble "has no legs and no eyes—just a small soft mouth. When stroked, it throbs and purrs. It loves being held and it loves the warmth of the human hand. . . . It is a simple life form with only two senses, a heat detection sense and a food detection sense.''

The most notable physical feature about the Tribble is, of course, the fur that covers its entire body. The presence of this fur suggests that Tribbles evolved in a mild climate which became cold at least part of the time.

Gerrold stated that a Tribble ''moves by pulsing and flexing its body, or by rolling, depending on how fast or how far it wants to go.'' In the episodes, we never saw a Tribble ''rolling''; therefore, we may assume that pulsing and flexing is the Tribble's preferred method of locomotion. Thus the Tribble's rate of movement is relatively slow, making it a very bad ground-dwelling animal—it simply would not have the speed necessary to evade predators.

Even if they could outdistance predators, Tribbles don't seem to have the ability to detect them. Bjo Tribble's *Star Trek Concordance* describes Tribbles as having ''no discernible feet, head, or other appendages.'' In *More Tribbles, More Troubles*, a Tribble was observed being eaten by a Glommer, a Klingon biological construct designed to be a Tribble predator. Two or three other Tribbles sat close by and made no attempt to ''roll'' away to safety. Apparently Tribbles do have only two senses (heat and food), for they could not detect a predator only ten centimeters away!

In *The Trouble with Tribbles*, Tribbles were clinging to the walls of the bridge, the rec room, etc. This ability to suspend itself at a 90-degree angle to the floor on a smooth surface proves that the Tribble is an excellent climber, able to climb and cling to almost anything. So we may then assume that the Tribble is a natural tree dweller, living on the sides of trunks and in branches. In such a position, the Tribble would be safe from ground-dwelling predators. This (plus the presence of fur) would lead us to conclude that the Tribbles' natural environment is a temperate deciduous forest, similar to those in North America. Thus, a Tribble would be more akin to an Earth squirrel than a rabbit.

But how would the Tribble, having only a sense of heat, know which way is up or down? Well, it really doesn't. It would use its heat direction sense to climb to the top branches of a tree during the day, moving closer to the heat of sunlight; at night it would move downward, closer to the radiating heat of the ground. (We can observe a similar action when a Tribble is attracted to the heat of a human hand.) This is called "positive thermotaxis," i.e., the Tribble will always move toward heat.

Perhaps one night on the Tribbles' world, Cyrano Jones was surprised by the sight of Tribbles crawling toward him from all directions, attracted by the heat of his camp fire.

Each of the Tribbles' appearances has coincided with some kind of grain (quadrotriticale, etc.). This has led to the common assumption that Tribbles are herbivores whose primary food source is grain. This is incorrect. In *The Trouble with Tribbles*, we observed Tribbles infiltrating the *Enterprise*'s food processors and eating, among other things, a "chicken sandwich and coffee." By eating the chicken, Tribbles have exhibited the apparent ability to assimilate protein and obtain nutrients by eating meat. Tribbles also devoured a Vulcan salad (Mr. Spock's lunch), demonstrating that they can exist on plants other than grains. In his book, Gerrold stated that in the first draft of *The Trouble with Tribbles*, he said, "What does it [the Tribble] eat? Anything that people can eat." All of these examples, considered together, reveal that Tribbles are actually omnivores—creatures that feed on both animal and vegetable substances. It may be fairly stated that Tribbles can eat everything nonpoisonous to humankind and more, for humans cannot gain nutrition from raw grain as Tribbles can. The fact that "Tribbles have no teeth" may explain why they would have a strong tendency to prefer plant or vegetable foods over animal flesh.

On its homeworld, the Tribble would be classified as a primary, secondary, and third level consumer in the trophic/feeding hierarchy. Because the Tribble is a tree dweller, a majority of its diet would consist of leaves, nuts, fruits, and tree-dwelling insects such as termites. At night, when the Tribble descends to the ground, its diet would increase to include grasses, fungi, other kinds of insects, snails, larva, worms, etc. Tribbles might even eat smaller mammals, such as mice. While a Tribble has no apparent way in which to capture such larger prey, it could utilize several as yet unrevealed weapons. One of these could be, theoretically, the use of its "tranquilizing purr" to affect the prey's nervous system, causing paralysis and unconsciousness. Perhaps they would seek out burrows where small animals have stored up food. Using its tranquilizing purr, the Tribble would devour the animal as well as its cache. Such a scenario reveals a grimmer image of the Tribble than we usually connect with the "harmless" pets they are normally assumed to be. Yet considering the Tribble's niche in its native ecosystem, the idea of a Tribble's being an omnivore and a predator is more plausible than assuming, as some do, that Tribbles need humans/humanoids to survive.

Tribbles, like all living creatures, would be affected by the changing of the seasons. In the spring and summer months, they would exist as described above. In the fall and winter months, however, it is a different story. It is doubtful that Tribbles are hibernating creatures. We all "know what happens if you feed a Tribble too much." This would effectively negate any efforts by the Tribble to store up fat for a winter's hibernation. Because of their defenselessness against predators and their slowness (not to mention their closeness to the ground, which would make it difficult if not impossible for them to move through deep snow), it is also unlikely that Tribbles forage during the winter months. One may only assume that Tribbles, like Earth squirrels, store up food for the winter months. Still, the Tribble would venture to the ground to search for food to augment its store and hence a greater number would fall prey to predators in the fall and winter months.

On a minor note, the *Star Trek Concordance* reports Tribbles have "a mouth on the ventral side." This is probably correct. There are several Earth creatures (flatworm, octopus, squid, starfish) which have mouths located on the underside/belly. What is curious about the Tribble's mouth, assuming that a statement made by Cyrano Jones is accurate, is that Tribbles have no teeth. When eating plants, grains, and animals, the Tribble must have some means of breaking down food, reducing it to smaller bits for digestion. Powerful jaws could do this in the absence of teeth, but Gerrold stated that Tribbles have "small soft mouths." If Tribbles cannot physically break up their food, perhaps they do so chemically. They may have highly effective digestive juices which, as acids, dissolve food into its basic nutrients during the process of feeding. This would limit the size of what the Tribble eats; however, each portion it eats and dissolves would be equivalent to a "bite," and judging from observations, it would be a speedy process. Another possibility is that the Tribble has a mutual symbiotic relationship with a colony of prokaryote-type bacteria (as Earth cows do with rumen bacteria). The bacteria would break down cellulose and transform the plants into useful nutritional material for the Tribble. Such colonies of bacteria could be obtained by eating insects (like termites) or simply transferred at birth.

It would also seem that a Tribble's metabolism is very effective in converting food into useful materials. This is suggested by the fact that we never saw any excrement ("Tribble droppings") despite the enormous numbers of the beasts that inhabited the *Enterprise* and other areas. Having an almost 100 percent food-to-nutrient conversion factor would coincide with the Tribble's reported ability to eat almost anything.

The most well-known fact about Tribbles is their ability to reproduce rapidly, geometrically increasing the local population. However, there are questions concerning the Tribble's "natural multiplying proclivities." For example, Dr. McCoy reported that the Tribble is "bisexual, reproducing at will." "Bisexual" means the Tribble would have both male and female gametes. In most higher-order bisexual organisms this would mean *two* Tribbles are needed for reproduction, each fertilizing the other. It is implied, however, that the Tribble can reproduce alone (i.e., it fertilizes itself).

Perhaps Dr. McCoy misspoke in saying "bisexual" and meant to say "asexual"—able to reproduce individually at will. Supporting this theory is the fact that McCoy was given one Tribble by Uhura in *The Trouble with Tribbles*; later we saw that he had "a lot of them." (Gerrold himself had McCoy saying the Tribbles are "asexual" in the story premise and first-draft script.) Assuming that McCoy was correct, however, it would appear Tribbles are unique in that they can perform both sexual and asexual reproduction.

In the Tribble, the need to reproduce appears to have a direct correlation with the amount of food it eats. With 50 percent of its metabolism devoted to breeding, the Tribble could have a very elaborate reproductive system, so there is no reason why there could not exist a biological mechanism which measures stomach content, then triggers the desire to reproduce.

If two Tribbles are close to each other at such a time, they would inseminate each other. If alone, the Tribble would perform self-fertilization.

Under these conditions, the spring and summer months would be the prime time for Tribble breeding because of the large amounts of food available. It would be during this time that a massive Tribble population explosion would occur. This large population would be thinned out by predators, especially during the winter months.

In *More Tribbles, More Troubles* we learned of a method to "spay" a Tribble. This involved having the Tribbles genetically engineered, including an injection of Neothylene, to slow down their metabolic rates. The process probably affects the organ which monitors stomach content and the Tribble's desire to reproduce.

THE TRUTH ABOUT TRIBBLES

The probable reason why Tribbles evolved to be so "highly prolific" is that their native ecosystem and environment made rapid breeding a necessary characteristic for survival. Mr. Spock suggested that Tribbles evolved in a "predator-filled" environment. This was purely extrapolation on Spock's part; probably only Cyrano Jones knows what the Tribbles' homeworld is really like. Under Shelford's Law of Tolerance, Tribbles could merely have evolved under very stressful conditions, such as Earth's tundra biomes. However, based on factors previously discussed, Mr. Spock's "predator-filled" environment seems correct.

Tribbles are perfectly adapted to serve as excellent prey for several levels of predators. Their high turnover rate (population size over a period of time) and their ability to eat almost anything nonpoisonous to humanoid life makes them a perfect species to support carnivorous species.

The Tribble, for all its lovableness, is a highly developed and fascinatingly complex creature. While we can enjoy watching their antics, it might be wise to remember that we, like the lowly Tribble, are often motivated by the desire for food, warmth, and reproduction. Which means, size and a little biological complexity aside, that we and the furry creature that is "the only love you can buy" are not too different from each other after all.

WHY SPOCK RAN AMOK

by Kyle Holland

Another subject which draws quite a few articles as well as a constant flow of letters expressing varying opinions is the state of pon farr; *in particular* pon farr *as experienced by Spock. In this article, however, we think you'll find that Kyle Holland has taken a rather unusual slant on the subject. We predict that this article will draw as much—if not more—mail as anything we've ever published.*

After reading G.B. Love's excellent "How and Why Vulcans Choose Their Mates" (*Best of Trek #5*), I was moved to comment on some of the particulars of Spock's *pon farr* experience. I am sure that many readers feel as I do: Spock did not undergo a genuine *pon farr*, but a false *pon farr*, one which was psychosomatically induced. Spock's own words, "Once I thought I had killed the captain, I lost all interest in T'Pring," leaves us no other conclusion. The object of *pon farr* is reproduction of the species; any Vulcan who, after seven (or in Spock's case, more) years of dormancy, loses interest because of an unhappy *Koon-ut-Kalif-fee* has not been through the real thing. Assuming this, we are only left to wonder how and why Spock's syndrome arose.

We should first of all note that the relationship between psychic and physiologic function in Vulcans, both male and female, is structurally different from what it is in humans. The Vulcan "hypothalamus" is much larger and more complex than its human counterpart, unmistakably indicating a more orderly evolution as well as the possibility that the Vulcan race is much older than our own. The superior mental and physical coordination of Vulcans, as well as their recuperative powers, is due to this phenomenon. Clearly, an emotionally distressed Vulcan would be subject to physical disorders of corresponding magnitude.

110

Spock, even though half human, possesses this more active physiology. In his youth, he began to feel that Vulcan was not the place where he could live his entire life. Outside of his immediate family, he found in Vulcan's ethnocentric society little tolerance of his human heritage. Not surprisingly, this rejection contributed to a form of self-hatred that made Spock himself intolerant of his human half. Upon joining Starfleet, Spock determined to "pass" as a full-blooded Vulcan, betraying no hint of his humanity—something he could never have done on Vulcan. For a time, this was easy to do, since in appearance and behavior he conformed to human preconceptions of what Vulcans should look like and how they should act. It is interesting to note that while Spock could hardly conceal his human connection, which was a matter of record, he attempted to minimize it, telling Kirk (in their earliest-known conversation) that an "ancestor" of his had married a woman from Earth. While not technically false, it was nevertheless a significant distortion.

We can only speculate about how much time passed before Spock began to regret his charade. Not all of Spock's shipmates felt kindly toward Vulcans; at times there were open demonstrations of suspicion and even hatred. The enormous task of maintaining a Vulcan persona in a non-Vulcan world was daily made more difficult by the baitings of McCoy and even Kirk, both of whom guessed at the frail foundations of Spock's pose. Only Montgomery Scott was unfailing in his admiration of the Vulcan's abilities and in trusting his judgment—but Spock would discover that under certain circumstances even Scotty could reveal the fear and hatred of aliens that affect humans in their weaker moments. Gradually, Spock came to feel that the Vulcan "phantom" he had been pursuing was costing him dearly, not only in terms of wasted psychic energies, but also in terms of his standing in the eyes of his shipmates.

At the same time, the pleasures of human existence were everywhere for Spock to see. His captain—whom Spock had, in his own mind, come to regard as his closest friend—was the very exemplar of human strength and joy: Kirk's vulnerabilities were only too obvious—a fact which at first disturbed Spock—but his pleasure in life never seemed to diminish, even in the most hopeless of circumstances. And Kirk was surrounded by warmth and respect—from his crew, from his colleagues in the fleet, and, when he was ashore, from women. Spock would eventually come to appreciate the deep pain that can be associated with love, but aboard the *Enterprise*, the lesson was clear: Friendship was the sustenance of daily life and love, or the hope of it, the guiding force of the species.

Spock's position slowly became untenable. He could not be wholly Vulcan, as he wished to be, and he could never become fully human, as normal life aboard the *Enterprise* seemed to demand. He could, perhaps, dimly see a future possibility of accepting and appreciating each feeling—simple or otherwise—for itself, identifying himself as the combination of diversities that he was, but for the immediate future, he was trapped by his hatred of an unresolved situation. Gradually his subconscious came to focus on the one great (but by no means the only) unresolved element in his life as a Vulcan—his bonding with T'Pring.

The external and internal pressures which impelled Spock toward a conclusion or abrogation of his arrangement with T'Pring are understandable enough. But these forces were long-term, and the fact is that Spock eventually reached a crisis wherein he could, apparently, survive only by consummating *pon farr* within seven or eight days. What factors, we are left to wonder, pushed Spock to the brink at just this time?

The psychic bonding of Vulcan children, according to Spock, took place so that both partners, no matter how far or long separated, would know when "the time is right." The "time," evidently, comes for Vulcans so infrequently and after so much metabolic preparation that the species would be endangered if many partners were caught by surprise; hence the sophisticated warning system expressed, physically, by *pon farr*. We may be sure, from Spock's remarks, that this is not a matter of chronometrically biological development triggered at the time of bonding. If that were the case, no one would need to "know" whether or not the time was right—he or she would simply appear at the right place, ready for events, confident that the partner would also be there. No, *pon farr* is very definitely a warning, a signal. But a signal of what, to whom?

The cyclical feature attributed to *pon farr* is critical. Throughout the galaxy, carbon-based life forms which have attained the mammalian or paramammalian stages feature cyclic estrus manifested in the female only. Male cyclicality (of which there are many examples) occurs only as a psychic or, in some cases, hormonally communicated sympathetic response to female estrum. This, then, is the basis for *pon farr*. The female, whose domination of a sector of the chosen male's parathalamus is effected at a point in childhood, is actually able to initiate the desired hormonal changes at the desired time.

Spock's susceptibility to T'Pring's signals was no doubt the result of the daily pressures to which he was subjected on the *Enterprise* and his unconscious desire to resolve, in some way, his relationship to his "wife." Nevertheless, the onset of *pon farr* did not come as a relief to him. He had hoped, he said, to be spared the whole business—meaning he had hoped that his betrothal could be dealt with in a logical and unemotional manner, and not in the way things were starting to go. His comment was revealing: He wished to avoid *pon farr*, but his subconscious conviction was that as a Vulcan he would be unable to do so. It is no wonder, then, that at the telehormonal urgings of T'Pring, the *pon farr* syndrome descended upon Spock with full force. Given what we know about psychosomatic dynamics, it is not improbable that he would indeed have died of some sort of mental imbalance had not a point of resolution been reached.

This point was indeed reached by Spock—not as it would have been by a Vulcan, with completion of *Koon-ut-Kalif-fee* and consummation—but upon his conscious realization that he had "killed" Kirk. Certainly, the conscious realization itself was enough to alert Spock to the fact that his state of mind was not, after all, rooted in Vulcan primal urges, but in his own subconscious conflicts and the immediate condition of his link to T'Pring. Madness, such as it was, was dispelled and Spock took his leave of T'Pring and T'Pau—desolated, but composed and coherent.

If we see *pon farr* in this light, we are in a position to answer several questions about Spock and Vulcan:

1. If this was a false *pon farr* and Spock was not in fact subject to the reproductive traumas of Vulcans, how could he be affected by T'Pring in the first place?

This takes us back to an old question: Which half of Spock is Vulcan? The answer, apparently, is half of every half. Spock's enormous psychodynamic recuperative powers indicate decisively that the structure of his parathalamus is in every way Vulcan; the telehormonal link with T'Pring was real. Nevertheless, some differences in the metabolic interlinks, possibly centered in the pituitary stalk, obstructed the total control of the adrenocortical system which she would have commanded in a Vulcan. It was not T'Pring but Spock who did the rest, probably as a result of a self-induced subconscious suggestion.

2. If *pon farr* is the sole sexual outlet of the Vulcan, and if it is permanent and exclusive, what was Stonn doing hanging around?

It has been convincingly suggested that bonding is only a social institution; natural love could occasionally arise between

Vulcans. This is apparently what happened to Stonn and T'Pring. Logically there is no reason why love (a source of shame to Vulcans) and sex (a necessary evil) should not be congruent, and for some Vulcans, the two obviously do go hand in hand.

If *pon farr*, as we have suggested, is not a natural and unavoidable condition of the Vulcan male but the result of telehormonal manipulation by the female, then the psychophysiological link is volitional on the part of the female and can be realized outside the institution of betrothal. The intense social sanctions on Vulcan intended to prevent such an occurrence proved to be ineffectual in the case of T'Pring and Stonn.

3. How could Sarek and Amanda have maintained a harmonious homelife?

Although much ingenious speculation has been lavished upon this question, the answer is really the simplest of all. Since *pon farr* is not a psychological but a social condition of the Vulcan male, it does not occur in the absence of a telehormonal link. We may, however, conjecture that the innate receptivity of the parathalamus to hormonal suggestion makes adjustment to the cyclical rhythms of non-Vulcan females quick and easy; it is primarily the social and philosophical intractability of Vulcan males which has prevented their developing an interest in interplanetary marriages.

4. How was Spock saved from future *pon farr* traumas?

This question, although it too has been "answered" in many ingenious ways, is no question at all. Spock never experienced a true *pon farr*, and his one false experience was enough to resolve many of the conflicts which had induced the syndrome. Moreover, his link with T'Pring ended, Spock would not be sympathetic to any female, all things being equal. Of course, for Spock, all things are never equal.

Had Spock truly experienced *pon farr*, his statement that "once I thought I had killed the captain, I lost all interest in T'Pring" would be rather alarming. In fact, Spock benefited greatly from his experience; ironically, the benefits sprang primarily from his seizing the opportunity to approximate conventional human acts of friendship. By inviting them to join him on Vulcan, Spock was able to inform Kirk and McCoy (in terms understandable and meaningful to all of them) that they were officially and publicly his friends. By confiding the nature of his "illness" to Kirk, he unwillingly conformed to human standards of intimate friendship. And by accepting Christine Chapel's *plomik* soup, he acknowledged an action considered warm by human standards, repugnant by Vulcan standards.

Not being human, Spock could hardly have taken unmixed satisfaction in sharing these things, but he was on his way to recognizing each on its own terms, beginning to come to a very unsteady compromise with himself. Far from the distortion of identifying his father as "an ancestor" who married a woman from Earth, he would later be able to say, "My father is from the planet Vulcan"—a more honest and, for Spock, a more difficult way of identifying things as they are.

A SAMPLING
OF "TREK ROUNDTABLE"

Letters from our readers

One of the greatest pleasures in editing our magazines and these collections is reading the comments sent in by our readers. Not only do we swell with pride at the compliments and cringe at the complaints, but we never cease to be amazed at the thought and effort that our readers put into their letters to Trek Roundtable. *We are justifiably proud of the fact that many fans consider* Trek Roundtable *to be fandom's major forum for expressing ideas about Star Trek, science fiction and related subjects, and the condition of the world in general. The high caliber of the mail we receive is illustrated by two simple facts: We never have nearly enough room to print all of the letters we receive; and many of our letter writers have gone on to expand upon their ideas and write full-fledged articles for* Trek *and other magazines. The following letters should give you a good idea of what goes on in a typical* Trek Roundtable.

Carol Newton
Valley View, Tex.

I enjoyed your issue of *Trek Movie Special #1* very much—yes, I would like to see further issues! (Food for a starving soul.) I am primarily a Spock fan, so I was glad to see several articles on him.

I was surprised to see so much written about Leonard Nimoy's supposed desire to have Spock killed. Whether true or not, the fact remains that he did play the role and has said that he looks forward to doing it again. I admire Leonard Nimoy a great deal as an actor, poet, and writer, and I wouldn't presume to pass judgment on his decisions. Perhaps the reason that Spock's complex and intriguing personality comes across so well is that the actor who portrays him is equally complex. Something to think on, anyway.

I loved *Wrath of Khan*; I thought the characters were more relaxed and true to form than in the first movie (but then I liked it too). Mainly I was glad to see Spock, Kirk, and McCoy enjoying one another's company again. There was plenty of suspense, laughter, and tears, and it left me with the warm feeling that my friends were back. And I plan on seeing Spock return!

I would like to say thank you for all the time and effort you have put in on your publication. It was darn well worth it!

Diane Draper
South Porcupine, Ontario, Canada

Having just finished reading your *Best of Trek* editions nos. 1, 2, and 3 for the second delight-filled time, I found myself staring at the advertisement on the last page of *BOT #3* in which you invite one and all to come and join the fun, and wondering why I have refrained from doing so until now. I mean, it's not as if I've been vacationing on Omnicron Ceti III, spending my days in a daze, nor have I been kidnapped by the local Klingon spy. (We do have one, you know—the dastardly troublemaker sabotaged the projectors both times I've been to see *Wrath of Khan*.) It certainly isn't due to a sudden revelation of the quality of *Trek*'s articles and their infinite diversity of comment and opinion, as that was apparent to me way back in *The Best of Trek* (#1). So why have I waited so long? Well, it may be that misery does indeed love company—and a shoulder to cry on.

That's what I said: misery. Not merely the misery of never—or only very, very rarely—finding someone who shares my love for Star Trek; that's a long-standing one I've come to terms with. It's not even the misery of having gone *five years* without seeing a single Star Trek episode (as it's not on local TV) that I speak of. No, the special anguish that compels me to write this letter is of more recent origin: *Star Trek II: The Wrath of Khan*.

Please don't get me wrong. In many, many ways *Wrath of Khan* was a joy to behold. In fact, for three-quarters of the movie I was absolutely beside myself with delight—even without the aid of a malfunctioning transporter—thinking, "They did it! They *finally* got it right! It's Star Trek again!" and breathing a sigh of relief that it wasn't another *STTMP*. (Sorry, Walter—I just can't agree with your glowing review of the first movie, though you raised some interesting points. I'd just as soon see it removed from the official annals of the Star Trek universe and forgotten. To me, its only justification is that it made a lot of money for Paramount and so encouraged them to take another crack at it.) I could write a whole 'nother letter on *Wrath of Khan's* good points: the humor, the depth of characterization, the long-overdue amplification of Chekov's role (which I hope will start a trend in the future for the other so-called "secondary" characters). Really, I was loving every minute of it—but then disaster struck and I was left in stunned, glassy-eyed shock.

I do not specifically mean the death of Spock. If the reasons for his termination do indeed lie—as vicious rumor would have it—in Leonard Nimoy's honest and irrevocable frustration with those pointed ears, my deep respect for him as an actor and a person prevents me from too harshly condemning his decision to remove himself from Star Trek. (But I don't believe that's the reason for a minute!)

Oh no, the bare fact of Spock's death didn't really bother me all that much (or Kirk either, it seemed). I witnessed it quite dry-eyed and unmoved, and therein lies my complaint—it is the *manner* of Spock's demise that I find unacceptable. This is how our beloved Vulcan is to be taken from us? In an anticlimactic, criminally understated, and emotionally sterile scene tacked onto the movie almost as an afterthought? It was a cinematic whimper when it should have been the most dramatic and heart-wrenching BANG! in all of Star Trek history, celluloid or print. Hey, Roddenberry, Bennett, Sowards, et al.: This isn't some anonymous ensign strolling down the corridor who won't even get his name in small print in the final credits you're killing off here—this is *Spock*, dammit, and if I have to sit there and watch him die I want it to *hurt*!

And it didn't . . . not nearly enough.

There was only one instant in that entire segment that, for me at least, evoked the merest flicker of the emotional impact it might have—*should* have—had, and that is when Kirk receives the summons to engineering and, glancing up, sees that Spock is not at his post . . . and we all realize, or at least guess, that he will never be there again.

I have wracked my brain trying to pinpoint just what was so wrong, so lacking, in the way his death was staged. Why did I feel so little emotional response—except for the nagging sense we'd been cheated somehow? I wanted to mourn. I wanted everyone in the theater, Trekkers or not, to be forced to grieve for this death as they have never grieved for any fictional character before. And what was their reaction? Guffaws at the incongruity of the bagpipes at the funeral, if anything at all. Oh, to be sure, it was a noble and gallant death, very much in the line of duty, logically necessary in order to save the *Enterprise* from certain destruction. And perhaps *that* was part of the problem. Spock's motivation for sacrificing himself was too matter-of-fact, too impersonal for anyone to relate to it. Would not Spock's death have had more meaning, more drama, would not it have better served his legend if he had given his life to save Jim Kirk's, and Jim's alone? In my opinion, it would have . . . and then I could have cried.

Which brings me to my next point. Not about my grief this time, but Kirk's—or rather the lack of it. Oh yes, there was his moving eulogy at the funeral, and, oh yes, he seemed properly stunned and grief-stricken in the engine room, but what's this? He's *smiling* at the end of the movie? Is there a Trekker alive who can honestly believe he could or would recover so quickly from what has to be the most soul-shattering loss he will ever face? No! They can deny me my mourning, but how dare they rob Kirk of his?

One last complaint: To add insult to injury we are left with the hint—vague, but it's there—that Spock just might not be dead after all, at least not forever and ever, amen. If it comes to pass that Spock is resurrected at the future convenience of Paramount and/or Nimoy, then his death in *Wrath of Khan* is cheapened even further to blatant manipulation and is a sadistic slap in the face to all of us who have given our love, loyalty, and support to Star Trek all these years. I have this horrible premonition—sometime in the future there will be a scene in *Star Trek???* that goes something like this:

Admiral Kirk, upon meeting Spock in a corridor, will say, "Aren't you dead?"

Spock: "As you can observe, admiral, I am quite well."

Kirk (sputtering): "Then you lied."

Spock: "No, Jim—I exaggerated."

Uh . . . my apologies; I think I got a little carried away. Thank you for the opportunity to speak my mind.

Live long and prosper (with apologies to Theodore Sturgeon) . . . though I fear Trekdom will do neither—they have killed our first officer and our friend.

Linda Kolman
Sunnyvale, Cal.

Has it only been seven weeks since I bought and read *Best of Trek #1-5*? Two months since I began my Trekking rampage, buying every store in the area out of Star Trek books, ordering any they didn't have in stock? Surely not; I've been a Trekker all my life—haven't I?

No, I haven't. (Oh, how it hurts to confess.) I've watched Star Trek while I couldn't focus on the screen (I was a bit young when it came out), and our family always made a habit of watching the reruns while eating dinner. Being born with functioning eyes, I learned to love the show (being born female, I promptly fell in love with William Shatner), but not so much its meaning. After *Star Trek: The Motion Picture* came out, and after reading the novel, I began to appreciate Star Trek's values. Still, it wasn't until *Wrath of Khan* that I became a devoted Trekker.

I believe, with all my objective talents, that *Wrath of Khan* was a work of art. Sure, errors can be spotted, but that is not what I'm talking about. They (those involved in production) managed to recapture the flavor of the original episodes and still add more dimension to the characters. Kirk became human, with strengths and vulnerabilities a little more visible. Spock noticeably softened, becoming more understanding toward humans. (After that scene on the bridge when the *Enterprise* cleared moorings, I again wondered if he wasn't an imp in disguise.) Even McCoy received better treatment in the second movie. He had a chance to do what he loves best—give unsolicited advice. Now *those* are the characters we know and love—and now they're even more believable.

One of the things I enjoyed most in the movie was Saavik's role. I consider her a worthy addition to the Star Trek cast. Kirstie Alley did a superb job of her portrayal. Vonda McIntyre's novel adaptation explained many things not in the movie—or did those scenes end up on the famous cutting-room floor? I hope that Miss Alley returns in *Star Trek III* as the mysterious Lieutenant Saavik.

I'd be curious to discover whether the budding romance between Saavik and David was originally in the script, or if it was an idea of Vonda McIntyre's to spice up the novel. It could cause an interesting conflict in the upcoming movie, should Paramount wish to pursue it. Hmmm . . .

One occurrence in the movie often argued about by fans is Spock's death. Really now, how many of you truly think he's dead? Some say that they would consider a resurrection of the captain to be an insult to their intelligence. I wouldn't be insulted in the slightest. The most likely way for the producers to "bring him back alive" would be to have the Genesis effect do its work on him. That planet's still evolving, you know. If that would insult certain fans, then surely the idea of a Genesis machine alone must be just as degrading. At any rate, there is always that cryptic "Remember" comment said during the mind meld. That should keep some people busy for a while. Besides, as everyone knows, he (Nimoy) has signed up for *Star Trek III*. Why fight it?

I'm sure that I'm not the first to comment on this, but did you notice that for Kirk's birthday, Spock gave Kirk a book and McCoy gave him the glasses with which to read it? I'm not a philosophy student, but it sure sounds like the old triad at work again. Spock usually provides the factual information on a situation, and McCoy offers his view as a humanitarian. Who makes the final decision? Kirk, of course. I won't go into the philosophical ramifications of the broken spectacles after Spock's death. Just think about it.

Judith Swanson
Santa Monica, Cal.

Two weeks ago I wolfed down what I had intended as a leisurely lunch, trying not to drown as I spluttered my coffee, and fled the restaurant, cackling through tears. Worried patrons eyed one another in my wake, questioning my sanity; I eat there almost every Saturday and always seemed normal before. Damn you, Kiel Stuart!!! That ought to teach me not to read while eating, but it won't.

In a nearby park, joggers collided as they gaped at the giggling madwoman under a tree; I finished "The Doom 'n' Gloom Machine," as well as the rest of *BOT #5*. and then spent the rest of the day tracking down the other *BOT* books. I now have all but the first one, and if that is still in print, I may even resort to (sigh) ordering it directly from the publisher.

Although I love Star Trek dearly, I was/am a dyed-in-the-pulps Science Fiction F*A*N first, and always tried to avoid the Trekker fanzines. I worked in a bookstore during college and was, of course, in charge of Science Fiction and Fantasy. "Don't throw me in the briar patch!" I read every book and magazine in my section and worked hard to make it the best selection of SF&F one could find in a chain store. So I squirmed when the manager gave in to a Trekkie's wheedling and consented to carry some fanzines for a while. True to my high calling, I read them and was nauseated. I have detested the ubiquitous "Mary Sue" since I first encountered her in seventh grade, when a fellow Star Trek fan showed me a "script" she had written, with the comment that her mother thought she should send it to NBC. Some mother! I still gag to think that an otherwise intelligent twelve-year-old would be so naive; the quality of the fanzines I saw was not much higher.

However, Trek looks like a lot of fun—intelligent fun—and my check is enclosed. After all, at age eleven, in my SF F*A*N purity I had refused to watch Star Trek when it premiered, because the first episode, which I missed, was praised by the same cretinous classmate who had once conned me into watching the lamentable *Lost in Space*. It was pure serendipity that I ever did watch ST; I happened to switch channels in the middle of "The Enemy Within" and joyfully realized that this was, at long last, televised science fiction! Just as it was serendipity that made me buy a *BOT* book to read at lunch, since nothing else in the SF section looked interesting.

Kiel Stuart, in fact, is highly contagious and should be quarantined. I have seen *Wrath of Khan* twice, and am now working on a parody of my own. Not of the whole movie; just biographical sketches of the various old and new crewmembers, as well as guest villain ("El Hunk," Ricardo Montalbod), plus a brief status report on the good ship herself (cackle, cackle). I have no plans to usurp Kiel's territory, but if she is going to rewrite any more episodes, here are some favorites—and others—that I would love to read after she gets through with them:

"The Powder Room—Where No Man Has Gone Before"

"The City on the Edge of an Earthquake Fault"

"The Ultima II Computer"

"Who Mourns for Adenoids?"

"Tomorrow Is Payday"

"The Trouble with Wookies"

"Divorce, Vulcan Style"

"For the World Is Hollow and Everything Else Is Boring, Too"

"The Intercourse Incident"

"Mother Knows Best" (sorry, D.C.)

"This Side of Parodize"

(I was going to include "Spock's Brain," which I hate, until I realized that it *is* a Star Trek parody, the greatest ever written—they even filmed it!)

As for the new movie: From *STTMP* I learned that a ST film makes more sense if you read the novelization. Vonda McIntyre's book of *Wrath of Khan* fortunately included scenes that were cut from the film (as well as others she invented) which cleared up some mysteries. For example, why did crusty Scotty get all torn up over the death of Peter Preston, who was surely not the only trainee killed? He was Scott's nephew, the book explains.

Or what is so special about the new crewmember, Lieutenant Saavik? (Great name.) The publicity surrounding the film mentioned that she is supposed to be half Vulcan and half Romulan; again, unless you can read, you wouldn't know. It was never mentioned in the film. Most reviewers referred to her simply as a new Vulcan character. Come on—with jade-green eyes and *arched* eyebrows?

Vonda McIntyre dropped hints as to Saavik's True Identity at least once every chapter, and I hope that she was working from inside information that will be borne out by the next film. I have always thought—with respect to Lieutenant Saavik's possible parentage—that where there was smoke, there was fire; but don't count on it. Paramount moves in mysterious ways its blunders to perform, and may well pass up a chance to develop Saavik as a character. And that would be a loss.

**Sue Dunlop
Pincourt, Quebec, Canada**

Okay, guys! You win! I surrender to you totally and irrevocably. I just can't fight it anymore. I am admitting to the world at large that I am an avid Trekker. My husband just clapped his hands to his head in total despair.

I rediscovered Star Trek over a year ago when I began buying Alan Dean Foster's *Log* books for my husband. David is a mild fan himself. One day, for lack of anything better, I picked one up and began to read. Well, the story I read was "Yesteryear," and you know that is one of the better of the animated series. Wham bam, thank you very much. I was hooked. I totally devoured every Star Trek book in the house and began to prowl about the bookstores for more. Every Sunday morning I was up at ten to watch my weekly fix of Star Trek. And fix is the most appropriate word. I was addicted, and how! Even the dog couldn't move while my favorite crew gallivanted about the galaxy. Since that time, I have collected almost every Star Trek book in print, seen reruns of all the shows, seen *The Wrath of Khan* twice (I had seen *Star Trek: The Motion Picture* when it first came out), and become an avid reader of *Starlog*, which always has an ST article.

Then came the internal struggle. Could a supposedly mature woman of twenty-five reconcile herself to being one of those crazy Star Trek fans? Should she even try? Finally I figured out that I was already one of those crazy Star Trek fans. I had only to look at the file of uncompleted Star Trek stories I'd written for proof. The battle was lost when I bought *The Best of Trek #2* and *#3* this weekend. I wanted to be one of those people privileged to receive that magazine with all those marvelous articles and essays and maybe one day (oh, dared I hope?) I would write something for it.

I must admit, like so many others, I adore Spock. Best thing since sliced bread. Beverly Wood's "I Love Spock" was a gem of the first water. I sense a kindred spirit there. At any rate, anyone who loves Spock is a friend of mine, and who can resist that so expressive eyebrow? I just wish, however, that Sondra Marshak and Myrna Culbreath would take it a little easy on the guy's psyche. In my humble and uneducated opinion, I think they get a little carried away with things in their *Phoenix* books. I much preferred their treatment of him in "Surprise" from *New Voyages 2*. I like to tell myself that it was Nichelle's calming influence.

Another of my favorites is Sulu. Something about the little guy intrigues me. He always seems to have the right comment at the right time, like during the countdown in "The Corbomite Maneuver." He is one of the reasons I enjoyed Vonda McIntyre's *Entropy Effect* so much.

Through the articles in the *Best of Trek* volumes, I have been able to see a new and deeper side to good old "Bones" McCoy. Twentieth-century everyman thrust into the advanced times of the twenty-third century. I only hope that I would be able to cope half as well. But even though his famed exchanges with Mr. Spock have a deeper purpose, I still find them great fun. I especially like his response to Spock's concern for Kirk in *Wrath of Khan*. You know the line: "Yes, Spock, *we'll* be careful!" Ah, Mr. Kelley is a wonderful actor!

Which brings me to *Wrath of Khan*. I loved it! I adored it! I enjoyed it no end! I cried like a baby both times I saw it. Finally, someone decided to treat the characters in a realistic way as they grow older (and hopefully wiser). It was just as I envisioned. Kirk poised and dignified in his elevated rank, but every now and then the mask would slip and there was that old glint of cocky, devilish mischief. And Spock. Ah, Spock! Comfortable at last with his duality, his two halves at war no more. A complete and peaceful Spock. Leonard Nimoy, I doff my hat.

And the new kids on the block. David, a James Kirk at nineteen if I ever saw one. His parents can be proud. Saavik could have done with some of the characterization that made her so special in the novelization, but I realize that some things have to be sacrificed in making a movie. I could grow to like the girl. After all, she hero-worships my favorite Vulcan, doesn't she?

All in all, *Wrath of Khan* was splendiferous! Yes, splendiferous. I once again realized the magnitude of talent that once graced our little TV screens. Shatner, Nimoy, Kelley. I'd give them all Academy Awards if I could. Ricardo Montalban, too. He was the epitome of mad revenge. But please, explain to me, Leslie Thompson, how come Khan's followers were all so young? They were too young to be original crewmembers of the *Botany Bay*, and too old to be their children. I'm a mite kerfluffled over that one.

Well, I could go on forever about our favorite ship and crew. As a matter of fact, I have on some occasions, much to the consternation of bewildered friends and family. Oh well, if I get committed, I hope they let me take my Star Trek collection.

Peggy Hartsook
North Platte, Neb.

Until now, I have never written anyone about Star Trek. I have always sat back and read other people's opinions and talked back to the paper if I disagreed with something. However, you guys asked for letters, so I fear that is all your fault. Here goes.

After *Star Trek: The Motion Picture* was lambasted by the critics and fans alike, I feared ST might finally be dead forever. I am a late joiner, having finally discovered ST in 1972 (through the Blish books), and it broke my heart to hear so many say they were through with Trek. (I was not acquainted with *Trek* magazine, where the true Trekkers are.) With a good measure of relief I heard there was finally going to be a *Star Trek II*. At Denver Star Con in 1981, George Takei said he thought this film would avoid some of the mistakes of the first, but it wouldn't be out until 1982. Sigh!

In April of 1982, I found *The Best of Trek #4* at the used-book store and decided to read it. (I ration my ST reading carefully— short feasts and long famines indeed!) Reading the book gave me Trek fever all over again. I couldn't wait to see the movie!

Finally, June 4 arrived and alas! Ye olde local theater had gotten *Star Trek II: The Wrath of Khan*. However, the friend I was going with called and said she had to work that night—could we go tomorrow night? With ill humor I said all right. That night, I took my dog for a ride. Can I help it if the car went past the theater to check the size of the crowd? I was stunned—hardly anybody was there! My God, I thought, don't tell me this is going to be a flop! I worried all night.

At last, June 5. What an endless day! Then I got a call, softball practice tonight! However, it drizzled rain all afternoon and even though it let up by evening, I couldn't risk life and limb on a slick, wet field, could I? Absolutely not! Happily, my friend and I went to *Wrath of Khan*.

What a magical night! The theater was full, not a seat to be had. And the movie was fabulous! Here, at last, was *good* ST. And also current. Rather than turn back time, the characters had moved with it. The acting was fantastic. We always get good acting from the Trek regulars, but also got excellent acting from the others. Ricardo Montalban was super. He is wasted in *Fantasy Island*. What a great villain! Bibi Besch—at last an intelligent, mature woman for Kirk. Paul Winfield—a small role, but he made it count. As for the regulars, William Shatner has always been my favorite, but in *Wrath of Khan*, I think he outdoes himself. He runs the gamut of emotions, from boredom to a near brush with disaster to a confident cockiness only to be brought down by a grievous loss. Yet, at the end, Kirk is back on his way to rebuilding his life again. Leonard Nimoy plays Spock with his usual quiet dignity, and yet I think he gets across a picture of Spock we've not seen very often, a happy, contented Spock. Both Shatner and Nimoy are to be congratulated on their restraint as well. The death scene was played perfectly when it could have easily slid into maudlin chaos. However, of all the Trek regulars, in this part of the country at least, DeForest Kelley's McCoy is picking up more fans all the time. McCoy's bluntness, humor, and exterior gruffness is endearing him to people who lost sight of McCoy in the rush for Kirk and Spock. Kelley richly deserves the applause.

Before I close I would like to get my two cents' worth in on the Spock controversy. As I said before, I am a Kirk fan, but all my friends are Spock fans and feel honor-bound to say that they think it just wouldn't be ST without Spock. I read David Gerrold's article in *Starlog* on why Spock should stay dead and I understand his point, about how Spock's death must not be cheapened and how through watching Kirk cope with his grief we can all learn to deal with life and death. But when I look at my friends—all of whom are inconsolable at the mere thought of Star Trek without Spock—and when I think of the tremendous team Shatner, Nimoy, and Kelley make, it seems a needless deprivation. Look, real life breaks up good things all too soon anyhow. For instance, the Beatles will never play again. Belushi and Akroyd will never make movies again. So if Leonard Nimoy is *willing* . . . why deprive ourselves of something we all enjoy, especially when all the people are there?

Well, I have rambled on far too long. Thank you very much for letting me have my say. Maybe I won't wait another ten years to write again, who knows? Again, thanks.

Linda L. Knight
Walla Walla, Wash.

Believe me, I am going to try to keep this short, but there is just so much I would like to say. First of all, I think an article on Spock's revival and the many ways in which it could be handled in the next movie would be very interesting. It just does not seem right that he is dead. So I guess making up different ways in which he comes back makes waiting for the next movie more tolerable.

This brings me to another subject, one that does not settle with me very well at all. It has to do with *Starlog* magazine. There have been a few letters from fans, comments in articles, and comments from the editor that they (Paramount) should let Spock rest in peace. They cannot be serious! Why? They say things like that it wouldn't be fair to the fans to bring him back because we already perceive him as being dead and it would be fooling with our emotions. I guarantee this Trekker will be extremely emotional if Spock is not brought back! How could any Star Trek fan even consider letting Spock remain dead when through the magic of science fiction we can have our beloved Vulcan returned to us?

How many of us, if we had the chance for a dead loved one to come back to us, would say, "No thanks, to me he's dead. Let him rest in peace"? Whose life is it, anyway? Especially if it was a young person in the prime of his life who was killed, like Spock. I know my example is extreme. Life, unfortunately, does not work that way. But science fiction can and has many times.

Which, I know, is another prime argument against Spock's revival. It has been done on Star Trek so many times before. Granted, it has been done on the television show, but the people involved are always brought back to life only a few hours after their supposed deaths. The possibilities for Spock's revival are numerous. The time span between his death and revival could be days, months, even years. It could go in many directions (which is why I think it would make for a good article). Can you imagine the scene when Kirk and Spock meet again? That alone would be worth the price of admission many times over! Star Trek is science fiction, Spock is a character in Star Trek and a very loved one at that. Let us not lose sight of this fact and take Spock's death so seriously that we forget what magic science fiction can hold for Spock's future. I could go on with this, but I won't. Hopefully, these people are in the minority. Can you imagine a "Keep Spock Dead" campaign? Ugh!!!

By the way, did you know that "by now everyone knows that the new Star Trek film is somewhat of a disappointment"? You didn't? Neither did I, which is why my mouth dropped open in shock when I read that in the latest *Twilight Zone* magazine. It is unbelievable. "Everyone knows"—everyone in the twilight zone, that is. Which is where these people have obviously been this summer. I do not know why I let that bug me, but it does.

Susie Baumgartel
Kingston, Ontario, Canada

This is what you might call an appreciation letter. I have just finished *The Best of Trek #5* and loved it, as usual. It's good to see that *Trek* is such an excellent magazine that it's had five edited books published. I especially loved *Trek Roundtable*—throughout it I kept agreeing and disagreeing, moaning and chuckling. I've heard this so many times before, but it's the same with me—I couldn't believe that there were so many people "out there" who felt the same way about Star Trek as I did; and they even mentioned some things that I thought no one but me noticed.

In particular, I'd like to point out that I agree with Rowena Warner (loved her poem!) in her letter concerning Kirk's reactions to Spock. I too noticed that he seemed to show less concern than Spock when the latter was in danger. Kirk does appear to be hiding his feelings for his friend much better than the Vulcan. This is something that has been ragging at my mind for ages, and now that someone has brought it to light, I would like to add my own thoughts.

In *Star Trek: The Motion Picture*, Spock tries to tell Kirk what he has discovered as the meaning of existence, the important essence of the human condition—feeling. It is a very touching scene, cut short by the crisis at hand. We see Spock struggling to explain his "feelings." He says, "I should have known." He has been aware of his deep friendship with Kirk but has never admitted it consciously and without artificial influence. He now admits this openly to Kirk, with Chapel and McCoy present, a great sacrifice for a being whose very soul demands the suppression of emotion; yet Kirk seems to be slightly unable, perhaps unwilling, to share this profoundness as openly as his friend. There is a silent "Yes, I understand" in his nod, but before long he is called to the attention of V'Ger. Granted the ship is his first concern, but after the crisis there is hardly any reflection on Spock's revelation.

Perhaps we want to see Kirk reacting the same way, even more so since he is a human and able to express his emotions easily. Perhaps it is not so much the case now as somebody said somewhere (I've looked all over for the quote but can't find it! I'm sure it's in *Star Trek Lives!*)—"We want to see Spock loving the captain." In a way we do; maybe it should be the other way around. Spock has progressed so far in associating with humans, to the point of even feeling emotion for his closest friends, that he should deserve more recognition for this great admission.

We know that Kirk loves his ship first and foremost, but when compared to Kirk's rather flippant relationships with the women in Star Trek, where he is in no way inhibited, it is quite possible to suppose that his relationship with Spock is so profound that he feels he will be hurt badly should something happen. Because of this possibility, he will not pass the boundary that Spock has passed. The Vulcan has not known that particular kind of pain and is not as familiar with it as Kirk is. Spock has never felt this close to anyone, and as a Vulcan, has never had the opportunity to be hurt. (I am not ignoring the feud between Spock and his father, Sarek—the bulk of that occurred before he even met Jim Kirk.)

It is human nature to cower away from what one fears most. James Kirk knows that neither he nor Spock will live forever, and it is for his protection against losing his best friend to shy away from such open reaction. This is quite natural for some of us; I know how it feels to lose a best friend and did not want to commit myself for fear of being hurt again. The duty of the subconscious is to protect the conscious mind. This is the case with James Kirk if Rowena Warner is correct.

It is interesting to note that this is not as true in written fiction. Kirk often shows an open commitment to Spock's friendship and reacts very emotionally time and time again. This is the way we want to see Kirk; the two are quite balanced in this respect, which satisfies us more, but may not be as realistic if we are to consider the visual episodes as seriously as the written ones. One exception (of course!) that I can remember off the top of my head takes place in "Winged Dreamers" in *The New Voyages*; consider the scene where the effect of the flyers has reached Spock. Once the Vulcan babbles on with the sudden revelation that he and Kirk can remain together on the planet forever, Kirk reacts quickly and rather violently, but only to *protect* their relationship from the rest of the curious bridge crew. He knows that in order to save Spock's pride, he must act violently by slapping him, a reaction which at first glance seems quite harsh, but is really rather protective for both him and his first officer.

Jim Kirk has been hurt many times—perhaps he should avert his reluctance and reveal his true sentiments before it is too late. Maybe this way he won't feel guilty for not letting Spock know that he feels the same way. Spock knows, of course, but wouldn't he feel less Vulcan if even Kirk, a human, wouldn't react as "emotionally"? And then . . . it is too late. The moment Kirk realizes what Spock has done at the climax of *Wrath of Khan*, we empathize deeply with him. The anguish, the anger, and the suddenness of Spock's death are felt by all—yet when Spock dies, I had the feeling that Kirk was even more anguished for not having revealed his feelings openly to the Vulcan before his friend died. He may regret this afterward and feel he should have helped Spock know it was all right. Knowing Spock, however, he may have already figured it out . . .

This is, of course, pure speculation and is simply something more to argue about. A great deal of this has to do with the actors themselves who have unconsciously conceived subtle idiosyncrasies that only fans pick up. Consider Spock's act of swallowing whenever Kirk is in danger, something Leonard Nimoy had never noticed until it was brought up by Sondra Marshak, et al., in *Star Trek Lives!* It is these little things that make characters even more unique and lifelike. To be able to do this without effort and be accepted by viewers is clearly another sign of excellent acting and dedication to one's work.

One more thing I'd like to mention concerns the "subtitle" of the third Star Trek movie, *In Search of Spock*. Obviously this is a takeoff of Nimoy's series, *In Search of . . .* , and is only an "in" joke, but the intent is there—why do we have to search for Spock? First of all, we know where Spock is, but why go out of our way to bring him back? Shouldn't we let him lie with the decency that he is known for? (Does he even want to come back?) Spock didn't die for a worthless cause, he died to save his ship and its crew, and though it would be great to have him back to appease our sentiments, is it in any way a "logical" thing to do? I don't think Spock would agree.

Michelle Woomert
Redwood City, Cal.

I am thirteen years old and I am a devoted Star Trek fan.

Last summer I was dragged to a movie by my mother and a friend. The friend thought I would like the movie because it was science fiction and this friend knew of my love for *Star Wars/The Empire Strikes Back* and George Lucas. The movie was *Star Trek II: The Wrath of Khan*. My mother was disgusted with Khan's little creatures, so she left, but I stayed. I watched in mild interest and decided it came in with *Star Wars/Empire/Raiders of the Lost Ark*, my favorites.

Soon after, I was given three novels, *Wrath of Khan*, *The Prometheus Design*, and *The Covenant of the Crown*. I loved *Wrath of Khan* but I did not understand the intros to the others and so I didn't read them until . . .

I was babysitting with a friend and we were watching television very late at night when we stumbled upon an ST rerun. So we watched it. I think it was "Amok Time," but I am not sure. I liked it very much.

I ended up watching another rerun one very late school night when someone accidentally left the TV on a channel that plays ST reruns. I really enjoyed it very, very much. It was "Wink of an Eye." It was then that I was "snatched" by "Trekkistism."

That was when I probably started watching ST every day and reading/collecting the books. I have not seen *Star Trek: The Motion Picture*; I have read the novelization.

I have been told that when I was very young I liked to watch Star Trek, but I do not remember.

I am sorry to be rambling on and on but I have so much to say and I can't help it.

I also write and perform my own stories like most ST fans. My best friends help me with my stories. We usually record the stories by copying the actors' voices like a radio program. We always have a narrator. I have gotten quite good at Chekov myself (even though I am a girl).

Paula Houseworth
APO N.Y.

So frequently it happens that people "jump on the bandwagon" and exploit something that is a sure moneymaker. But you people at *Trek* have an obvious deep and abiding love for the phenomena of Star Trek that has *always* shown through in your publications. Again, my deepest thanks and appreciation to you all.

Just today I received and devoured your first *Trek Movie Special*. Please publish another soon! The article by Walter Irwin (God love him!) said all the things I have thought about the movie. (I've seen it eight times—but only so far! I wonder how long until it will be available in video?)

The other articles were also of the quality and depth that I have come to expect from your publication.

But your Roundtable! I take gross exception to the letter you published by Ms. Draper and the letter by Lynette Wood. (You must have chosen those two in particular because they were sure to elicit a response from your readers.) Ms. Draper obviously missed the entire point of Mr. Spock's demise; and Ms. Wood was looking for a poor movie when she went to see it, or while watching she'd have been as totally enthralled with our beloved world of Star Trek as the majority of us were. It would have been impossible not to be—*Wrath of Khan* is Star Trek at its best and growing.

STTMP was a joy only in that it reopened doors for millions of starving Star Trek fans. Unfortunately, in spite of having seen it countless times, I can't really say more than that for it.

But *Wrath of Khan*—that was what we had waited years so faithfully for. It fulfilled every expectation, and then some. It was a logical growth from the series, the "lost fifteen years," and *STTMP*; the latter seen in a more—but not too—human Mr. Spock. I only pray that *Star Trek III* (there *really* is a *Star Trek III*, isn't there? Being stationed with the Army in Germany we are so terribly out of touch. I only got to see *Wrath of Khan* last month!) will continue to allow ST to grow in the fashion we all expect and hope for. There is so much potential for greatness to continue, particularly with the addition of characters like Saavik (she is Star Trek born and bred, for sure!) that I cringe at the thought of another misconceived venture like *Star Trek: The Motion Picture*.

A small comment off the top of my head on the new uniforms: In *STTMP* the uniforms were a contrivance. They were a change made for the sake of change that grated on my nerves every time I watched the movie. But the new uniforms in *Wrath of Khan* looked like they belonged. In *STTMP* I longed for the return of the velour shirt. But now I hope they never again mess with the Starfleet uniforms. They got it right this time. (They got *everything* right this time!)

Please keep on Trekkin' and publishing until we have reached the ideals Star Trek achieved. Unfortunately we will probably all be long dead and gone before then. . . .

Rick Jones
Argos, Ind.

To my immense pleasure, I recently discovered *Best of Trek #5*. Each volume has been excellent, although I was disappointed at the lack of original artwork in this book.

I have noticed several articles which leave me grumbling, and true to the tradition of fandom, I've decided to grumble to anyone who'll sit still long enough to listen. And you have to—it's your job! (Well, part of your job, anyway.) The Star Trek Mysteries series has begun to stray from the true puzzles of Star Trek into inconsequential trivia. The mysteries of phaser control and the shuttlecraft absence in "The Enemy Within" are the proper subjects for this series—problems which, at first glance, seem to prove Star Trek inconsistent. But there are all kinds of explanations for the colors in the corridors or the elevator system aboard the *Enterprise*, and while the fate of Kirk and Spock in the "Mirror, Mirror" universe is up for speculation, there are many better topics for Mysteries.

I also wish you would caution your readers that the statements found in Trek are your views on areas of Star Trek, and not "the official word." For example, you say that no shuttlecrafts were deployed in "The Enemy Within" because of upper-air turbulence. Fair enough, but one may also explain this matter by saying that none of the shuttlecraft were operational because of damage to the hangar in an untold battle.

Jennifer Weston's article "Of Spock, Genes, and DNA Recombination" was good, but I wondered if another theory had been considered: Human and Vulcan DNA is compatible because the two races are related, even as Vulcans and Romulans are apparently branches of the same line. There is still the problem of Amanda's carrying Spock through pregnancy, but we must remember that twenty-third-century medical knowledge is involved.

G.B. Love's article on Vulcan mate selection suggested that

Surak lived in an era of technology surpassing Earth's mid-twentieth century, primarily because they needed the spacecraft capable of settling the star systems now containing the Romulan Empire. That assumes that the Romulans descended from Vulcans from the planet Vulcan, but suppose both groups came from yet another group of Vulcans? A crash landing on Vulcan, followed by a loss of technological skills, could have resulted in the nomadic tribes pictured in much fan literature.

The article which bothered me the most was "Approaching Evil." Joyce Tullock claimed that Star Trek's theme concerning evil was that "evil" is only our label for "different"; evil is lack of knowledge. Most of the evidence for this theory came from *Star Trek: The Motion Picture*. Why? And then there's the assertion that Star Trek rarely dealt in the absolutes of good and evil! What, then, was that red ball of energy that nearly transformed the *Enterprise* into a flying gore factory? How about Jack the Ripper? Sure, we learned through Star Trek that sometimes we arbitrarily label the unknown as evil, but we also learned that evil does exist and must be defeated. Besides, who ever said that *Star Trek: The Motion Picture* was addressing the subject of evil? In my view, Star Trek taught us that evil is real: Witness Redjac. And evil isn't simply confusion: Witness Khan, who knew both good and evil (when we first saw him) and chose evil (in *Wrath of Khan*). The lesson of Star Trek is not a deeply philosophical one to be slowly unearthed from obscure sections of one motion picture. Rather, it is presented plainly, and forcefully, in one of the better-known statements from "A Taste of Armageddeon": "We can admit that we are killers . . . but we are not going to kill today." Evil is real. Evil is inevitable, because we're human. But the manifestation of evil is not inevitable, again because we're human, because we have the ability to say "We're not going to kill today."

By the way, I'd like to offer my solution to "the great Klingon debate": *Star Trek: The Motion Picture* is the first time we ever saw full-blooded Klingons. Just as Spock is referred to as a Vulcan, when he is actually a Vulcan-human hybrid, all those TV Klingons were actually the result of Vulcan-Klingon ancestry. The bony-headed Klingons are to the TV Klingons as Surak is to Spock. And why not have an entire bridge crew of the "new" Klingons? The Federation gave a whole starship over to Vulcans!

I've noticed that people are trying to decide which Star Trek novels fit into the universe of the Star Trek series. I haven't thought about that one, except to note that they can't all be in the same universe because both *Vulcan!* and a story from *New Voyages* claim to record Spock's first mind meld with a nonintelligent life form. I have come to the conclusion that while the original series shows us what really happened to Kirk and crew, the cartoon series was an example of twenty-third-century fiction. Those stories were all made up about the famous crew of the *Enterprise*.

Sorry I took up so much of your time rambling about *Best of Trek #5*. So that I don't sound like a total cynic, let me add that I did enjoy much of the latest installment of "Mysteries" and look forward to future articles of this sort ("Star Trek VII: The Wrath of Mysteries Solved"?). The bios of McCoy and Scotty, as well as the article on cinematography, were excellent, and "Doom 'n' Gloom" was outrageous! I'd like you to bring back original artwork (only put some clothes on Spock's ensign) and include more of that wonderful poetry!

Parting shot: Wasn't Vulcan shown once with two moons? And didn't Spock once say that Vulcan had no moon? How about solving that mystery? I'd suggest that the two "moons" (assuming they aren't figments of my imagination) were actually artificial satellites housing scientific projects, which were orbiting Vulcan because that planet had little water and would be relatively unaffected by the gravitational forces introduced.

Mary Ann Williams
Madill, Okla.

I seem to have the dubious ability to discover Star Trek items too late. For example, I have just recently found a few of the photonovels, and since I was very impressed with them, I wrote to Bantam and requested information on purchasing the remaining books to complete my set. Imagine my disappointment when I received their reply informing me that the books were out of print. I will just have to make out with what I have, I suppose.

And then, I found *The Best of Trek* series in my local Waldenbooks! I read each of the four books from cover to cover, and then read them all again. And, of course, I sent my order for a subscription the minute I read the ad in the back of *BOT #4*. Then I waited with greatest anticipation for my first issue to arrive. Today when I found that package in my mailbox, I thought I had been whisked to heaven on Earth. I can assure you that these Trek magazines have been given an honored place in my bookshelves and they will be treated with the respect they so richly deserve.

I also noticed the note at the end of *Trek* No. 19 inviting reader comments. I'd just like to say that I thought it was a great magazine. Very polished and professional. Since I am employed with a newspaper, I know the trials and tribulations of publishing, and the horrors of dealing with the U.S. Postal Service. Ours is a mutual dislike relationship, sort of like Tribbles and Klingons! I also know the horrors of putting out the finished product and discovering an error when it is simply too late to correct or explain. It hurts, very much indeed.

I would like to put back into Star Trek, for others, the joy it has given me. That, I think, is the major force of Star Trek—the caring, the sharing, the love between all concerned. Also, I'd like to be able to communicate with fellow Trek followers. Currently, my close friend Julia Davis and I seem to be the only Trekkers in Marshall County, Oklahoma. My younger brother and my grandmother are marginally interested in Star Trek, and that's only due to my hard work in getting them to finally watch it. Julia and I, however, are committed. We bounce trivia off each other, trade books, and go to the movies together. Speaking of movies, we've seen *Wrath of Khan* twice so far and plan to return as soon as possible. Our conversations are peppered with Trekkisms, and our families and friends seem to think we are the aliens!

In regard to *Wrath of Khan*, we both thought it was fantastic. The story, the ship, the uniforms, and especially the relationship between the Big Three—everything was just perfect. We laughed, we cried, and we vowed to keep Star Trek forever in mind. The funeral scene was very effective, most notably the playing of "Amazing Grace" with bagpipes. It caused a rather large lump in many throats, judging by the reaction in the theater. And the magic of the final moments, with Leonard Nimoy reciting the Star Trek introduction, was unforgettable. Imagine sitting in a darkened theater and hearing those words, and then hearing countless soft voices speaking with that of Nimoy. Unforgettable!

Judy Knowlton
Anoka, Minn.

I have been buying and reading the *Best of Trek* books and enjoying them thoroughly. My brother, two sisters, and I have been closet Trekkers for years now, expecting at any time that we would outgrow our love for Star Trek, but it only seems to get worse, and since I saw the new movie yesterday, I am finally moved to write to someone, admit that I'm a Trekker, and pour out some of my feelings about my favorite science fiction.

Would you believe I find myself in mourning for someone who doesn't really exist? I've been telling myself not to be too caught up in the spirit of Star Trek, to keep my balance—after all, I'm a rational adult, I hope—but my throat continues to choke me with a lump in it as big as the Rock of Gibraltar and my heart insists upon feeling battered, bruised, and broken. I feel as though I've lost a dearly loved teacher and father. Watching Spock die was painful, but it was like tearing something loose inside to see his body hurled into space away from the *Enterprise*. I believe other fans must know what I'm talking about. In the theater where my sister and I saw the movie, there was complete silence during these scenes, almost a stunned silence, and it was broken only by a lady nearby who kept murmuring, "I can't believe it, I just can't believe it." When we were shown that Spock's resting place is on the newly formed living planet caused by the explosion of Genesis, there were sighs of, "Ah, there he is!" I wonder if anyone felt he would like to take up a watchful vigil beside Spock in that lovely place, to be there when he comes to life again. Imagining this seems to ease the pain a little for me.

The movie as a whole was wonderful. It was like seeing the old Star Trek, full of humor, warmth, lots of action, and it was, of course, delightful to see Kirk and Spock in action together again. This was Star Trek all grown up—adult, realistic (as much as SF can be). I suppose the development of the characters is what makes for the realism. However, it was a little daunting to see Kirk as a middle-aged weary man, being taught some lessons that he had managed to evade until now. I guess we want our heroes to stay forever young and triumphant. Still, the movie gave more depth and rounding out of the character of Jim Kirk, and in a way that's very satisfying.

Was it my imagination or did Spock seem more relaxed and at peace with himself? It would seem as though his experience with V'Ger really did help him.

I see that Ricardo Montalban had no difficulty in recreating Khan. We could fully sympathize with Chekov's terror at the thought of being caught on the planet by Khan, and it sure turned out his fears weren't groundless!

There are a great many things I'd like to write about concerning the movie, etc., but I won't take any more of your time. I wish I had the talent and know-how to write an article, it would be such fun. At any rate, my brothers, sisters, and I look forward to reading what those who are more articulate will say about *Wrath of Khan* and on any other subject related to Star Trek.

Dawn Jellison
Jacksonville Beach, Fla.

Surprise! I actually got up the nerve to write a letter! I wrote one much like this to another Star Trek fan, and then decided I like it enough to write another one to *Trek*.

I'm fifteen, and I've been a total ST fan since about the third time I watched the show, about three years ago. My favorite character is Spock, who is and ever shall be my friend. He may not know that, but I can manage. As heartbreaking as it was to lose him, I do agree with most fans that the death scene was, well, powerful. I don't know if I should be proud of myself or very ashamed that I did not cry during this scene (or, for that matter, during *E.T.*). It must be that I've considered myself a Vulcan for too long, and now it seems shameful to Spock to shed human tears over his death. No wonder my father doesn't like my watching the show!

I have conflicting views on whether or not they should resurrect Spock. As much as I love him, I also recognize the fact that this wasn't just some simple "blow of the phaser and goodbye" death. This was *Spock*, giving his life, as he nearly had countless times before, in the line of duty. But this time it wasn't simply to save James Kirk, or any other single person, but to save the *Enterprise* and the hundreds of people onboard from a most certain destruction. Also, after sacrificing himself so much in that horrid radiation, how can they, after so much glory and honor given to his deed, bear to bring him back? It's like saying, "Here he is again, our indestructible Spock, back to go through how many other pointless deaths until James Kirk doesn't care anymore, and walks around the corner each day to meet Spock and say 'Aren't you dead?' and never know when the final death is coming."

Well, I guess I went a little nuts in that paragraph, because (to be on the other side of the argument) I really do want Spock back very much; for selfish reasons, of course, because I just can't imagine Star Trek without him. I suppose I'd be happy with whatever Paramount decides to do, but I wish they hadn't backed themselves into a corner like this in the first place.

It is always debated whether or not Spock will come back from the dead, but what about the Spock in "Mirror, Mirror"?

What if he decided he *was* part of a very illogical Starfleet, and that he *should* do what our James Kirk asked? What if that Spock succeeded, or, more likely, helped that universe to change, maybe not in his lifetime, but in another? He could be running for his life out there, and somehow (only Spock could figure it out) move from his universe to ours! I admit that it certainly wouldn't be the same Spock, teacher of Saavik and friend to James Kirk, but at least our Spock could remain the way he gave his life to be, and not be risen from the dead like some sort of fantasy. It might even be that McCoy's "Remember" was meant for the other Spock?

BIAXIAL WARP PODS—THE "NEW" WARP DRIVE

by Philip Davies

Articles discussing the "technical" side of Star Trek are among the most controversial we publish. Fans are divided almost fifty-fifty—they either love them or hate them. But we think this first effort by Philip Davies, which discusses the new configuration of the Enterprise *as seen in* Star Trek: The Motion Picture *and* Wrath of Khan, *will please even that nontechnical 50 percent of you out there.*

It is generally accepted in both Star Trek fandom and by those producing the films that the warp drive engines of the *Enterprise* work by producing a magnetic vortex that leads into a wormhole, or superspace channel that bypasses linear distance in conventional spacetime. We also know that no spaceship has been seen in Star Trek with more or fewer than two warp pods; it has therefore been suggested, and it may be considered accepted, that two warp pods are necessary to maintain the "proper harmonies" for controlled wormholing. At no point has it been made particularly clear what that necessary harmony is—understandably, because the mechanics of Star Trek is based on a system of physics centuries ahead of us. Or is it?

After all, Zefrem Cochrane "discovered" the space warp two centuries before Star Trek, while everyone else was using *SS Valiant*-type galactic survey ships, which were probably derived from or were in fact DY-500 class ships. In "Space Seed," Lieutenant Marla McGivers points out that the achievement of interplanetary travel alone took years, until "around 2018." Therefore, lightspeed/light-plus impulse drive is at most thirty years away; knowledge of space warp characteristics about the same; and achievement of warp drive per se is less than a century distant. Therefore warp drive is probably a direct product of quantum physics as we know it today, with, of course, technical refinements.

The following theoretical model of warp drive derives in part from specific references in Star Trek and in part from Jescoe Von Puttkamer's wormhole explication in *Starlog* magazine. One other major assumption is made: Everything built by Starfleet is built with operation in mind, with no regard merely for appearance. (Hasn't it ever nagged you that the primary hull is a disk and not a more functional sphere?) This theory will attempt to integrate every facet of *Enterprise* design, from twin warp pods to engineering redesign to nacelle configurations to relocated or modified weapons to the various cooling surfaces. For, to quote Larry Niven, "There Is a Tide," and for Federation starships, the chief threat to their survival is the tide.

It is important to keep in mind that warp/wormhole theory requires a "unification of powers," so to speak, in the form of supergravity. In this perception, all electromagnetic phenomena, however different their apparent behavior, are levels of activity in a magnetic field; that field being a volume of energy, or in Wheelerian terms, the magnetic field being a distortion of the curvature in spacetime. That is, light, heat, gamma, and so-called cosmic rays are all variations in the same basic process that causes gravity, and if Einstein is correct and gravity is an electromagnetic field that imparts energy of motion, then ultimately there is a connection between electromagnetic and kinetic energy. Since we are interested in moving the *Enterprise* from here (our solar system) to there (the galactic rim, for example), the relationship between electromagnetic and purely kinetic forces is our immediate concern. We can characterize the difference between conventional electromagnetism and gravity as essentially energy in two quantum states, albeit one exponentially more active than the other. This approach allows us to speculate on the use of supergravity machinery—machinery functioning on principles comparable to "normal" magnetic field characteristics.

The wormhole effect is, to reprise, a vortex in spacetime that has its "entrance" at one point in space, and does not in fact have an exit, although it can be diagrammed as if it does; such a diagram is more a representation of ends than means. The ship will have traveled past a certain linear distance *as if* navigating a channel, but in fact it has traveled "inward" a distance along the radius of a spherical vortex, a vortex surrounding a centerpoint of infinitely contracting radius. The nearest relative to this effect is the so-called black hole, which should give some inkling of the energy scales in question—it is no surprise that antimatter is the required power source. One can model the *Enterprise*'s warp pods to create the vortical distortion of space along the starship's axis of motion.

As observed, the centerpoint of the vortex is infinitely contracting, causing the spherical vortex to be of infinite radius, ergo infinite circumference. Of course, the vortex cannot be of infinite circumference, lest it consume the entire universe; one can fly around a vortex, but not through it, because as a gravity well, it must stretch the contained space to provide the necessary infinite distance to the center. From the gravity-well model, the farther one proceeds into the vortex, the more dramatically the radial distance is stretched.

It is this radial curve that the *Enterprise* navigates at faster-than-light velocities. Needless to say, the faster one proceeds along the radial curve, the more rapidly the degree of radial distortion will increase. This radial stretch should extend the time factor in covering even the most minute radial distance (actually a great distance in "real" space), thus explaining the curiously long delays for lightspeed/light-plus weapons to impact with their target during warp maneuvering. (Examples of this are the delay between firing and contact during the M-5 wargames in "The Ultimate Computer"; the creeping approach of NOMAD's warp 15 torpedos in "The Changeling"; and the amount of time the *Enterprise* had to retreat when the Romulan flagship fired its implosion-plasma bolt in "Balance of Terror," a bolt which outraced the *Enterprise*'s emergency warp speed, Warp 8.) The minutes experienced on the *Enterprise* would amount to seconds, fractions of seconds outside the warp effect.

Which is why the crew doesn't die of old age in the covering of a mile in normal space terms—they *don't* cover that mile, they just look as if they're covering it. In fact, they bypass it, covering, say, an inch (or less) of radial distance. Under such cicumstances, warp maneuvering may be impractical over extremely short distances because of the time extension effect. Impulse at sublight may in fact be superior for in-close maneuvering, in-system or in such a place as the Mutara Nebula.

In view of certain elements in the series, we must assume that impulse drive is capable of faster-than-light speeds, perhaps employing a warp-type vortex, without warp drive. This brings us to how the warp effect is generated, what exactly warp drive is, and thus to the "tide."

Warp vortices are, in part, an easy problem to solve. The vortex is created by a hellishly powerful supergravity torus, or "magnetomic" coil, to borrow from Star Trek jargon. Such a torus will have to be a superconductor (for reasons to be developed later), and will generate the gravimagnetic field by utilizing the complete power output of the antimatter reactor, or most of it anyway, operating in a field so strong the heat will be in excess of 100 million degrees absolute. Therefore, the superconductor is probably a synthetic molecule, extremely loosely bound in its structure to damp out random or heat vibration to a level less energetic than the vibration set up by the unresisted Cooper electron pairs. Indeed, it is not unrealistic to suggest that the warp torus would in effect be one colossal molecule.

Warp drive, per se, utilizes the warp field to provide kinetic energy. How? Simple (sort of): One can compare the warp drive to a linear induction motor, in which the magnetic field along which the magnetic flux propels the ship is the field of the vortex, along the radius. This is achieved by extending the torus into a toroidal coil, or helix. Our one humongous superconducting molecule is even larger, and it is not surprising that it took at least a century to make it work.

Under such a system, an increase in power should increase the centripetal force, or inward attraction of the vortex, as it acts upon the ship (to reverse course, reverse the current flow along the helices). For now, let's just say that the warp factors are most likely quantum levels in centripetal attraction as the power channeled from the antimatter banks through the helix is increased.

The tide is a characteristic of most vortex effects and is particularly inevitable in the construction of our warp helix. The power flow, you see, not only travels along the helix, it travels in a spiral path along the flux-generating magnet. It therefore has not only linear energy, but tangential or rotational force. This linear pull combined with rotation creates a tidal force like that which tears any object approaching a black hole into basic particles. This is the kind of energy used to propel the *Enterprise*. By definition, alas, the *Enterprise* must be torn into snarks and boojums by her own engines. With such energy absorbed into her matter, the ship will truly explode.

Such a problem is far from new. Steam-powered ships suffered from similar turbulence created by single waterscrews until stabilizers, gyros, and contrarotating waterscrews were incorporated; the helicopter utilizes the same principle of countervailing forces.

So the logical conclusion to keep the *Enterprise* from being destroyed is to employ a countervailing warp helix. There are two ways of doing this.

The first is a by using a double helix. The double helix is very attractive and might even be practical in the impulse-drive single torus. However, Starfleet engineering is not all-powerful, and to build two 100-million-degree super-molecules into one shell, with one cooling system, can safely be considered an engineering impossibility. Very possibly the ion drive that lit the lovelight in Scotty's eyes in "Spock's Brain" used plasma created by a medium of ionized gases to maintain and control a double-helix warp drive. The heat radiated from each helix could have increased the electrical activity in whatever ionic medium was being used, effectively converting the heat into an electric current, carried out to provide ship's power—or even cycled right back into the warp helix!

The remaining, and necessary, configuration for maintaining a countervailing warp helix on a starship is twin warp nacelles. The simplest version of this structure would be the Klingon warship, or the USS *Reliant*'s class of starship. (The *Reliant* is clearly an earlier-model starship than the Constitution class, although her registration is NCC 1864, later than that of the *Enterprise*. Probably the *Reliant* class is the Model T or jeep of starship design, a simple, efficient basic configuration that has not needed to be changed in perhaps a century.)

In a starship, the massive tidal forces must be balanced against one another to create a subspace vortex; or, rather, two integrated superspace vortices, an ellipsoid effect. This requires that the warp helices be perfectly synchronized—there is no space for even minute error. Since the antimatter is housed in the warp nacelles, a safe, jettisonable distance from the populated hulls, it is safe to assume that the energy produced in the reactors is beamed down to the engineering section in some coherent form. Once there, it is run through a group of dilithium crystals, through which it is monitored and maintained, then projected back up to the nacelles.

Now that we've kept the *Enterprise* from blowing herself up, we surely don't want her flailing off course. The warp effect, while created in a linear area, acts as a radial section of a spherical field. However, while such an engine will innately be oriented toward the centerpoint, the specific radial orientation of the axis, in terms relative to external space, is not dictated by the warp helix effect.

Logically, the *Enterprise*'s internal navigation system would operate in much the same way as the warp drive. If one were to construct a large, double-helix torus oriented 90 degrees across the cortical axis it would act in the same manner as a gyrocompass. Let us call this mechanism the gyrosynchronous torus. The "gyrosynch" would have to be synchronized with the warp helices, and in view of the Constitution class's six dilithium crystals (the number burned out in "Mudd's Women"), it is safe to suggest that there are two crystals assigned to each helix group, two to each warp helix allowing backup and rescue potential, but only one to each lateral coil, because loss of the lateral magnets would result only in going off course—provided both coils in the lateral torus remained in synch.

Conceivably, the gyrosynch would curve space sufficiently to help the fusion motors cheat the Einsteinian laws of light speed. The vortical mechanics would be more complex than, and less efficient than, the pure warp drive. In such a mechanism, the impulse-drive vehicle, in a warp ship unlike a DY-500, would navigate a chord across the vortex, a chord that would be in fact a parabola.

It should now be clear that the lateral torus in question is built into the disk-shaped primary hull. The inward flow into the doughnut-shaped hole of the torus of the magnetic field, heavily damped by nonmagnetic insulators or diffracting transmissions, acts to provide the simulated gravity in the primary hull, and that similarly reduced power fields operate in the secondary hull.

Note also that the primary hull is midway between the secondary hull and the warp nacelles. This arrangement keeps everything within the fields of the vortical ellipse and the gyrosynch, the secondary hull being necessitated by design size limits of the gyrosynch (as is the aft superstructure of the *Reliant*). As already described, the closeness of the coils in a double-helix configuration creates considerable engineering problems, probably increasing with size.

Now that we've established the design of the Constitution class, an investigation into the design and engineering limits should clarify the circumstances surrounding the reconstruction of the warp nacelles. It has been observed in Star Trek that *structurally* a starship cannot exceed Warp 10. On a ship that can survive, structurally, a point-blank nuclear detonation? Too long at Warp 8 and she'll blow up? Yet, with a little not so-gentle-help from the Kelvans in "By Any Other Name," the *Enterprise* exceeded Warp 15; put through some kind of mass-conversion/reconstruction in "That Which Survives," she exceeded Warp 13; and in "Let That Be Your Last Battlefield," she ran around in circles at Warp 10.

As we have constructed her, the *Enterprise* is a maze of delicately balanced, highly energetic fields. The point is, there is no such thing as a perfect machine, and even if the *Enterprise* was designed to an accuracy of within .001 percent, when you are dealing with forces in terms of eight or nine exponential quanta above light speed, you've got a considerable amount of random energy running around guided only by Finagle's Constant (or Murphy's Law). What we're talking about is cumulative design or material imperfections, the limits of engineering precision. In effect, a safe measurement at Warp 6 will start to show problems; "cracks" at Warp 7; and by Warp 8 these faults are crevasses, because warp factors are *exponential* quanta. Slight fluctuations in the vortical fields become leaps and bounds in energy levels; minuscule imperfections in the balance of countervailing forces, one-molecule impurities in a dilithium crystal, may cause the tidal forces to slip out of synchronization, and only a marginal shift in the balance would instantly vaporize the ship.

In the old-style circular-section nacelles, the stability of the nacelles is maintained by the ship's frame and the counterbalancing tidal force. The two pods, in neutralizing each other's tide, create a no-tide region where the helices are kept in line by warp struts. This alignment is subject to the stresses of maneuvering; the torque in turning, the audible vibration created by the flowing energy in engineering channels, the kick of the impulse engines, weapon impacts. The trititanium hull is not perfectly elastic, and the original configuration is never quite regained. These are cumulative flaws, worsening over a period of time.

At any given time, however, the warp pods' fields are stable only along one axis, that of the ship's motion. They do not directly relate to the gyrosynch because that is mostly tied in with navigation, its impulse-drive function being almost coincidental. If the warp pods could be built with some means of further stabilizing them, balanced between two linear axes instead of just one, it would be like a ladder having two legs for stability instead of just a central single stem. Also, such a configuration would expand the diffracting no-tide zone, allowing more structural give-and-take in combat and in other stress situations, as well as during the ongoing stresses of operation over long periods of time. Increased "give" would compensate for engineering limits of accuracy and then some, not only allowing a wider safety margin, but the potential to extensively upgrade one's power system, so that the new maximum speed is much greater.

What, then, should be the helix construction for increased vertical field stability and expanded diffraction/countervailance region? To build two separate helices in one housing would lead to many of the same operating difficulties as the double-helix design, not to mention duplicating the power control and synchrony-maintenance difficulties. An ellipse or rectangular winding would still produce a roughly circular field effect. The logical development is, therefore, a figure-eight or bi-axial winding. The needed shell configuration for such a section would be rectangular, slightly constricted around the middle. It is worth pointing out that the side grilles on the Constitution II class ships are located in the middle of the diffraction zone (inside) and on the totally unmodified, nonbalanced warp field zone diametrically opposed to the diffraction zone. Probably these grilles relate to synchronization, or optimum countervailance, while the outer grilles' fields act as the two main field-induction paths, like rails. Otherwise, they are colossal cooling surfaces.

In *Star Trek: The Motion Picture*, the wormhole accident was clearly the product of a matter-antimatter imbalance made possible by the expanded helices having a slip in countervailance caused by (a) one reactor's having a slip in its normal ratio of matter to antimatter, (b) one reactor's upping its power output too soon to allow a balanced warp effect, or (c) both reactors' failing to maintain synchronized interface reactions between matter and antimatter. That this did not destroy the *Enterprise* instantly is because the expanded countervailance system was flexible enough to briefly allow the imbalance to exist. The reason the wormhole did not throw the *Enterprise* far off course is that she was in the wormhole for seconds at most, at a low warp factor.

It was erroneously stated that because the warp factors available have increased from eight to twelve, the power output of the *Enterprise* engines doubled. No, the increase in relative velocities between warp factors is not arithmetical, but exponential. In such a model of warp drive wherein the factors are a quanta of warp maneuvering power, there is absolutely no basis in extant quantum systems to suggest that the required increase in power to step up a quantum level would be anything less than exponential. Therefore, the increase in *Enterprise* reactor capability is an increase of four quantum levels, four exponential measures of the power generated. The increased amount of available power would have immensely improved deflector strength, improved sensor range, and allowed that much more power to be available for such ship's services as science laboratories. If photon torpedos are products of available antimatter, then their availability and effectiveness would also be greatly enhanced. As we can see, the uprated warp designs have made possible a whole spectrum of improvements.

Our study of warp design can even shed new light on the phaser. I for one have never been particularly won over by the theory stating that phasers are integrated laser/fast proton streams. (It is worth pointing out that back in Captain Pike's day, the *Enterprise* used lasers.) I strongly suspect that "phaser" stands for Panchromatic Helix Accelerated Stimulated Emission Radiation. In other words, the phaser is a quantity of energy that can be polarized, focused, and transmitted in any frequency or energy state (e.g., infrared to cut, full spectrum to disrupt, a stream of electrons imparting a fair electric jolt to the nervous system to stun) and then accelerated or amplified in a sense by being channeled along a small double-helix channel. In the handgun or weapon version, the supermolecule helix may not radiate enough heat to be of great difficulty when employed in coaxial form. If this is the case, channeling the phasers through the warp-drive helix in addition to the weapon helix would lead to one godawfully powerful weapon!

So there we are, that is the rundown on the new engines and the way they work. The rankling thing is that the Klingons had the biaxial warp helix first. This is why their otherwise inferior ships proved so stunningly effective in action against the Constitution-class cruisers. Their firepower has rarely proved superior, but their speed has been noted at up to Warp 10. This strongly suggests that they also have learned not to put their phasers through the warp-drive system; but the greater output potential of their nacelles has led to a consistent and often devastating reliance on photon torpedos.

ANOTHER LOOK AT CAPTAIN KIRK'S PERSONALITY

by Deanna Rafferty

When submitting this article, Deanna asked, "My memory fails me. Have you run an article called 'A Look at Kirk's Personality'? If not, how can I call this 'Another Look'?" Our memory failed us too, and to be frank, we didn't check, for when one considers that Star Trek: The Motion Picture *and* Wrath of Khan *indeed gave us "another look" at Captain Kirk, the article's title becomes entirely appropriate. Deanna is quickly becoming one of our most faithful contributors, as well as one of the most insightful. See if you agree.*

Much has been written about the various changes seen in Spock's personality in *Star Trek: The Motion Picture* and *Star Trek II: Wrath of Khan*. Making the debates even more interesting and exciting is the night-and-day difference in his personality displayed in each film. But the same thing is true of Kirk's personality, and although this fact has been quite overlooked, understanding it is vital to our enjoyment and understanding of both films and "current" Star Trek in general.

To understand the connection between *Wrath of Khan* and *Star Trek: The Motion Picture*—a connection which, frankly, many fans have found to be almost nonexistent on the surface of things—we must go very far back and examine the state of James T. Kirk's personality at the end of the original series.

Kirk, although he had suffered through at least three debilitating love affairs, the deaths of his best friend, his brother, and his lover, several bouts of disease and injury, two courts-martial, a literal splitting of his good and evil natures, and much, much more, did not really seem to learn anything from his trials. We could see Spock grow throughout the course of the series in a number of ways, but Kirk was apparently the same no matter what astounding, nerve-racking, or horrifying thing happened to him. At the beginning of the series, Jim Kirk was a cocky, womanizing, self-centered—dare we say it?—boor. Worse, we could see that Kirk indulged very little in introspection and self-examination or self-evaluation—at least not publicly. Not for Jim Kirk was the kind of heart-to-heart talk we saw Chris Pike share with his ship's doctor. No, for good or ill, Kirk kept his own counsel. At the end of the series, he wasn't much better.

However, we know that Jim Kirk is not an unfeeling and insensitive boor. He is deeply caring, deeply committed, a person who not only affects events around him, but is affected by them. No boor could make the kind of impassioned speeches Kirk made on a number of occasions—speeches which if they did not succeed in intent, at least gained him the respect and attention of friend and foe alike. These were not just words to Kirk, but his personal beliefs, his soul if you will, pouring out in a torrent of ofttimes beautiful oratory. And, as always, actions speak louder than words. We saw innumerable instances of Kirk's love, his compassion, his simple, innate desire to help and serve others even at the cost of his own life. James Kirk's words and his actions had such a seemingly powerful influence upon everyone with whom he came in contact that one could fairly describe him as *mesmerizing*. Why, then, did he apparently not heed his own example and grow through his experiences, change for the better? Why did Jim Kirk remain the same person when any other man would so surely have been forever transformed?

The answer is, of course, that Kirk *did* change. Being human, being a caring, compassionate person, being *Kirk*, he couldn't help but change. But also being a starship captain, being the one who shouldered the burdens, the griefs, being *Kirk*, he could not allow himself to show the changes within himself.

Here we have an uncanny parallel between Kirk and Spock. Spock, as everyone knows, has fought a lifelong battle to suppress and disguise his human half, his emotions and reactions. It is also common knowledge that—at least since the *Enterprise* and Jim Kirk—Spock's battle has been a losing one. Kirk, on the other hand, seemed to be the archetypical human—wearing his emotions on his sleeve, savoring life and its physical pleasures to the fullest. We thought we could always tell what Kirk felt, what he was thinking. Except in the rare instance when he was working undercover or in secrecy, Jim made little secret of his feelings. We grieved with him, rejoiced with him, felt fear with him. We even, on occasion, got drunk with him.

Not so Spock. Our knowledge of Spock's emotions and feelings were limited to those infrequent instances when dire straits or unnatural influences caused them to break free. Oh—and a number of other times too . . . when Kirk *told* us what Spock was feeling. It was always Kirk (gleefully aided and abetted by McCoy) who was trying to move Spock along, to loosen him up, to get him to act "more human." If anyone in the universe was responsible for the changes in Spock, however slight in the original series or however drastic in *Star Trek: The Motion Picture*, it was Kirk. (It is important to add that Kirk was so desperately forcing Spock toward humanity for dual reasons: First, he truly felt it better for Spock to experience and benefit from his human half; second, Kirk knew that the more Spock allowed himself to acknowledge emotion, the more likely he would be to continue and strengthen the friendship between them, a friendship desperately necessary to Kirk.)

It is ironic that, being so intent upon making Spock change, Kirk himself displayed so little growth. Since we know that Kirk was not the kind of person who could ignore the people and events thundering through his life, we can only conclude that he, much like Spock, both consciously and unconsciously suppressed the mental changes and influences that events forced upon him. Indeed, Kirk seemed (toward the end of the series) almost to become a parody of his old self: a supermacho man, parading around with chest puffed out, speechifying and pontificating at the drop of a hat, the very model of a modern starship captain. It was very strange, very un-Kirkish, to coin a phrase—and it was all ballyhoo, all bluff. If the truth be known, Kirk was probably pretty damn near the end of his rope by this time.

The adventures of the *Enterprise* related in the animated episodes must be taken with a grain of salt, since they are severely truncated and sometimes unreliable concerning characterization. But in even the small glimpses we were allowed into Kirk's mind in these episodes, we can tell that he did indeed begin to change a bit during that, the "fourth year" of the *Enterprise*'s five-year mission. And it is not a change for the better. In the animated series, Kirk is colder, more militaristic, more intellectual than ever before. Doing exactly the opposite of what he has been continually pushing Spock to do, Kirk becomes less human, less emotional. But considering what he has been through in the previous three or four years, this is perhaps an understandable reaction.

Kirk, like any good commander, has always been able to compartmentalize both his intellect and his emotions. He will feel that it is necessary and good for his crew to take frequent rest leave; he will feel just as strongly that he must not. He will feel that a man must temper justice with compassion; as a captain, he must obey and implement the rules, no matter what the result or who is hurt. And so on. In each of these instances and many more, Kirk sees no dichotomy, no inconsistency in his feelings. It is part of his work, what he does, what he believes in. So it is understandable why he could feel that Spock should loosen up his emotions while at the same time suppressing his own.

We may assume that this phase did not last long. Kirk is naturally too ebullient and volatile a person to successfully suppress his emotions. Even so, the realization that he was doing so probably came as a bit of a shock to him—he would simply not have considered the question, so unused was he to examining his own feelings and motivations. This discovery probably did not cause him to change in any discernible manner beyond the unsuccessful and short-lived suppression of emotions. What it did do was lead him into the first of the number of serious periods of depression which were to mark both his personal and professional life for years to come.

(There followed a number of missions in the "fifth year" of the voyage, some of which are related in various novels and other formats. The fluctuations in Kirk's mindset and sometimes even in his behavior are accurately portrayed in these novels; the comment that Kirk's personality seemed to change from book to book was more than an idle observation.)

The euphoria that seized Kirk upon the successful completion of the *Enterprise*'s five-year mission and the offer of promotion to admiral lead him into making the disastrous decision to accept the promotion and shoreside duty. McCoy, who had certainly been carefully monitoring Kirk's mental state for quite a while, desperately argued against acceptance; he understood all too well the precarious mental trap into which Kirk was gleefully strolling.

Inevitably, the boredom of Earth duty caused Kirk to regret his decision. His work was unsatisfactory, his friends scattered who-knows-where, even the obligatory love affair soon paled. Most hurtful of all, he felt as if he had been abandoned by Spock and McCoy.

Kirk probably wouldn't have admitted to taking either McCoy or Spock for granted, but when one looks at many examples from the series, it is clear that he did so. Perhaps this stemmed from a confidence that he knew them well enough to predict their actions. So it was entirely likely that he expected them to join him at Starfleet Headquarters—after all, Spock could just about name his spot, and any medical facility in the world would be happy to have McCoy. Kirk must have felt pretty good, feeling that he had just about reached the pinnacle of his profession and he would have his "family" at his side to share in the glory and, finally, the safety of Earthside duty.

McCoy, however, angered by Kirk's refusal to heed his advice and pretty much fed up with Starfleet service in general, resigned his commission in favor of researching the vast medical knowledge of the Fabrini. We can only speculate on the conversation in which McCoy informed Kirk he would be resigning, but it is a pretty sure bet that it ended acrimoniously, for when Kirk and McCoy first meet in *Star Trek: The Motion Picture*, there is a palpable tension between them. For a moment, it seems as if McCoy will refuse to take Kirk's proffered hand of friendship; he is naturally angered that Kirk had him recalled to active duty, but there is little doubt that much of his unfriendly attitude stems from their previous angry parting.

Kirk would have been deeply hurt by McCoy's action, but he would have been able to understand it. The doctor had originally joined Starfleet in order to escape hurtful memories, and he shared little of Kirk's enthusiasm for space travel and exploration . . . he shared none of Kirk's need for danger and excitement. Starfleet was never really McCoy's home, no matter how comfortable he seemed to become in his position or how satisfying the work. It was and always had been a refuge, a place where men and women traditionally took a newcomer at face value and asked no questions, made no judgments beyond a person's work. This was not an attitude which McCoy the humanist would have appreciated, but he would have been quite grateful for its existence. It was perhaps this one-step-removed attitude about Starfleet (as much as his personal knowledge about Kirk) that allowed McCoy to accurately predict that Kirk would soon tire of the pomp and empty duties of the admiralty. Onboard the *Enterprise*, Kirk had a large amount of freedom and autonomy; in the upper reaches of Starfleet, he would be just another small fish in a big pond, resented by those who had spent their lives working toward his newly awarded rank, neglected by those who did not include him in the "club" of old-line officers who ran Starfleet in name and deed.

McCoy and Kirk had a bitter argument (probably a series of increasingly acrimonious ones), but it is doubtful that that alone would have led McCoy to resign Starfleet and, literally, leave Kirk. As mentioned above, McCoy knew of Kirk's increasing tendency toward depression; that, coupled with the ever-increasing bitterness and resentment he could see looming for Kirk on the professional horizon, may have made McCoy decide he could not stay and see his old friend be destroyed in small stages. Of course, he knew that his absence would probably only help to accelerate the process, but we may be sure that had McCoy felt there were *any* chance that his presence could have prevented Kirk's decline, he most certainly would have remained at his side. Bones often talked like a pessimist, but he is the ultimate optimist—so when he gave up on Jim Kirk, it should have been obvious that he considered him a hopeless case. It should have been most obvious to Jim Kirk.

Perhaps it was obvious to Spock, as well. We know that the Vulcan made up his mind to resign and return to Vulcan quite a while before the end of the five-year mission. However, we also can deduce that his decision was made sometime *after* the adventure related in the final animated episode. Spock, of course, noticed Jim's colder, less emotional attitude during the "fourth year," and it may well be that he felt his own unemotional stance was unduly affecting Kirk. (Spock must have felt ironic amusement when realizing this, for Kirk and McCoy—and even he, at times—had always felt that it would be the other way around.) Unwilling, as always, to allow his captain to come to any harm because of him, Spock would have logically decided that the best way to remove the hurtful influence was to remove the cause— himself. This proved not to be necessary, for Kirk soon abandoned the unemotional attitude, but the thought would certainly have stuck in Spock's mind. As much as he cared for James Kirk, Spock could, and probably would have, come up with hundreds of chillingly logical reasons why his presence was debilitating to Kirk. But as long as they continued to serve on the *Enterprise*, the problem remained moot. Kirk reverted back— with occasional lapses—to his previous personality and attitudes, and although Spock must have been concerned, he did not need to take any kind of action.

This all changed, of course, when the five-year mission was complete and each member of the *Enterprise* crew was faced with the start of a new phase of his or her life and career. In previous instances, the choice had been simple for Spock: reassignment to the same or another ship, perhaps a promotion, and new, more taxing and interesting duties. This time, however, Spock faced a more difficult choice. He was not oblivious to the scuttlebutt that claimed Kirk would be offered an admiralcy, the *Enterprise* would be retired for two or three years for refitting, and the officers and crew retrained for the "new" ship. Spock could choose from several options: He would have been immediately granted a captaincy of his own (we may assume the *Enterprise* was his for the asking); he could have remained as science officer under a new captain; or he could opt to remain at Starfleet in any number of capacities.

Spock could not see fulfillment in any of these choices. His oft-stated disdain for command was real. And there was no longer any reason to remain aboard the *Enterprise*, or any ship for that matter. Spock had failed to find what he was seeking when he joined Starfleet. The most attractive option was probably that of accepting an Earthside position at Starfleet. There were many jobs which would provide him with challenge and intellectual stimulus—research, design, training and teaching. And he would be near Kirk, if not actually working with him.

None of this was set at the time Spock made his decisions, of course. The Vulcan would simply have taken into account human nature and the needs and exigencies of Starfleet politics and accurately predicted the offer and Kirk's acceptance. He may even have predicted McCoy's refusal to remain. (If so, it would have made his decision to return to Vulcan and leave Kirk literally alone all the more difficult.) It is unlikely that Kirk had at this time made up his own mind, although, like Spock, he would have heard the gossip and rumors. As a matter of fact, the longer the rumors flew, the more likely they were to have a salubrious effect on Kirk, making him all the more likely to accept the offer once it was officially made. (Could the fine, wily hand of Nogura have been working months in advance?) So, having time to think, Spock would have sat down and logically considered the pros and cons of the matter.

What his internal mental arguments were, we will never know, but we can get a hint of the kind of turmoil in his mind by the flood of feelings which almost overwhelms him upon his return to the *Enterprise* in *Star Trek: The Motion Picture*. Spock is surprised not at the existence of these feelings, but instead at their intensity after two years of intensive *Kolinahr* training. So if he has no problem admitting to these feelings' existence at such a trying time, we can only assume that he acknowledged those feelings and carefully examined them at another time. Surely he would have done so during the "cleansing" rituals of *Kolinahr*, but it's a good bet he also did so during his meditations about what to do after the end of the five-year mission.

Probably it was a combination of factors that led Spock to decide in favor of *Kolinahr*—his discomfort with his feelings for

his human friends; his dissatisfaction with a life-style he had
spent almost twenty years building over the objections of family
and culture; the inevitable mental letdown that comes at the end
of a personal era (and, if Vulcans have such things, a midlife
crisis); the realization that all of his searching had not helped him
to bring either side of his personality into prominence and control . . . *and*, like McCoy, an unwillingness to stick around and
see Jim Kirk be destroyed.

For that is surely what was happening to the Jim Kirk we saw
at the beginning of *Star Trek: The Motion Picture*: He was a man
lost, defeated by, ironically, his own blazing success. Even if
Spock or McCoy had remained, it is doubtful that Kirk would
have been any happier or more satisfied. Indeed, their presence
might have only served to remind him all the more of the
freedom that he gave up when he accepted promotion. Without
them, without either of them, he didn't have a chance.

Because of the anger with which Kirk and McCoy parted, they
obviously did not contact each other during the entire time
between Kirk's promotion and the arrival of V'Ger. True, McCoy
was working in an isolated laboratory, but in an age of transport-
ers and high-speed people movers, the other side of the world is
only a short ride away. Of course, it was impossible to contact
Spock, even if Kirk had wanted to. It is unlikely that even
someone on Vulcan could have easily reached him, for the
Kolinahr grounds are a remote retreat, far from any Vulcan cities
or services. From the manner in which Scotty, Sulu, and the
others greet Kirk upon his arrival at the *Enterprise*, we may
assume that he has had no contact with them, either, except
perhaps for an occasional passing in the line of duty.

This tells us something very significant about the time between the promotion and V'Ger. Jim Kirk had purposely, almost
determinedly, cut himself off from all of his *Enterprise* crewmembers and associates. No matter how angry and bitter the
words at their parting, Kirk and McCoy could easily have patched
things up over a few drinks; it would only have taken one of the
two proud and stubborn men to make the overture. And surely
Scotty, who probably had his opinions about the wisdom of
Kirk's actions but had kept them to himself, as both duty and
prudence would require, would have been happy to continue his
infrequent, but memorable, binges with Kirk.

Instead, Kirk isolated himself, with (if we infer correctly
from the novelization of *Star Trek: The Motion Picture*) his affair
with Lori Ciana as his only social contact. It was only natural
that Kirk would shun the company of his former *Enterprise*

mates, not wanting to be reminded of the satisfying berth he had abandoned. It was quite unnatural, however, for him to take on the role of "faithful lover"—just as it was unnatural for him to happily fly a desk.

Kirk was role-playing during these two years, desperately fighting off the ever-growing realization that he had made a dreadful mistake, a mistake which—seemingly—could never be rectified. At the time we first see him in the novelization of *Star Trek: The Motion Picture*, Kirk is vacationing. The vacation is the first in years he feels he really needs. The pressures and boredom (the two are not mutually exclusive) of his job have worn him down much more than captaining a starship ever did, and he is feeling very low.

Although Gene Roddenberry does not point it out, it is obvious here that Kirk is on the verge of cracking. At the very least he will slip into deep depression; at the worst he would have a complete nervous breakdown. He is too closely confined by his job, his position, his rank, his affair. He no longer has his freedom, his powers, his friends, or his self-respect. We have the merest hint, the tiniest between-the-lines implication that perhaps Kirk doesn't really intend to return from this vacation— the manner in which he reflects upon the height of the power station gives us the impression that he's stood there before . . . contemplating what?

The command alert signal captures Kirk's full attention immediately; whatever his current state of mind, he has not been so far gone as to ignore the clarion call of duty. It is probably a call which he has been praying for, for now, at last, here is an opportunity for action—and, almost unbelievably, an opportunity to regain command of a starship.

It is at this point, when the thought of having himself put in command of the intercepting vessel first enter his mind, that Jim Kirk goes slightly mad. Idle thought quickly becomes hope, hope becomes determination, determination becomes obsession.

One of the major facets (or flaws, if you will) of Kirk's character as displayed throughout the various Star Trek series was his propensity to become obsessed with a goal. It mattered little what the goal was—vengeance, thwarting the Klingons, outmaneuvering a rival lover—Kirk often pursued it with a single-mindedness that bordered on mania. It is only to be expected that after having been virtually one of the living dead for over two years, he would seize upon a chance at command with all of the implacable determination he possesses. And Lord help anyone who stands in his way. . . .

The Kirk we see in *Star Trek: The Motion Picture* is a Kirk we have never seen before. Yes, we have seen Jim during his periodic obsessions, but always when he has entered such phases he has done so from his customary position of power and pride. Not so now. Kirk, although indomitable, is in the position of supplicant. It is likely that he literally blackmails Nogura into giving him command of the *Enterprise*; it is a fact that he bullies Decker unmercifully upon taking that command.

He is sharp-tongued, vindictive, confused, and, most horrifying and saddest of all, scared. In his obsession to command, to get "out there," he has abandoned or forgotten the virtues that made him such an excellent commander in the first place. He has forgotten the lesson which was so graphically illustrated to him in "The Enemy Within": His dark side is what makes him strong, but it is his compassionate side that makes him able to use that strength constructively. The overweening ambition, the braggadocio, the downright ruthlessness of Kirk come out full force thanks to his manic desire to escape the prison of his own making—a prison built of the bricks of ambition and the bars of political expediency. In truth, Kirk is much more than obsessed, he is literally fighting for his life. If he fails at this, his last chance for a command, his last chance to escape from that prison, his last chance to return to the stars, then he will surely die by one means or another. It is this desperation which unleashes the animal side of his personality, the side which will fight and claw and take whatever it can—whatever it wants. And in this case, what it wants is command of the *Enterprise*.

Once he has achieved this goal, Kirk's animal side once again creeps back into its hideyhole and his rational side takes command. Immediately, however, he runs into problems. Simply put, he just no longer is qualified to command a starship. He's too rusty, he's lost that vital edge, he's too damn old . . . or so he thinks. This attitude, coupled with a few early and entirely understandable and easily overlooked mistakes, plus the emotional letdown caused by "caging" the animal side of his nature, once again causes Kirk to suffer a massive bout of depression.

It is unlikely that Kirk and the *Enterprise* would have survived the mission had not Spock arrived in response to V'Ger's "call." Not only did the Vulcan's technical expertise and an eventual mind meld help them to contact and understand the Intruder, it was only his sheer physical presence that enabled Kirk to shake off his mounting depression and take firm command of the ship. Even when Spock acted coolly toward him and McCoy, even when he was confused and hurt by the Vulcan's truculence, just knowing that he was *there* made all the difference in the world to Kirk.

Although Spock's presence and the subsequent increase in action and shipboard activity serve to rid Jim of his depression, he is still severely troubled throughout the mission. Deep inside, he realizes that he has practically stolen the ship from Decker (and just in case he might have rationalized otherwise, McCoy is there to remind him about it), and that the joy and exhilaration he should feel are absent. The two things which have been missing from his life, the two missing facets of his being which kept him from being complete—Spock and the *Enterprise*—are his once again. But still he is unhappy, unsatisfied. We can see this distress in every action Kirk takes, in every agonized decision. He feels that his life is a failure, is worthless, for he has violated his principles, his moral code, his friendship with Decker, and, perhaps, even his Starfleet oath in an obsessed attempt to recapture the *Enterprise*. Now it is his, Spock and McCoy are again at his side . . . and he feels empty. No wonder he seems so eager to operate the code sequence which will merge his essence with that of V'Ger.

Then Spock returns from his attempt to mind-meld with V'Ger and reports that the creature is barren—it has found what it searched for, but is empty, unsatisfied. It wants the eternal "more." In short, it and Jim Kirk are in the same boat. Kirk is pleased and touched by Spock's recognition of the "simple feeling" and will be even more so when he later takes time to reflect upon what it means to both of them. But when Spock reports on V'Ger's thoughts, Kirk hears only one part of it—that V'Ger is searching. In a sudden insight, Kirk realizes that life is searching, that every living being spends his entire span of existence wanting "more" and asking "Is this all there is?" It is man's eternal nature to never be satisfied.

Such insights are, of course, shallow and simplistic, but nonetheless true for that. But at this particular time, to a Jim Kirk feeling as lost as a soul can be, they are as the secrets of the ages. Unknowingly and inadvertently, Spock has brought the means of his friend's salvation—the simple knowledge that he is not alone in his pain.

Of course, Spock also learns from this knowledge, but he absorbs it intellectually (although in no less of a flashing insight) and immediately interprets it in terms of his own emotional crisis.

This one instance shows us once again how very, very much alike Kirk and Spock really are. We may assume that when the

V'Ger affair was over and the two men sat down for the first heart-to-heart talk they had ever shared, they must have been amazed to discover that the personal crisis of each of them was so similar in result, even though worlds apart in cause. Too, each of them would share with the other the calm acceptance of fate and circumstance that the insight had given them.

Some of this acceptance is already evident in the film's final scenes. Spock speaks of transcendence in worshipful tones, as if he longs to experience the release of his soul from the half-breed body and curse of emotion and flow into another dimension or plane of existence. Kirk is able to experience that transcendent beauty with all of his senses and understand it, just as moments before he fully understood what Decker meant. Even McCoy is awed, but, typically, he makes the entire experience understandable by boiling it down to humanistic terms: "It's been a long time since I've helped to deliver a baby."

Spock announces his decision to remain, and we may assume that McCoy also will stay. But what of Kirk? At the end of *Star Trek: The Motion Picture*, there is little doubt that all of his mental problems have been solved, and he fully intends to keep the *Enterprise* under his command and return to space as her captain.

What, then, happened between the end of *STTMP* and the beginning of *Star Trek II: The Wrath of Khan*? Why did Kirk return to ground duties? (One may assume his temporary reduction in rank to captain was just that, temporary, but even if he had to sacrifice his admiralcy to keep the *Enterprise*, there's no doubt which he'd have chosen.) Why is Spock now captain of the *Enterprise*?

First, we must remember that in Star Trek time, something on the order of ten years passed between *Star Trek: The Motion Picture* and *Wrath of Khan*. That's a long time, and any changes that took place in that time would be at least logical in a time-frame reference. People grow, people change. But Kirk didn't change, at least not that much. In a couple of the very first scenes in *Wrath of Khan*, both Spock and McCoy chastise him for surrendering his command and accepting a desk job.

What is interesting about this is that in neither instance is the event spoken of as something that happened long ago. It is entirely proper to assume that Kirk did indeed take command of the *Enterprise* after *STTMP* and hold that command for some years; it is just as likely to assume that Spock, McCoy, and many others in his crew remained with him.

Although Kirk and his friends regret his decision to surrender the *Enterprise*, none of the anger and acrimony we saw in *Star Trek: The Motion Picture* is evident. It's obvious that they, like any good friend would, tried to talk Kirk out of it, but they accepted his decision with good grace. This time all of them remained close friends, staying in contact. But how close could that contact be if Spock and McCoy were serving on the *Enterprise* and Kirk was based on Earth?

The obvious answer is that outlined in several articles in *Best of Trek #6*: The *Enterprise*, thanks to the development of newer starships (like the *Reliant*), has been "retired" and now serves as a training vessel. Spock, as a teacher at Starfleet Academy, has served as the captain of the ship on training cruises; such cruises probably last several months, for even without venturing near hostile territory, much of their corner of the galaxy could be traveled. Such extended voyages would explain why Kirk would be prohibited from serving as captain of the trainee ship; for he too was associated with the Academy. It is quite likely that he was commanding the Academy, a most prestigious position. McCoy would be serving dual duties—teacher, doctor on call, training ship surgeon—and therefore would be based at Starfleet, as would Spock. So while the two of them would spend a large part of their time in space, they would still be serving under Kirk . . . a most satisfactory solution.

At least Spock and McCoy seem satisfied.

McCoy, as he is fond of pointing out, was always a simple man with simple desires—to be out of the way of trouble, to keep busy without being responsible for lives, to have a soft hammock and a cool drink. Teaching—the instruction kind, not the classroom kind—would come naturally to Bones, and the academic life-style would appeal to the puritan side of his nature. (The wide range of available nightlife in San Francisco would appeal to several other sides of his nature, we may be sure!) McCoy would probably agree that teaching might get a little boring at times, but it's one hell of a lot better than getting shot at by Klingons.

Spock too seems finally content. Somewhere along the line between *Star Trek: The Motion Picture* and *Wrath of Khan*, Spock has accepted his duality and learned to live with himself and for himself. (Probably it took him years to achieve this inner peace and balance, and it is probably also an ongoing process.) He can now freely and unashamedly acknowledge his friendship and concern for Kirk; we assume he would do so for McCoy if the need arose. In any case, Spock need not carry his mental burdens around with him any longer.

The only one of the three who is still having problems is Kirk. This time he's once again on the verge of that same old chasm of depression; this time the cause is the same—and yet it is not.

Although he freely gave up his command to rejoin Starfleet Command, Kirk did so this second time under radically different circumstances than before. The first time he was much younger and therefore more easily dazzled by the fame and adulation that was his for the asking. In the novelization of *Star Trek: The Motion Picture*, Kirk reflects bitterly on the way Admiral Nogura manipulated him into accepting the admiralcy and how he was being used as a publicity figurehead, but it must be admitted that it probably wasn't very hard for the old man to pull Kirk's strings.

The second time, however, Kirk probably talked himself into the move. He might have reasoned that his return to the *Enterprise* after *STTMP* and his service upon her for several more years proved to others as well as himself that he could command a starship under any circumstances. The offer of commanding the Academy (although it was a position in which he could make a difference, as opposed to the paperwork admiralcy he had held before) would not alone have lured him to return to Earth, but the possibility that Spock and McCoy would also sign up for Academy service would have. Since we may assume from the events before and during *Star Trek: The Motion Picture* that Kirk would never again allow himself to be used (or misused) by Starfleet, we know that he would not have again "retired" from active duty without very good reason indeed. And he had good reason, in his mind perhaps the best: By transferring to Starfleet Headquarters and/or the Academy in his wake, Spock and McCoy would be *safe*. No longer would Kirk have to worry that his friends would meet death somewhere in space, nor would he have the incredible burden of having to feel responsible for that death. Earth was safe for all of them, and at that time in the life of a man with very few friends and family, safety was more important than freedom.

Again, although we are not told how long it has been since Kirk gave up his command and began "flying a computer console," we may assume that it has been only a few years, at most. That has been long enough, however, for Kirk to again become dissatisfied with being earthbound. (We really don't have any indication that he is dissatisfied with his work this time; it just seems that there isn't enough of it. McCoy's crack about a computer console may have been unjustified—Kirk could have had myriad duties, many of which could have been interesting and fulfilling.)

The problem, as it will always be with Jim Kirk, is that he is totally addicted to space. He must be "out there," he must be in command, and, most important and saddest, he must have that element of constant danger to feel alive. It may even be that he must have those he loves in danger, as well, to feel totally alive; his own life is not valuable enough to him to fully stir and engage his emotions.

Kirk refuses to (perhaps cannot) recognize this, for to do so would again prove his decision to accept Earth duty wrong, and might also again trigger the manic determination to regain command that plagued him in *Star Trek: The Motion Picture*. It is a sure bet that Kirk remembered how he felt and acted during that time and he has no desire to ever fall into such a mental state again. But he is once again trapped by his oldest and most malevolent enemy: depression. This time, thanks to his refusal to see that he should be in space combined with the actual passage of time, he fixates upon his age. He not only feels old, he feels useless and left behind by events and life.

This is not true, of course. Kirk, like anyone, can make of his life what he chooses. Such an ability is within our grasp; so much more so would it be to Kirk in his time. We see no indication of it in the dialogue of *Wrath of Khan*, but there are more options open to Kirk than he is willing to admit. Although Starfleet has been his life, he is not unbreakably tied to it. He could easily gain command of any number of commercial spacegoing vessels; he could just as easily obtain financial backing to go into business for himself. This would probably not satisfy Kirk, however; ferrying passengers or cargo along safe, well-traveled routes would not be exciting or dangerous or challenging enough for him. The only advantage would be being in space, but that would very soon pale and become as boring and routine as his Starfleet duties. He could also take command of a trading ship, one of his own or one owned by someone else. This would allow him the opportunity to travel widely about the galaxy pretty much as he chose, avoiding the ennui of regular runs. However, it is likely that Kirk would find the rituals of trading as alien and ultimately repugnant as the rituals of diplomacy. He might, for a short while, enjoy the bargaining, but would soon be feeling that he was nothing but a glorified merchant.

The only non-Starfleet spacegoing position which would satisfy Kirk would be to command one of the small commercial exploration vessels which seek out minerals, habitable planets for colonization, etc. Being able to go beyond established Federation perimeters, often in the wake of the first starship explorations (knowing Kirk, it would sometimes be before them!), would satisfy Kirk's need for danger and excitement and his love of the alien and unknown. Too, he would feel as if he were actually accomplishing something in this work—finding a new planet that could become a home for millions or feed millions more, or a valuable new source of dilithium crystals for Federation ships, or a new race with incalculably valuable knowledge— that would be something to live for, work Kirk could be happy doing.

So why wasn't he? For one thing, he was feeling too old, too used-up to start over in a new career. In his depressed state, he had convinced himself that space was a "game for the young," an area in which an old retread like himself could not successfully compete. Too, even if he had felt up to starting a new career, he would have been loath to ask Spock and McCoy to abandon the careers they had established at Starfleet—the *safe* careers which he would be asking them to leave to again face the dangers of deep space. And it wouldn't be any fun to go alone, would it? Being alone was also a game for the young—it was a curse for the old.

So at the beginning of *Star Trek II: The Wrath of Khan* we see James T. Kirk enmeshed in the same trap as before: bound to duties he is no longer interested in, barred from deep space, feeling old and discarded. There's no indication of it in this film, but we may also assume that there was another in the long line of failed love affairs somewhere not too far back in Kirk's past as well. His loves always seem to end badly; that too has been one of the contributors to his bouts of depression over the years.

Kirk "came alive" to a certain extent once he had taken command of the *Enterprise*, but he was almost immediately confronted with evidence that his instincts were very rusty indeed. Although he and Spock managed to avoid complete defeat by a combination of knowledge and trickery (always skills best used by Kirk), the effect must have been jarring to Kirk, bringing back to him unwanted memories of the wormhole debacle in *STTMP*. Worse, the ship was being attacked by Khan, an old enemy for whom Kirk felt responsible.

The subsequent events of *Wrath of Khan* served to pull Kirk from his depression, but presented him with an entirely new raft of problems. He was again confronted with Carol Marcus, and although we are not told any of the details concerning their long-ago affair, we can assume that they were deeply in love. The result of that affair, David, is also something new in Kirk's life. Although the evidence tends to substantiate the fact that Kirk was always aware of David's existence, it is hard for us to believe that Kirk would not demand that he have a hand in raising his son. The only possible reason for Kirk's acquiescence would be that he too shared Carol's desire that David *not* follow his father's footsteps into space. Seeing how unfulfilled a spacefarer's life has left him, this is an action we can understand, if not totally agree with.

Now, however, it is a different story. David has accepted Kirk as his father and expressed pride in him and his work. He is also no longer a child; he is a trained and extremely talented scientist, fully capable of making his own decisions and career choices. Kirk would be willing to have David serve with him now—not only because David is his son, but because David would be a valuable member of the crew. More important, he would have interests and values removed from Starfleet; his "world," being wider than that of his father, might not prove nearly as constraining. There is a better-than-even chance that David would find service both exciting and rewarding.

This acceptance, however, does not come to either of them until after the disastrous death of Spock. We have yet to learn the full effect of this upon Kirk. He seems to take it well, in an accepting, philosophical vein. It looks as if he will avoid depression this time, and it is entirely possible that he will be able to do so forevermore in the future. This would be perhaps the greatest good to come from Spock's sacrifice.

Aside from his grief, the greatest effect Spock's death will have on Kirk will be the absence of that link between them, that symbiotic relationship which they shared for so many years. It has been said that Kirk and Spock and McCoy were three facets of a single integrated personality. The question is, will that personality be able to function now that part of it is gone?

The answer is, of course, yes. Kirk will not have the intellectual and pragmatically moral advice of Spock to guide him any longer, but much of that will now come from Kirk himself. Having conquered his fears about growing old, he will be able to use his age, his experience to advise himself and others. Before *Wrath of Khan*, it is unlikely that Kirk ever used his age as a measuring stick of wisdom—it would have sounded too much like an old salt complaining that no one minded his elders anymore. He will now freely admit to his age, pointing up that it is only wisdom and experience that allows a person to survive fifty-odd years of deep-space exploration.

Admitting to being older will help Kirk to act older—no more young girls, no more risky missions, no more posturing poses and cocky speeches. Feeling younger, however, will allow Kirk to act younger too—no more depression, no more false hopes of safety and security, no more denial of what and who he is.

Kirk has finally reached maturity. He regrets, as do we all, that it took the death of his dearest friend to help him achieve that maturity. He is, however, now content with himself and his life for the first time in many years. And those things with which a man can never be content—such as the loss of Spock—he now accepts as an inevitable part of life. No longer does Jim Kirk chastise himself for such things; he goes on, regretfully, sorrowfully, but he goes on.

SECRETS OF
STAR TREK

by Richard Mangus

It never ceases to amaze us how readers can see the same episodes we saw and glean from them knowledge and information which eluded us completely. In this article, which sees some of those hidden facets as secrets, both literal and figurative, Richard Mangus discusses things from particular episodes which give them an entirely new and sometimes far different meaning. After reading this article, we think you'll look at Star Trek in an entirely new way.

From the earliest episodes, secrets have played a major part in Star Trek plots. Sometimes these secrets were straightforward bits of information hidden from the viewer, but becoming clear as the story unfolded. Instances of this include the plot to capture the Romulan cloaking device in "The *Enterprise* Incident" and the dangerous secret of Talos IV in "The Menagerie." At other times the secret was only part of the background of the episode, never exactly being revealed during the plot, but all the same there helping to make it more interesting and intriguing. Stories of this type make up such episodes as "Where No Man Has Gone Before," "The Squire of Gothos," and "The Ultimate Computer," among others.

In "Where No Man Has Gone Before," the secret lies in the reasons why the *Enterprise* was sent to the edge of the galaxy at that particular time and with that particular crew.

The existence of the recorder buoy that the *Enterprise* picked up en route to the edge of the galaxy was unknown to the crew and was not in the computer records. Although it was known that the *Reliant* was lost in the area, the mission doesn't seem to be to investigate the *Reliant*'s fate, but instead only to penetrate the galaxy frontier. The buoy was found only by accident and too late to allow the *Enterprise* crew to adequately prepare for contact with some sort of barrier at the edge of the galaxy. (Given Kirk's propensities, however, it is likely the *Enterprise* would have gone on anyway, regardless of any warnings received.) After being badly damaged by forces beyond the understanding of even twenty-third-century science, the *Enterprise* managed to reach a robot mining installation in only a few days using impulse power.

It seems unlikely, if the mine was that close to the galaxy rim, that no other Federation ships would venture beyond the edge of the galaxy. There would be no lack of ships in the area, either: Finding the resources would require survey missions; determining that the resources could be mined would require geological missions; and finally the building and starting up of the station would be a project taking many months and involving dozens of ships and hundreds, perhaps thousands, of workers. Still, even with all this traffic so close, the *Enterprise* had no record of any ships exploring beyond the galaxy frontier—a frontier so close to Delta Vega that even an old impulse ship could have reached it in days, a slow warp-drive commercial ship in hours.

A further hint about this secret in "Where No Man" lies in the addition of Drs. Dehner and Piper to the *Enterprise* crew for this mission. Elizabeth Dehner was assigned to observe crew reactions under difficult conditions—she just happened to have a remarkably high ESP rating, as did Gary Mitchell and Mr. Spock. And instead of McCoy, the ship's doctor is an older, perhaps more experienced and hardened doctor who doesn't have the same rapport with crew and officers as did McCoy, a more aloof and objective medical man. It is very likely that Starfleet had a good idea of what it was sending the *Enterprise* to investigate.

It is probable that since the disappearance of the *Valiant*, a number of ships had visited the area of the galaxy rim. Most of these were probably destroyed, as was the *Valiant*, either by the force of the barrier itself or later by individuals who acquired strange new powers and either wrecked their ships or were destroyed by self-destruct systems. Possibly a few ships or survivors returned; perhaps more modern recorder buoys were left to relate the strange tales of ESP and danger. This information would be classified by Starfleet, and the area surrounding the edge of the galaxy would be declared off limits.

For years, nothing more would be done to explore the area. Wars and other serious problems and projects would mean that few ships could be spared to investigate the barrier—especially since they would likely be destroyed. Finally, in a time of peace, the *Reliant*'s recorder buoy was detected, and the *Enterprise* was sent to penetrate the barrier. Without being given a proper briefing, Kirk and his crew were sent forth, expected to research the problem, survive, and make a full report upon returning.

The inclusion of Dehner, along with Mitchell and Spock, would make sure that at least a few of the crew had enough latent ESP powers to be affected by the energy in the barrier. The exclusion of McCoy and his replacement with Piper helped to deprive Kirk of a necessary sounding board, compounding the problem; as would the fact that one of those affected was his best friend, and another could very well be his first officer. The deck was certainly stacked against Kirk in this instance. It almost seems as if Starfleet was willing to sacrifice the *Enterprise* and her crew in order to gain information. It would be safe to say that the survival of the *Enterprise* through this mission made Kirk's reputation with Starfleet. More important from his standpoint, however (as well as ours), is that the events led to the first tentative overtures of friendship from Mr. Spock.

It would seem that in later instances Kirk and Spock were not quite as much in the dark. In ''The Squire of Gothos,'' we wonder why the *Enterprise* putters along at Warp 3 if it is carrying needed medical supplies. The secret of this episode is apparently that Kirk and Spock knew of rumors and wild stories of strange aliens in Napoleonic drawing rooms capturing humans and had been sent by Starfleet to investigate. Thus the *Enterprise* moves along at a speed slow enough so that she might be mistaken for a freighter and also slow enough to easily hit with a transporter beam and confiscate a couple of crewmembers.

The keys to this episode's secret were mostly in the teaser: Kirk claims they are in a hurry, but they have been trundling along at Warp 2 and are only now accelerating to Warp 3, not fast at all by starship standards. Spock notes the presence of Gothos before the highly trained starship navigator sees it; it is as if he knew his reading meant that they had come upon what they were looking for. After Kirk vanishes, Spock apparently does not consider looking for him any other place than on Gothos, a very un-Spocklike action. Spock is also unsurprised at what they find on the surface of Gothos. It is as if he and Kirk had been told what to expect.

If this was indeed the case, they could not have known the truth behind Trelane, of course. But having prior knowledge of his irresponsible and irrational actions certainly would have helped them to face him more confidently and objectively.

In "Mirror, Mirror," we see an instance wherein secrets must be kept after the events of the episode. Starfleet would certainly suppress information about the alternate universe (and how to travel back and forth between the dimensions, something which Scotty apparently found the key to doing). Further research could lead to further contact with a potentially dangerous adversary, possibly leading to inter-universe war and resulting devastation. It is likely that Spock-2 would suppress the information for the same reasons, as well as to protect himself.

No starship may ever visit the planet Talos IV. To do so is to incur the only death penalty remaining on the books; if you go there and come back, you get "zapped." The *Enterprise* went there twice.

The first time really doesn't count, for no one had ever before visited the planet and learned of the dangers there. The ban was issued because of what Christopher Pike and his crew discovered about Talos IV. Thus even the existence of Talos IV was kept secret.

The *Enterprise*'s second voyage to Talos IV was also unplanned, at least by Starfleet. Spock reputedly planned and instigated the voyage to give Captain Pike a "second chance" at life. Once again Kirk was kept in the dark about what was going on, dragged along first by a falsified message, then by a phantom instilled in his mind. It was always Spock and the Talosians in command, never Kirk. He never knew what was really going on and never had much choice in the matter, even over his own actions. Still, he showed fortitude, decision-making ability, and an aptitude for getting at the truth which threatened the plans of even the monstrously powerful Talosians.

Regardless of the altruistic motives of Spock's actions, he and Kirk should have been arrested, tried, and probably executed upon their return from Talos IV—unless Spock was acting with the knowledge, and perhaps even the approval, of Starfleet.

The fiction of the court-martial in which the events of Pike's visit were revealed proved that the Talosians' mental powers were vast indeed. They were not isolated in their little system after all, and a ban on visiting the planet would do little good if the knowledge of thought-casting could be learned without physical contact with the Talosians. Having probably learned this during Pike's mission (when the *Enterprise* intercepted the false SOS radio message), the Federation needed to have Pike and Spock return to Talos to be sure that the Talosians were sincere in their vow to keep their knowledge to themselves. Kirk was not told of the mission so that if Spock failed, Kirk could be exonerated of charges and Starfleet would not lose its best captain. Spock did succeed, however, so the secret that he and Starfleet acted together in the affair remains a secret.

Kirk, on the other hand, had the ability to get himself into trouble without anyone's help. Whether in space or on a planet, whether on a mission or just passing by, whether willingly or unwillingly, Kirk entered adventures in the strangest ways.

In "Arena" he was planning to beam down to Cestus III to have a friendly dinner and ended up in the opening shots of a war. The rescue mission to Omnicron Ceti III in "This Side of Paradise" was supposedly routine, but Kirk nearly ended up losing his ship and crew. These and many other examples show that there would have been opportunity for plenty of adventure and dangers even without Starfleet's intervention.

In the early part of "The Ultimate Computer," Kirk seems to be asking himself one question: "Why me?" The answer, of course, is his ability to pull hats out of rabbits, to come back from hopeless situations after desperate struggles. Of course, Kirk, being a hero, leaves the meaningless question behind him as difficulties begin to appear and starts acting heroically. The only reason for his behavior, however, is that Starfleet gave no answers, no explanations, no warning that there could be dangerous problems with the M-series computers. When the exercise began to go wrong, the onboard crew once again faced a life-or-death situation with no information from Starfleet command.

It could be suggested that in this case Starfleet again chose not to reveal possible flaws in the M-5 in order to observe how the computer could be overcome in an emergency. As with the events in 'Where No Man Has Gone Before," such actions would lead one to believe that Starfleet is more than willing to sacrifice a ship and crew for a little knowledge. To be fair, however, in each case the knowledge gained could be immense—a particularly ESP-sensitive person such as Gary Mitchell could, if unchecked, eventually threaten the entire galaxy; and the M-5, if it could be properly controlled, could be the ultimate deterrent against Klingon and Romulan aggression. In either case, we can easily visualize both Kirk and Spock gladly giving their lives to protect the safety of the Federation.

Secrets form the beginning and ending of "Metamorphosis." The existence of Zefrem Cochrane, discoverer of warp drive, on asteroid Gamma Canaris N is a secret from everyone—he was assumed to have died many years before. Kirk and Spock assume that he will want to go back with them to the Federation, where he will be greatly honored, for it is to him, more than any other individual, that Starfleet owes its very existence. Too, knowledge of past centuries from a human instead of a Vulcan point of view would be useful. And who knows what new discoveries have been brewing in Cochrane's mind since his isolation 150 years previously? He had little to do except think, after all.

Once the Companion had merged her essence with that of Nancy Hedford and Cochrane had decided to remain with her on the asteroid, however, everything changed. Spock, Kirk, and McCoy promised to keep his secret, and they have done so.

This brings us to another secret of Star Trek, one which again involves Starfleet Command. Evidently, Starfleet has existed for some time, at least a hundred years since the war with the Romulans. But in "The Menagerie," the *Enterprise* is described as the first space cruiser on its mission in space, thirteen years before the time of the series. On Elba II, Kirk, Garth, and Spock discuss the foundation of the Federation as an event that they remember during their lifetimes, not as a distant event from history books. Garth was evidently partially responsible for it, a great leader at a crucial point in history. After that, Starfleet was not just an Earth force, but accepted people from other planets as well—such as a young half-breed Vulcan who was one of the first aliens at the Academy and later shipped out on the first purely Federation cruiser.

The question remains, however: Did Starfleet force the union of worlds? It could have been that the Peace Mission of Axanar ended a war and began the United Federation of Planets.

Forcing meetings of worlds may be something that Starfleet is experienced in from its very beginnings, an old talent and a weapon for averting war and saving lives. Who but Starfleet would send one starship to pick up all of the diplomats attending an important conference and ship them together to the meeting? It was inevitable that much of the discussion of the Babel conference would begin onboard the *Enterprise* long before the meeting officially started, and that might have been the point of doing it. But one may assume that at least a few of the ambassadors would have objected. Were they forced to go anyway? We are not told.

In any case, gathering all of these important and influential delegates together on one planet is dangerous—to do so on one starship seems rather foolhardy. Yet, this is exactly what Starfleet did. Kirk seemed to be aware of the gravity of the meeting, but curiously unaware of the full seriousness of the situation. Also, Starfleet, with its wide range of devices (and presumably people) to spy and observe, couldn't have been completely unaware of a plot that required such massive preparation. Again, Kirk and his crew were uninformed of a potentially dangerous situation.

It is possible that Starfleet gambled that Kirk could deal with any threat (if indeed a threat arose), for his track record was pretty good, and the experience of having faced danger and seeing how desperately their enemies wished to stop admission of Coridan to the Federation would have caused the ambassadors to reach agreement. One may only assume that Starfleet favored admission of Coridan for strategic reasons, and allowed events to occur in a fashion that would favor that admission. Such interference is probably against Starfleet's charter from the Federation; if nothing else, it would be repugnant to many Federation member planets. Any such involvement would have to be kept in deepest secrecy—secret even from the captain and first officer of the starship involved.

The story of Khan Noonian Singh and his followers is rife with secrets. The secret of Khan began long before the beginnings of Starfleet or the Federation when Khan and his people boarded a ship, perhaps the first starship, and headed into space. As Spock said, knowledge that Khan had escaped would have been kept from war-weary populations, since any further threat from Khan was remote. And since no notes were kept, there were no warnings for someone in the future who might encounter Khan's ship.

Once he had regained his ship from Khan and exiled the "supermen," it is obvious that Kirk intended the group should survive on Alpha Ceti V. The conversation between him and Spock at the end of "Space Seed" suggests that both of them fully expect Khan's people to make a new beginning and a success of their world. And it is entirely possible that Kirk intended to stop in occasionally and see how Khan and his people were doing.

Perhaps Starfleet had different ideas. Knowledge of the existence of Khan could have been censored and Kirk, Spock, and the others ordered to remain silent about the existence of the supermen, as well as to keep away from Alpha Ceti V. No doubt surviving records of the carnage wrought by the supermen in the twentieth century, the still-active prejudices against genetic manipulation, and the terrorizing manner in which Khan acted immediately upon awakening aboard the *Enterprise* acted to convince the Federation and Starfleet that the best course was to keep Khan and his people completely isolated. It was always possible that he could again take over a ship.

It is even possible that some of the more violent and callous members of Starfleet could have gotten their way and seen to it that Alpha Ceti VI exploded. Perhaps it was intended that Ceti V be the target; perhaps it was thought that the resultant devastation would be enough to wipe out Khan's threat forever (with no risk whatever that blame could ever be laid upon Starfleet). The unlucky *Botany Bay* herself could have been used as the weapon of destruction.

While such a scenario is horrifying to contemplate, it must always be remembered that the primary jobs of Starfleet are exploration and protection. Many fans tend to overlook the protective functions of Starfleet except when the *Enterprise* or some other ship is attacked, but by its very definition, protection is more than just battling aggressors. It is also Starfleet's job to see that more subtle threats, such as Khan, are defused or eliminated. Since no organization can know everything or be everywhere, it is sometimes only realistic to take fate into one's hands and see to it that events take place in favor of the good guys. Taking care of citizens of the Federation isn't always a clean or nice job. More often than we would like to admit, perhaps, Starfleet has to get its hands dirty and play the game according to someone else's rules.

Perhaps it isn't always a good idea to tell officers all of the information available. Prepared for one danger, looking toward one aim, they might be surprised by something completely unexpected. Knowing nothing, expecting anything, they will seldom be caught unawares. Then there is always the possibility that information could leak out—either inadvertently or on purpose—with disastrous results. Plans can be completely ruined when officers approach them with preconceived notions. What is a starship crew for if it doesn't have to face dangers and solve problems?

Secrets in Star Trek take many forms and involve the crewmembers of the *Enterprise* in many ways, some good, some bad. But it is the job of the officers and crew to face problems so that others don't have to, to meet challenges and fend off dangers. The fact that Starfleet sometimes sends them in, confident that they will succeed, without full information, or with ulterior motives, demonstrates the trust that Starfleet has in its people, rather than a lack of trust. And the opposite is sometimes true, as well: Kirk, Spock, and others have been known to keep secrets from Starfleet and the Federation. Again, it is not a lack of trust that causes them to do this, but instead a conviction that they have been chosen and trained well enough to make such decisions.

Star Trek's secrets are not always earth-shaking, nor do they always cause our heroes great danger. In the majority of episodes, no secrets of any import exist at all; in many others, small subtle secrets serve as textual background, making the episodes richer and more realistic. (There is no need to delve into such secrets, they are better left unexamined as part and parcel of Star Trek's "universe.") In any case, secrets in Star Trek have helped to provide us with some of the most interesting episodes of all.

LOVE IN STAR TREK—
PART TWO

by Walter Irwin

As stated in the first half of this article (Best of Trek #5), *Star Trek showed us in many ways that love is a universal constant. This concept was carried on and further developed in the two feature films. But, as is ever true with Star Trek, such development did not always go in the direction that we expected it to. In this concluding part of his article, Walter examines these further examples of love in Star Trek and explains what the differences are and what they mean.*

Love in Star Trek, as in life, takes many forms. Throughout the course of the series' run, almost every type of love which one sentient being may feel for another was presented. The need and desire for love was presented as an everyday, natural part of the characters' lives, just as it is of our own. Sometimes love was the focus of an episode, as in "Requiem for Methusulah"; other times the tug of conflicting loves was the focus, as in "City on the Edge of Forever." Other types of love than the romantic were also pivotal to many episodes: brotherly love ("The Empath"), love of freedom ("The Menagerie"), paternal love ("The Conscience of the King"), and even love for inanimate objects ("This Side of Paradise").

Star Trek is, of course, based on love. The underlying theme of the series is the assurance that man will one day overcome his own humanity and learn to live in peace and brotherly love not only with his own kind, but with myriad other sentient beings throughout the universe. The love of freedom is also a very important part of the Star Trek concept. Each person is allowed the right to be free and desires that that same right be extended to all others. It naturally follows that love of individuality is the one theme which ties both of these together. This is embodied in the

Vulcan philosophy of IDIC (Infinite Diversity in Infinite Combinations), which states that it is the differences between beings which must be revered, not the samenesses, and that tolerance and understanding between all life forms can only result in love. Stated as it is in such terms, we can see that the Star Trek concept was an extremely optimistic one—especially when we consider the turbulent times in which the series was first developed and introduced to the viewing public. In order to make his message of tolerance and love more palatable to a public which had so often heard the word "love" bandied about in conjunction with everything from antiwar protests to tennybopper cosmetics that it had become virtually meaningless, Gene Roddenberry wisely incorporated healthy doses of adventure, exploration, mystery, danger, and the lure of the unknown into the Star Trek format—a form of "sugar-coating" the messages, as it were.

(It must be noted, of course, that these same elements are prerequisites for any successful television series, and Roddenberry did not coldly and cynically include them simply to trick viewers into watching his programs. When speaking of love, it must be remembered that the average human loves nothing more than excitement, danger, mystery, and the scary unknown—especially if all of these can be experienced in the comfort of his living room.)

Even though Gene Roddenberry's firm guiding hand was absent from the third-season episodes, and a number of the philosophical elements which had made the series so rich in texture and depth were sadly absent, both the concept and practice of love permeated many of these third-season programs. Indeed, although many of the basic plotlines in this season are generally acknowledged to be among the series' weakest, many of the strongest affirmations of the concepts about love were presented in third-season episodes. It was the only season during which Kirk, Spock, McCoy, and Scotty *all* enjoyed brief encounters with love.

Spock was the first. In the second episode of the season, he became involved with one of the most fascinating and mysterious characters ever seen in Star Trek—the Romulan commander. (Yes, she has a name. It is rare and beautiful and incongruous when spoken by a soldier. And we never learn it.) Nor do we learn much of anything about the commander. She is undoubtedly one of the most complex and conflicted characters appearing in Star Trek, and that is probably even more of a reason for her lasting popularity with fans than her involvement with Spock.

But we must not forget that any woman who can so intrigue Spock is also irresistibly intriguing to us. . . .

From one standpoint, the commander can be seen as the archetype of woman as presented in film and television—the cold, seemingly emotionless "female executive" who finds that her intrusion into "the man's world" has left her lonely, frustrated, and vaguely unhappy. She doesn't realize *why* she's unhappy, of course. It isn't until a dominant, virile male comes along and sweeps her off her feet into the bedroom—or kitchen—that she discovers all she ever *really* wanted was to be a complacent and compliant hausfrau. (You've seen it a zillion times in Doris Day movies.) It's very easy to view the commander as a lonely, frustrated, and vaguely unhappy Romulan warrior who doesn't discover the True Meaning of Life until Mr. Spock comes along and sweeps her off her feet. She then discovers that all she ever really wanted to be is a good little Vulcan wife.

But, as always, Star Trek adds a little twist. The commander is no spinster pining away in lonely isolation at the top, compensating for the lack of Mr. Right through power and ambition. She is a vital, willful, and highly intelligent woman who has risen to her present position by being *more* vital, willful, and highly intelligent than the men around her. She, like her male counterpart in Starfleet, Kirk, is obviously smitten with a desire and need for command, and she is highly proficient at her job. After all, her ship was chosen as the vessel to test the cloaking device and Federation defenses, so the Romulan High Command must have confidence in her. Her position is not compensation for a lack of love in her life; it is a result of her intelligence, skill, and ambition. She likes to command, she likes being a warrior.

We can only surmise the details, but judging by the take-charge manner in which she becomes intimate with Spock, the commander has an active and satisfactory sex life. In this, as in her position as a commander, she is complete. There is no question of compensation or sublimation of her desires in any area. So why does she seemingly go ga-ga over Spock?

Simple . . . she doesn't. At all times during their "affair," *she* is the one who is in control, the partner who is dominant. If there was any seducing done in those scenes we didn't see, it was *she* who did the seducing. In a coolly calculated manner which would draw a whistle of admiration from Kirk, the commander leads Spock into her boudoir and into her arms. Spock, as we all know, was acting out of duty—playing along for the purpose of buying time. But he certainly didn't look unhappy with his duty. In fact, we get the distinct impression that he was downright enjoying it. Although the commander was understandably upset and unhappy when Spock's true motives were revealed, she didn't moan and groan . . . she quickly and efficiently ordered his immediate execution. However much he may have touched that soft, sensitive, and feminine part of her (and that is not a repressed part, by any means; she revealed it quite willingly and naturally), Spock wasn't nearly as important to the commander as was her career. Or her revenge.

If she wasn't in love with Spock, however, then why did she beam aboard the *Enterprise* with him? It was an act completely out of character for her. She wasn't afraid or panicky—she is much too haughty and controlled for that—and surely she didn't have a wild desire to remain with Spock "under any circumstances." The only possible explanation for her action is that she couldn't bear the thought of Spock's getting away without her being on hand to prove to Kirk that Spock's deception was not totally successful. Kirk (and in her mind, Spock) might be able to gloat about stealing the cloaking device, but she was going to make damned certain that they wouldn't be able to gloat about Spock's putting one over on her. It was pride, pure and simple, that sent her to the *Enterprise*.

Spock *was* affected by the commander to a certain degree, but it was probably most likely the unaccustomed physical closeness to a female that affected him. (It has been suggested that the wily commander slipped an aphrodisiac into Spock's drink. Romulan fly, most likely.) Spock would probably have reacted to any Vulcanoid female under similar circumstances, and the results would have been the same. It was an uncomfortable and somewhat unnerving experience for him, but his control of his emotions (and presumably his libido) and his loyalty to Starfleet completely obliterated any chance that he would become the least bit involved with the commander. It is more likely that the reverse is true—the commander would have been drawn to Spock's integrity (an attribute highly prized among Romulans) and perhaps by the challenge of "unfreezing" a Vulcan. There was respect between them, yes, perhaps even admiration. But not love.

We can only assume that the wily commander managed to convince her superiors that her journey to the *Enterprise* justified her "capture" and that she was restored to her command. Chances are she's out there somewhere today, fighting battles, advancing her career, and helping to spread the many good things that are part of the Romulan Way.

* * *

Miramanee, the Amerind maiden of "The Paradise Syndrome," was one of the most charming and appealing women to have graced Star Trek. It is little wonder that Kirk/Kirok fell in love with her at first sight. Although he had suffered an almost complete loss of memory, Kirk still retained his basic personality and knowledge, as well as his sharp eye for a shapely female and his recently expressed yen for a life of peace and quiet. In Miramanee and her people, Kirk found both, and while he remained ignorant of his true self, he was more happy than we had before or since seen him. He loved Miramanee totally, but even that love was not enough to keep his dynamic personality in check for long. Unable to be content with the simple life-style of the Indians, Kirk suffered from "strange" dreams and urges; by the time the asteroid arrived, he was pushing the Indians into civilization. Miramanee instinctively knew that their love couldn't survive a resurgence of the suppressed memories represented by the dreams of "the lodge that flies through the sky"; once Kirok's satisfaction with the simple life turned to boredom, his satisfaction with his and Miramanee's idyllic marriage would end as well.

Unfortunately, it ended in tragedy. Although Kirk was saddened by the death of Miramanee and their child, it is doubtful that he felt any regret for the loss of their life together. His love for Miramanee was deep, but it could not, under any circumstances, have lasted once he regained his memory. As Kirk or Kirok, the captain simply could not be satisfied (at that period in his life and career) with the simple pleasures of a wife and family.

Other examples of love are seen in this episode: Salish, the ousted medicine chief, loved Miramanee, and his jealousy led him to attempt murder; another example of how twisted love invariably leads to evil in Star Trek. Spock, on the other hand, remained completely in control of his emotions, even to the point of suppressing his worry about Kirk, and concentrated totally on the problem at hand. To Spock's logical mind, love was the necessity of saving as many beings as possible from the threat of the asteroid, even though that meant abandoning Kirk temporarily to an unknown fate. It must be noted, however, that both Spock and McCoy felt that Kirk was still alive on the Amerind planet, and that much of the cause of Spock's obsession with halting the asteroid could have been prompted by his knowledge that Kirk would surely die if the asteroid struck the planet. McCoy, naturally, misunderstood Spock's logic and fretted unendingly about Kirk.

* * *

In "And the Children Shall Lead" the evil "angel" Gorgon twists the affection of children to his own ends. As the love of children is a pure, innocent love, such manipulation is a definite no-no in Star Trek. Gorgon's powers of illusion force the children to forget the deaths of their parents, and they naturally transfer all of their boundless love to the most convenient and kindliest-seeming adult figure available—Gorgon. His hold on them was probably strengthened by his illusory powers; he could have appeared as one of their parents or any other beloved figure, or he could have supplied them with the fulfillment of their childish fantasies. It is only when Kirk and Spock remind the children of the true love they shared with their parents that the children can see Gorgon for the evil being he really is and are freed of his influence. As is always true in Star Trek, real, natural love is more powerful than artificial, unnatural love. It is interesting to note that (again) it is Kirk's love for the *Enterprise* and his command and his fear of losing them that provide the key to defeat Gorgon.

Another love triangle appears in "Is There in Truth No Beauty?" but this time it is a slightly different one: Larry Marvick loves blind telepath Miranda Jones, but she is deeply involved with Kollos, an alien so hideously ugly—or beautiful—that to see him will drive a human insane. The question that lingers from this episode is, of course, if Kollos and Miranda actually shared love. Marvick thought so, but he was unbalanced to begin with (again, jealousy is condemned and punished), and we get a definite feeling that Miranda, for her part, wanted to love Kollos. It was her uncertainty about this that led her to fear and resent Spock's ability to mind-link with Kollos—and his ability to actually *see* Kollos. It is this which bothered Miranda the most, for she was unable to see the object of her affections, and Spock—her rival in a sense—could. It was not so much jealousy that prompted Miranda's resentment of Spock, but instead her fear that Kollos would find her lacking—and therefore undeserving of his love—after melding with the intellectual Spock. Not only was Miranda reluctant to help Spock, but in an indirect way, she was also responsible for Marvick's madness and the plight of the ship. She was spared punishment, however, because she saw the error of her ways and performed heroically to help restore Spock's sanity. It is interesting to note that it is only *after* she helps Spock that she is able to form a permanent link with Kollos, leaving us with the impression that Kollos desired to share love with her, but required that she relieve herself of her irrational behavior and attitudes before he would commit himself. One could even suspect that Kollos took the opportunity provided by Marvick's attack on him to place the ship deep into the energy zone and force a situation wherein Miranda would be forced to face herself.

"Spectre of the Gun" reaffirms Star Trek's dictum "Love thy fellow being"; that peace and the refusal to kill are values highly prized by superior beings and that our acceptance of this philosophy is a first step in the maturation of our species. An interesting sidelight in this episode is Chekov's instant and somewhat overanxious attentions to the dancehall girl, Sylvia. Looks as if Chekov was overdue for shore leave.

Again, love for others was the lesson in "Day of the Dove," but in this instance we saw a more tangible and horrifying result of hatred—the alien entity that "fed" off of enmity and violence. Here, we see Chekov's inner demons take the form of a sexual attack on Mara . . . the boy was *way* overdue for shore leave!

It was, in the minds of many Star Trek fans, high time for Leonard McCoy to have a true love affair. In "For the World Is Hollow and I Have Touched the Sky," he not only had his affair, he ended up married! True, in Star Trek fashion, McCoy was not truly "himself" during this period. Suffering from xenopolycythemia, McCoy wasn't functioning mentally on his usual level. So when he discovered a mutual attraction with the beautiful Natira, McCoy decided to grab what happiness he could and agreed to stay with her on Yonada. In his mind, a few months of wedded bliss was a fair trade for the million-to-one chance of finding a cure in space. This seems like a rational decision, but had McCoy been acting normally, he would never have agreed to remain with Natira; regardless of his illness, he would not have given up so easily. We've seen him work many sleepless hours to discover cures for literally dozens of diseases, and he knew he would have the full support of Spock and Kirk in his search. Too, McCoy would not normally have been so callous as to marry a woman knowing that he would shortly die and leave her bereaved. He has seen too much pain to so casually inflict it upon another.

All of these considerations aside, McCoy *did* choose to remain with Natira, so we may assume that the shock of discovering he was doomed seriously affected both his judgment and his consideration for others. If nothing else, a normal McCoy would have quickly realized that Natira was simply not his type. She was a strong-willed woman, used to command and control, and would thus have been totally unsuited to McCoy's laid-back life-style. McCoy may have been drawn to her beauty and gentle mien, but he would surely have balked at the first sign of her iron will. (As a matter of fact, the moment he was cured, he jumped back aboard the *Enterprise* and flew away without so much as a quickie divorce!) To be fair, McCoy would certainly have realized that a marriage between himself and Natira could never work, and he used the excuse of her duty to break it off quickly and cleanly. Bones is basically a decent and straightforward man, and he would never have asked her to marry him (no matter *what* the circumstances) if he hadn't truly felt something for her. We can only hope that Bones someday finds Yonada again, and that he and Natira have a lingering and mutually satisfactory reunion.

"The Tholian Web" is notable for its reaffirmation of the Friendship. Kirk, via prerecorded computer cassette, instructs Spock and McCoy to look to each other for strength, guidance, and friendship. It is the first time we are given any indication from any of the Big Three that they are mortal and can die—but that their friendship can continue even if one of them dies. Thus, the Friendship is elevated into the realm of love, for love does not require the presence or interaction of the loved one, and love remains, can even grow, after death.

Also in "The Tholian Web," we get an interesting glimpse into the psyche of Uhura. It has long been conjectured by fans that Uhura is deeply in love with Kirk (and perhaps vice versa). During the time that Kirk is trapped in the interphase, it is Uhura who seems to feel the loss most deeply when he is presumed dead. It is also she who first sees the phantomlike visage of Kirk. It is left up to the reader to decide if Uhura's love for Kirk enabled him to partially return from the interphase dimension and thereby be saved. Or was it just coincidence? Was Uhura only mourning the loss of a good friend and her captain—or was it very much more?

Well, in "Plato's Stepchildren" we get a little more evidence. When the Platonians cause two women to be beamed down to participate in the "entertainments" with Kirk and Spock, it is Uhura and Chapel who are summoned. So we have something more to add to our conjecture: Were the women picked because they were the most handy? Or were the thoughts of Kirk and Spock somehow scanned and the most suitable partners chosen for them? More likely, however, because of the presence of Christine, it was the thoughts of the *women* that were scanned— and, again, it was Uhura who showed the greatest affinity for Kirk. When she and Jim are forced to kiss, Uhura is almost on the verge of tears . . . but are they tears of humiliation or are they caused by the fact that she has longed for such a moment (as did Christine with Spock) but is shamed by having it forced upon Kirk? Again, we can only speculate.

The Platonians, because of their mental powers, had lost the capacity to truly love; they instead turned their passions toward decadent and humiliating entertainment. Here we see another tenet of Star Trek. Love cannot survive within a stagnant society; it is only when man continues to strive, to better himself and his fellows, that love may flourish. Of all the Platonians, it is only the dwarf Alexander who shows any compassion or affection for the *Enterprise* crewmembers; it is only he who has not gained the telekenetic power; it is only he who has remained active and growing throughout the years.

Deela, queen of the Scalosians in "Wink of an Eye," wants only to have Kirk (or any suitable male, for that matter) impregnate her. In the process, however, she succumbs to Jim's charms as so many others have done, and although she truly loves Rael, she develops quite a liking for Kirk. It is unfortunate the mores of the time prevented full exploration of the desperate existence the Scalosians were forced to endure, for the interplay between Deela and Rael only hinted at the pain and embarrassment they suffered. It is quite amazing that Star Trek was able to get away with as frank an exploration of sexual matters as is seen in this episode. Male sterility was hardly acknowledged to exist within the world of network television in the 1960s, much less a sterility which forced the females of the species to mate with any being they could, literally, "get." Even more shocking is the concept that these females were acting with the full knowledge and approval (however grudging) of their male counterparts. The thought of being impotent is horrifying enough to the average male viewer. The further thought of having to sit helplessly by while another male, a healthy, virile male, makes love to his woman . . . It's a wonder the plotline didn't give the network boys the screaming willies and cause them to quash the show while it was still in script. This was extremely strong stuff for television in the '60s and another indication of how Roddenberry's science fiction format allowed discussion and examination of themes which would be completely taboo in an everyday dramatic presentation. It is a shame that this ability—this power, if you will—was so often misused or frittered away by silly plots and endless moralizing.

Self-sacrifice is the greatest expression of love, and its undying importance was constantly reaffirmed in Star Trek in many ways. But never more so than in "The Empath." It is only through an act of self-sacrifice that the beautiful mute empath Gem can save her people, but (according to the Vians) such an act is completely alien and unknown to her race. (One can only wonder how a people can even begin to approach the fringes of civilization without such behavior as a working part of their value system; perhaps Gem's race had some sort of religious or social taboos against self-sacrifice.) In order to meet the Vians' specifications for survival and have her people rescued (a goal Gem probably does not even know she is seeking), Gem must not just sacrifice her life, she must *learn* to do so. This she has been unable to do until the arrival of Kirk, Spock, and McCoy. It is through their example, their willingness to die for each other if need be, that Gem learns the value of friendship and love, and she is finally able to make such a choice by and for herself. She has not been able to learn this from the Vians, who (in true Star Trek "villain" tradition) are a stagnant, inbred race no longer capable of feeling or loving. (Gem has also obviously been incapable of learning from the researchers, but we don't know if they were unwilling to exhibit self-sacrifice, or if they simply didn't last long enough under the Vians' tender mercies to teach her anything.) Gem learns her lesson very well and as a reward is spared. Her race, through her, will be deemed deserving by the Vians and thus rescued. Perhaps too the Vians will reconsider their life-style and morality, and if they are able, will try to imbue their race with a little more compassion and understanding . . . which, if they are successful, will eventually restore their ability to know love.

Also in "The Empath" the Friendship is again affirmed, this time through the example of each man's love for the others. Each is quite willing to die (or worse) to spare his friends, and the other two, together and separately, are equally as adamant that their friend will not make such a sacrifice. It must also be remembered that Gem learned from these three about the joys of *living* and gained that spark of human spirit and will which keeps humans from surrendering. Gem was taught not only how to sacrifice herself for her fellow man, but, more important, how to *live* for her fellow man. It was this which allowed her to live after healing McCoy; it is this which will allow her people to begin again after the traumatic shock of being transplanted from one planet to another by the Vians. The program is a warm example of all that is best in man, and a solid and visible example of the love and respect underlying the characterizations of Kirk, Spock, and McCoy.

Kirk falls in love with the haughty and volatile "Ellan of Troyius," but he does so because of a strange psychophysical "love potion" contained within her tears. Ellan is hardly the lovable type under any circumstances, and it is not hard for us to believe that Kirk could so easily throw off the effects of the tears. Spock, however, in his usual perceptive way, offers another explanation: Kirk's antidote for Ellan's "magic" is the *Enterprise* . . . and in his particular instance, there is no cure.

Also in "Ellan of Troyius" we saw a rarity in Star Trek—the use of marriage as diplomacy. It is not hard to imagine that arranged marriages exist on many worlds in the galaxy (it seems to be the practice on Vulcan, for example), and it is one easy step from that to arranging marriages between members of two races or two planets or even two species. Even so, Star Trek seemed to shy away from portraying love and/or sex as a tool to be used in such a fashion—which is, when you think about it, a curious thing, for sex was portrayed as being an integral part of life in every other area, affecting the outcome of many battles, personal problems, captivity situations, etc. Apparently when dealing with political issues, Star Trek preferred to use such broad strokes, such elusive and nonidentifiable allegorical mirroring of our society that the question of sex would be of minor import. According to Freud, sex is the root of every human action. According to the Network, however, sex is the root of everything except business and government.

Marta, the Green Orion slave girl in "Whom the Gods Destroy," has an unusual hang-up: She must kill those she loves . . . and the lady falls in love *very* easily. She is, of course, quite insane, but we can see in her character a restatement of the Star Trek position that love must be pure—i.e., untouched by insanity or loss of control, without perversion—to be true love. The case of Garth of Izar is a curious one, for he received his injuries and subsequent madness because of an action taken to help others. Perhaps Garth was unstable to begin with and his actions were prompted more by reasons of personal aggrandizement than by altruistic motives.

* * *

Although Star Trek lauded self-sacrifice as a viable and sometimes desirable course of action, we saw the occasional instance wherein self-sacrifice was represented as being unnecessary and meaningless. Nowhere was this more strongly stated than in "The Mark of Gideon," wherein the beautiful Odona is to become a casualty of Vegan choriomeningitis (a culture of which is taken from Kirk's blood) and will die as an example to her people that voluntary death is a solution to Gideon's horrifying population problem. It is not, of course, necessary for Odona to die—any more than it is necessary for *any* of Gideon's inhabitants to die. Only their bizarre prejudice against birth control keeps them from stabilizing their population. And if they felt that custom must be preserved at all costs, many of the inhabitants could simply leave Gideon and colonize new worlds. The introduction of a deadly plague to a world where death is unknown would not be inspiring to its populace. Instead, there would probably be mass panic, leading to the eventual destruction of Gideon society. Even if the people were conditioned to accept this solution, it is entirely possible that the epidemic could get out of control, and soon destroy everyone on the planet. This episode tells us that altruism, like love, can sometimes be carried to ridiculous lengths.

Losira ("That Which Survives") must have been a wonderfully warm and loving woman. So much so that her computer replica feels regret and pain at being forced to kill, causing the hesitation that eventually enables Kirk and Co. to defeat the computer. We saw how Kirk and McCoy reacted to the replica (and even Spock to an extent), and it would be interesting to see how they would have responded to a flesh-and-blood Losira.

Because of his disappointing experience with Carolyn Palamas, it wasn't any surprise that it was quite a while before Scotty let himself feel anything for a woman again. (Indeed, his shattered, one-sided affair with Carolyn probably contributed to his temporary distrust of females as seen in "Wolf in the Fold".) So it was nice to see him once again interested in a lady in "The Lights of Zetar." Mira Romaine, the new object of Scotty's tender affections, seemed to be much more his type: She's intelligent and somewhat technical-minded, and unlike the glamorous Carolyn, Mira is a woman of mature and gentle loveliness. Although she wasn't head over heels in love with Montgomery, she did care about him and returned his affection in a tender manner that indicated she could grow to love him very much. Indeed, her greatest fear about the aliens was not that they were invading her mind and body, but that they might prove harmful to Scotty. If you read between the lines of Alan Dean Foster's *Log* series of adaptations of the animated series, you get the impression that he believes Mira and Scotty eventually married, and share an open marriage which allows both of them to pursue their respective careers. We can only hope that this is true, for if anyone deserves happiness, it is Scotty.

Throughout the course of Star Trek, we saw Captain Kirk fall in love many times, but always under unusual circumstances or when his reasoning faculties were impaired: He had a false memory of love for Helen Noel impressed upon his mind by the neural neutralizer; he was misplaced in time when he fell in love with Edith Keeler; his dependence on Dr. Janet Wallace was caused by his loss of confidence when he grew unnaturally old; he was suffering from amnesia when he wooed and wed Miramanee; and his passion for Ellan was caused by the "magic" of her tears. Not once did we see Jim Kirk fall naturally and completely in love with any woman while in his normal state of mind under normal circumstances. This has, naturally, given rise to speculation that Kirk is unwilling—or unable—to fall in love in the normal, everyday manner. He must, many fans say, have to be "out of his mind"—or at least have extraordinary circumstances as an excuse—to bind himself to a woman.

We know that this is not true. We were told of several instances in Jim's past when he was very much in love with certain women, and none of those instances could be described as unusual. It's just that during the particular time of his life that is portrayed in the series, he didn't happen to meet the "right woman"—in this case, the term being applied to a woman with whom Kirk would be willing to share a long-term relationship and not necessarily a marriage partner or a "true love." And who knows what happened offscreen?

Kirk is a warm, loving, compassionate, virile human male, and whatever his failings may be in affairs of the heart, being unwilling to love is not one of them. It may very well be that he is often *too* willing to fall in love . . . and under "normal" circumstances, guards against it.

But we have a quandary presented to us in "Requiem for Methusulah": Kirk, while seemingly himself and in control of his emotions, fell deeply in love with Reena Kapec. She was, unbeknownst to him, an android, which might seem to be the "unusual circumstances" seen in every other case, but Kirk didn't discover this fact until well after he had acknowledged and declared his love. It didn't make any difference in any case, for he continued to respond to her as a "real" woman even after he learned the truth. So why did this happen? Was Reena the right "woman" after all?

Probably not. Kirk fell in love with her too quickly, too totally. While apparently a warm, innocent, and undeniably beautiful girl, Reena simply would not be the type to whom Kirk would be irresistibly attracted. As we have seen, it is always the strong-willed dynamic female that catches Jim's fancy, and Reena, while highly intelligent and versed in many talents, had all the personality of a doormat. Kirk might have found her naiveté charming in small doses, and probably lusted after her lush form, but he wouldn't fall in love with her.

Yet he did. So there must have been a reason, an outside influence which caused Kirk to succumb so quickly. It could have been that Flint used some sort of "love potion" to affect Kirk, causing him to fall in love and (hopefully) arouse the corresponding passion and emotions in Reena that he, Flint, had been unable to awaken. (Some fans have speculated that Flint speedily programmed Reena to "match" Kirk's psychological profile so completely that he couldn't help but fall for her, but this is highly unlikely. Flint had no knowledge of Kirk's psyche, and besides, Reena was to be *his* "ideal woman." He would hardly have wanted her to be a "love match" for another man.) Flint could have introduced the drug/elixir/potion in any number of ways (most likely in the drink he served Kirk), or Reena herself could have exuded some sort of artificial pheromone that affected Kirk.

Flint would not have capriciously selected Kirk. Spock is a Vulcan, which automatically eliminated him, and McCoy was a bit too old. He would have been a bit too much of a father figure in the mold of Flint. And don't for a minute think that Flint didn't know that Reena loved and respected him as a father; he was too experienced in love and life to have made that kind of mistake. Reena's earth-based education would have provided her with an intellectual aversion to incest, which is why she never had any kind of passionate feelings for Flint, and he knew that the only chance he had of overcoming her prejudice was to have Kirk awaken her sexuality. Then, once Reena had become a fully functioning and sexually active woman and Kirk was gone . . .

Spock must have suspected the artificial source of Kirk's feelings; it would otherwise have been unthinkable for him to delve into Kirk's mind without permission and pull out memories in such a wholesale fashion. Spock is no stranger to emotion, even love, and he would know that even in an unhappy love affair, part of the human need is to hold on to the memory, even if the majority of memories are sad ones.

Flint, on the other hand, tried to create love. As Star Trek often showed us, the only kind of love which is acceptable is that which is natural and mutually shared. It cannot be created, forced, or bargained for. The greatest irony is that Flint had already gained Reena's love—the love of a daughter for her father, the love of a student for her teacher, the love of a friend for a friend—but in his single-minded quest for an immortal sexual partner, he was blinded to the virtue and value of a loving and devoted daughter. Flint paid for his aberration with the death of Reena and, eventually, his own.

Spock is strangely drawn to the nonviolent principles (but not practices) and the "free love" of the space hippies in "The Way to Eden." His experiences on Omnicron Ceti III probably caused him to feel a little nostalgic at the mention of an "Eden"; he probably also sympathized with the youngsters' alienation. Kirk, on the other hand, dismisses it all as sheer nonsense; he has little use for an Eden, as his actions on both Omnicron Ceti and the Amerind planet showed. Regardless of the interests of the principals involved, Star Trek again used an episode to illusrate the folly of meaningless, and ultimately loveless, existence.

The Vulcan embodiment of "love," Surak, makes an appearance in "The Savage Curtain." Hailed by Spock as the father of all that Vulcans are, Surak is completely nonviolent, preaching the value of brotherly love and sharing ever the self-defeating practices of fighting and distrust. As in our own civilization, the principles of nonviolence are fine until the time comes when men must fight to preserve freedom. This is something Spock understands (and most other modern Vulcans as well; Vulcan is a full participant in Starfleet), and he disappoints Surak when he chooses to remain with Kirk and fight the villains. The difference in the attitudes toward their respective idols shown by Kirk and Spock is revealing: Kirk considers Lincoln a great man, someone to be admired and emulated; Spock seems to feel that Surak is almost a god, someone to be worshiped. While both replicates die bravely, it seems to be Kirk who is less disappointed by meeting his idol "in the flesh." Spock, while he still reveres Surak for what he was and what he accomplished, is forced to admit to himself that Surak's principles are not always correct or reasonable. This was perhaps Spock's first great revelation: The Vulcan Way is not always the right way.

Spock, like Kirk, never fell in love while "himself"—although that would, in any case, be a heck of a lot less likely to happen with Spock than it would be with Kirk. But in "All Our Yesterdays" the circumstances were such that Spock *was* himself—at least the self he would be if all psychological and social restraints were removed; the Spock he would have been had he been born thousands of years in Vulcan's past. As a result of not having been "prepared" by Mr. Atoz's atavachron, Spock reverted to the psychic demeanor of his ancestors (or his contemporaries; it's all in how you look at it) and began to fall victim to temptations of the flesh. And succulent temptation indeed was the enticing Zarabeth. Freed of his emotional constraints, Spock was able to eat and enjoy meat, became angry to the point of violence with Dr. McCoy, and fell in love with Zarabeth.

Which wouldn't be too hard for any normal, healthy male, be he human or Vulcan. Zarabeth was a beautiful, intelligent, and self-sufficient young woman, just the type that Spock would approve of as an excellent example of her species. Once Spock had reverted, however, all he cared about was that Zarabeth was a woman. (It is interesting to speculate why Dr. McCoy did not revert to a more savage mien as well. Perhaps he, as a human, was *already* acting as savagely and emotionally as were his counterparts on ancient Earth.) Although Zarabeth was lonely to the point of madness and desperation, still she was a warm and bright individual, completely lacking in the coyness and martyr- dom that flawed Leila Kalomi's personality. She and Spock, even in the throes of his artificial passion, made an attractive and well-matched couple. We cannot help but get the feeling that he would have had an interest in her even under normal circumstances —and we also get the feeling that he will not forget her as easily as he would like to have Dr. McCoy think. We can only trust that nine months or so after her visitors from the future departed, Zarabeth had a pointy-eared little toddler to ease her loneliness.

Was Kirk once in love with Janice Lester? Surely she was in love with him to the point of becoming quite insane when they split up. Perhaps they were too much alike. Janice, in her madness, reflects in a warped and unhealthy manner many of the qualities that we find in Kirk: ambition, obsession with command, vanity, ruthlessness. Or maybe she just aped these things in her insane desire to *be* Kirk, taking them to extremes because of hatred and illness. Revenge, not love, was Janice's motive, but the root cause of all her trouble was her unrequited love for Kirk. We can't blame him, of course; he was very young and didn't desire to remain in an affair that would have destroyed them both. He was also too young and inexperienced in true human emotions to realize how deeply Janice was hurt; a more mature Kirk could perhaps have found a way to end the affair without such bitterness and rancor. In any case, he could not have predicted that Janice would be so disastrously affected by the breakup.

Dr. Coleman loved Janice. Yes, it doesn't make sense for a man to help the woman he loves become another man, but love often doesn't make sense. Probably Coleman felt that once Janice had achieved her wish to be Kirk, she would realize that she was happier as a woman being loved by Coleman, and would reverse the mindswap. Coleman seriously misread both Janice's degree of insanity and her intentions, but then he wasn't the most stable of personalities himself. He allowed Janice to use him at every opportunity, worrying only about the consequences of their actions, never about the morality of them. As we said, love in Star Trek takes many forms—and not all of then are logical or healthy.

The animated Star Trek episodes, while well done within the budgetary and time limitations imposed upon them, were nonetheless sorely lacking in character development and exposition. Thus many of Star Trek's attitudes (both stated and implicit) about love and examples of the same were absent from the animated shows. However, several episodes did manage to sneak in a few instances, and those are worth mentioning in this article.

"Yesteryear" showed us a young Spock who had great respect and affection for his parents, but a lovely and purely innocent love for his pet *sehlat*, I'Chaya. Thus we learn that Spock was no different from little boys everywhere: He felt misunderstood by his parents, he fought with his friends, he ran away from home, and he had a "dog." But it is when I'Chaya is severely wounded and young Spock makes the decision to have him put to sleep rather than suffer constant pain that we see the beginnings of the adult love and compassion our Mr. Spock displays in abundance.

*   *   *

In adapting the form of Carter Winston, the Vendorian shape-changer also assimilated many of Winston's characteristics, including Winston's love for Anne Nored. The more he is around her, the more he is drawn to her—a combination of Winston's memories and feelings, and the alien's own need for acceptance and affection. When he finally reveals himself and admits to his treachery, he is surprised to find that Anne is willing to accept him as Winston and he eagerly agrees to her suggestion that they "talk it over."

"Mudd's Passion" introduced a love potion onboard the *Enterprise,* and naturally it was poor old Spock who got the biggest dose of it. (Most of the other crewmembers got to share in the fun as well when the potion got swept into the ship's ventilation system.) Of course, Christine would never have agreed to mess with Mudd and his schemes if she thought the potion would actually work; when it does, she is more surprised and aghast than anyone. An amusing side effect of the potion is that it causes the folks who fall in love because of it to hate each other violently for several hours afterward . . . kind of the same feelings this episode engendered in most fans.

The longtime love of Robert April and his wife, Sarah, is one of the few instances of a successful, mutually enhancing marriage we saw in Star Trek. No greater indication of the happiness of their union can be thought of than their decision to revert to their true ages, and their reason for doing so: The only life worth living over is one which has left you unfulfilled. As Robert and Sarah are very happy indeed with the lives they've led together, they do not require "a second chance." It is a nice affirmation of what love should be and one of the finest moments in animated Star Trek.

Of course, many other animated episodes contained instances of love at its best as postulated by Star Trek. Kirk's unwillingness to kill the cosmic cloud creature in "One of Our Ships Is Missing" and its corresponding reluctance to harm the *Enterprise* crew; Dr. Keniclius 5's desire to bring peace to the galaxy ("The Infinite Vulcan"); and the examples of acceptance of difference seen in "Magicks of Megas-Tu," "The Terratin Incident," "Time Trap," and "BEM."

So we may see that although the limitations of the animated form did prevent the series from achieving the richness of characterization and interaction that made the original series so involving, the concepts of Star Trek were so overridingly *right* that even the kid-vid mentality of Saturday-morning cartoons couldn't destroy them.

Star Trek: The Motion Picture contained many examples of love, some of them quite startlingly different from the kinds of love previously displayed in the Star Trek universe. Many fans have commented that Gene Roddenberry's view of Star Trek and its universe seemed to somehow change during the years-long layoff, seemed somehow to have become cynical and embittered, seeing the *Enterprise* as a harsh mistress rather than as the demanding and unforgiving, but ultimately supremely rewarding, lover that she was in the series. This, of course, resulted in a drastic change in the characterization of Kirk (who, as always, may be seen as Roddenberry's alter ego); changes in Kirk's character resulted, not unsurprisingly, in changes in supporting characters. Most important of these was the change in Spock. The changes in Spock were valid and logical within the emotional framework which had been built over the course of the series (these changes will be discussed in depth later), but it may be simply stated for the purposes of this argument that Spock's characterization changes and actions were performed so as to completely alienate Kirk, allowing his total aloneness to be the core around which the film's plot was built. A Kirk deprived of the three things he loves most—his command, his ship, his best friend—is a Kirk lost, a Kirk unlike any other we have ever seen. In causing this to happen, Roddenberry immediately supplied himself with a plot premise guaranteed to grab the emotions of every fan, and he also enriched and furthered the characterization of Spock and Kirk (and, resultingly, those around them) to a degree which would have otherwise been unthinkable.

Kirk, as we were shown innumerable times during the course of the series, coveted the *Enterprise* and the power and prestige afforded to him as her captain. This was, except in times of mental distress or, rarer, total honesty, expressed as "love" for the ship. This is quite an unusual way for Kirk to feel, especially toward an inanimate object. Kirk seldom, if ever, displayed the type of personality which would attach feelings to (or attribute them from) an inanimate object. On the contrary, from what we learn of and can see of Kirk's personality, he is a man who encumbers himself with as few possessions as possible, denoting a distinctive lack of sentiment. Aside from a few ancient books, his medals and awards (which he does not display), and some works of art, Kirk's cabin is almost spartanly bare. One cannot help but feel that his soul is in similar shape. So why, then, do fans so insistently declare that Kirk passionately loves the physical being, the nuts and bolts, the "stem to stern" reality of the *Enterprise*? It is simply not logical and is certainly not backed up by fact or statement.

There is sentiment involved, of course—fan sentiment. Not wanting to admit that their beloved Kirk can be less than perfect, they choose instead to cloak his perfectly natural and understandable passion for command in a more romantic desire for "a tall ship and a star to sail her by." This fiction is harmless enough— one even suspects that Kirk himself has used it to good effect now and then during the course of a love affair or two—but it must have particularly rankled Roddenberry, who originally conceived Kirk as a Horatio Hornblower surrogate; not a romantic or a dreamer, but instead a hardheaded, professional spacefarer who was tempered by compassion, love, and dreams, not ruled by them. When preparing *Star Trek: The Motion Picture*, Roddenberry could have seen this new film as the opportunity to rectify this misapprehension of his main character in a most dramatic and detailed manner. The result: the harsh, demanding, almost obsessed Kirk we saw throughout much of the film.

This was not a "new" Kirk by any means—we had seen him a number of times previously acting in just such a roughshod and domineering manner. The difference in *Star Trek: The Motion Picture* was that Kirk was, for the first time in our experience, acting from a position of weakness, not a position of strength. Deprived of the confidence and authority of legitimate command, the very worst side of Kirk's passions revealed itself. No, this was nothing like the sneering, brutal "evil side" of Kirk we saw in "The Enemy Within" . . . the Kirk in *STTMP* was a man floundering, desperately grasping for a last chance at—what? Life? Love? Freedom? Perhaps all of these.

But it is love which is our consideration here, and it was through an act of love that Kirk regained his self, his true identity. But Roddenberry wasn't going to be that obvious. It would have been easy to allow Kirk to suit up and go after Spock, unconscious from his encounter with V'Ger. (Indeed, we are teased with a shot of Kirk donning the EVA suit.) Spock, however, was sent back to the ship by V'Ger, depriving Kirk of a "typical Kirk self-sacrificing scene" in this film. There would be no easy catharsis, no simple heroics to put things aright. Kirk would have to face his own humanity and failings in the face of his friend Spock. It was obviously not only the Vulcan who was experiencing the joy of that "simple feeling"—as Spock felt, for the first time, what it meant to *know* that loved ones care, so too was Kirk's own self-worth reaffirmed in the love that Spock shared with him.

Spock formed a new link with humanity, and through his humanness, Kirk reformed his broken link. Thus, we learn that the power of love and friendship enables men to transcend doubts and fears. In sharing feelings, they are able to become more than the sum of their parts.

Spock's actions at the end of the original five-year mission are almost incomprehensible to most fans. Denying all that he had learned about himself and his own humanity, he left his human friends and Starfleet and thrust himself into the harsh Vulcan *Kolinahr* discipline. We may assume that this was a case in which love was not enough—Spock felt so incomplete and so dissatisfied with his life that the love and respect of his friends was unfulfilling. Eventually, however, the love Spock held for them, especially Kirk, betrayed his ambitions to achieve a state of total absence of emotion. The dullest schoolchild could have told Spock that you can't forget those you love, no matter what kind of mental disciplines you use. Those you love are too much a part of yourself to deny.

One of the most charming and/or exasperating things about Spock, however, has always been his stubbornness about admitting the extent to which emotions affect him. Once again, he denies their strength, and upon arriving on the *Enterprise*, affects a mantle of cold aloofness which fools no one, but exasperates everybody. This time, however, Spock is not simply standing back and remaining uninvolved. He must, for the sake of his own sanity, keep the onrushing emotions from taking control. Having for so long attempted to eradicate these emotions, he must have found it devastating to find out how completely he had failed. Any lesser man would have been crushed. The cold logic of V'Ger is, Spock feels, his last hope. If he can only discover what the secret is, how the entity can be so free of emotion, then perhaps he can salvage something of his ambitions.

Of course, Spock ultimately learns that the very logic of V'Ger's mind causes it to be barren of hope and beauty and faith and all of the other million-and-one intangible things that make human life so interesting and exciting. Or so Spock says.

Consider this: V'Ger was compared, by Spock, to a child . . . questioning, seeking, wondering who it was and where it was going. These are not cold, logical concerns. They are the stuff of self-awareness, of burgeoning humanity. If V'Ger could seek something greater than itself, then it could at least understand the concept of faith, even if it could not accept it.

Spock, in his abortive meld with V'Ger, would have seen all this and more. It probably was more like a look into his own mind than anything else, and it could have been this realization which led him to an appreciation of the "simple feeling" of shared human love and friendship. Spock, being Spock, still could not bring himself to simply admit he had been wrong. So he sort of colored the situation a bit in his own favor. And that is more than enough proof that he accepted and embraced his humanity.

Love in *Star Trek: The Motion Picture* is seen, above all, as a healing force. Not only are Kirk and Spock flawed, Decker and Ilia are also. Separated by the dual demons of duty and honor, they are each incomplete without the other.

(It is a curious statement that Star Trek makes in regard to "mixed" love between partners of different planetary species: in every example seen, the love shared is unusually strong and pure, as if the very action of overcoming the taboos and strictures against interspecies romance forms stronger, more passionate bonds.)

Ilia is incomplete simply by virtue of the fact that she must (by oath!) refrain from sexual contact while serving in Starfleet. For a being as sexually oriented as are the Deltans, such abstinence must be as debilitating as the lack of proper sleep or food would be to us. One cannot help but feel that Ilia is punishing herself in some way by agreeing to such an existence. The most natural supposition, of course, is that she joined Starfleet both to forget Decker and to serve penance for having committed the crime of falling in love with him. If so, then her choice of career was a rather strange one, for chances were that she would eventually come across him again; a classic case of self-fulfilling disaster.

Decker, on the other hand, is more of a "young Kirk" than is at first evident. At the time of his unconsummated affair with Ilia on Delta, he was more concerned with his career than with his happiness. Or, rather, he made the same mistake as did Kirk of confusing ambition with gaining happiness. Will tells Ilia that had he attempted to tell her goodbye, he would have been unable to leave. This, too, evokes echoes of Kirk, who also often seemed to be at a loss when ending an affair—probably because, like Decker, he feared that he would be unable to say a meaningful goodbye. By the time of *Star Trek: The Motion Picture*, Will has achieved his desire: captaincy of a starship. But he is probably not totally happy, no more than was Kirk when commanding the *Enterprise*. He, perhaps unconsciously, yearns for something more, to be a part of something greater. We may assume that Ilia was inextricably wound up in this desire; it may even have centered around her. In any case, when they again met aboard the *Enterprise*, Decker's decision to remain with her, in whatever fashion, became a certainty. Neither of them would have been able to bear parting again. Indeed, so strong was Decker's love for Ilia that he transferred it to the V'Ger-created simulacrum. So strong was her love for him that it survived even within the circuitry of that being and kept it from becoming totally a machine and a creature of V'Ger.

Decker and Ilia, like almost every major character in *STTMP*, are seriously flawed, and it is only when they are literally merged with each other that we see them as complete beings. We are never flat-out told that they are "two halves of a whole," that would be too easy, too much a cliché. But it is a definite impression we gain through their actions, their scenes together. The two of them, together with the "soul" of V'Ger, come together to forge a new life form, one which must, of necessity in this Star Trek universe, contain the best—and worst—of each of them. Even though unthinkably advanced, it will still be a living, conscious, loving being . . . one with the galaxy and with all things.

Star Trek II: The Wrath of Khan presented us with an abundance of love, not only through our old friends, but through the introduction of new characters and situations.

Once again the story revolves around Kirk, and once again he is unhappy. This time, however, his unhappiness is caused by the fact that he feels that life is passing him by. He would much rather be back in space, in command of the *Enterprise*, but we get the impression that it is not so much the ship and the power of command that he covets, but instead any opportunity to do something meaningful with his life. His overweening concern with age is caused more by a surplus of time in which to sit around and think about it than by any physical symptoms. He is bored and lonely. He feels old and useless. He feels unloved.

For Kirk, love has always been inextricably tied up with his career and the resulting respect and admiration gained from it. He has rarely, if ever, entered into a one-on-one relationship with a lover or a friend on a basis of equality. Even when he lost his memory and fell in love with the Indian maiden, Miramanee, Kirk was considered to be a god by her and the members of her tribe. And now that he is more or less stalled in his career, "flying a desk," his status is no longer a bulwark to his confidence. Although he holds high position and has achieved great honor,

Kirk obviously feels that he is little more than a civil servant. And when confronted by his friends, he feels out of things, hopelessly left on the sidelines as they, and life, pass him by. For the first time, we see Kirk surrounded by *things*, albeit beautiful, meaningful things, but inanimate objects nonetheless. It is the mark of how much Kirk has changed, of how he considers his life to be forever set upon a single path. Kirk's antiques and souvenirs tell us that he expects to spend the rest of his life in those rooms, eventually becoming, as McCoy warns, one of the antiques himself.

This is not strictly true, of course. The chiding that McCoy gives him as a kind of backhanded birthday present lets us know that it is still possible for Kirk to get a deep-space command simply by asking for it. Why he does not is the deepest mystery of the film. We can casually assume that he would not feel comfortable unless he captained the *Enterprise* and was surrounded by his old crew, but that would be wrong. As much as Kirk respected and admired and depended upon these people, he could, and would, successfully serve without them. No, the reason why Kirk would not obtain another ship is a mystery which will only be solved when we learn the story (or stories) relating what happened during the years between the films.

In any case, once Kirk is forced by circumstance to take command of the *Enterprise*, he soon becomes his old self—rusty to the point of danger, perhaps, but still *Captain* Kirk. It is important to note that Kirk did not actively desire to wrest command from Spock—regulations required that he do so. And when he went to the Vulcan's quarters to inform him, Kirk sounded genuinely regretful and apologetic. Spock, as usual, had the perfect response and we saw immediately that their friendship, so painfully affirmed in *Star Trek: The Motion Picture*, remained intact and stronger than ever.

There are no problems between Kirk and Spock (and McCoy) in *Wrath of Khan*. They are close friends and associates; McCoy even serves on the *Enterprise* under Spock! The triad is complete— but somehow a little less interesting than before. . . . Perhaps the loss of the tension caused by Spock's adamant refusals to admit to his human side is more debilitating than we ever thought it would be; perhaps each of them is just a little older and a little more sedate and less interesting. In any case, we see three men who have aged well, each growing richer through the others. Except for Kirk's dissatisfaction, we could say that they had reached a kind of Star Trek nirvana.

Even if Kirk were not feeling old, he still is actually growing old. And the one inevitable fact of life is that by living it, we leave a trail behind us, an unalterable past, full of our follies and wisdoms. If we are lucky, our pasts will never catch up with us. James Kirk, although it would be inaccurate to call him unlucky, *is* something of a magnet for trouble. And in *Wrath of Khan*, we basically see the story of what happens when several large chunks of Jim Kirk's past present themselves to him all in a few days. . . .

We may assume that Kirk loved Carol Marcus and that they spent quite a bit of time together; they may even have had a short-term marriage contract. But we get the distinct impression that their parting was not as amicable as their present behavior would lead us to believe. Kirk speaks bitterly to McCoy of "reopening old wounds"; we do not know if this refers to the circumstances of their parting or Carol's insistence that David be raised free from Kirk's influence. In any case, Kirk's feelings for her have survived relatively intact through the years, as his comment to McCoy and his tender mien to her unmistakably display. It might be too strong a statement to say that he still loves her, but he definitely still has a soft spot for Carol, and probably easily could fall in love with her again.

Of course, Kirk's feelings for Carol are inextricably tied up with his rather ambivalent feelings for David. Kirk says flat out in the film that he stayed away because she wanted him to; it is possible that he transferred some of the resentment he felt toward Carol to the child, a perfectly natural response, and one which would allow him to justify the fact that he was not around when his son was growing up. (It's interesting that in her novelization of *Wrath of Khan*, Vonda McIntyre softens Kirk's position, leaving a question in our minds as to whether or not he knew of David's birth.) Deep in his heart, Kirk probably knows that he would have made a lousy father, what with being absent most of the time and not possessing the temperament for home life anyway. What is rather amazing is that Kirk did not attempt to keep track of David. Knowing how possessive and obsessive Kirk could become under certain circumstances, it is hard to believe that he could so totally divorce himself from the life of his child. We would expect Kirk to gain information, in one way or another, about David and even, in whatever ways possible, to influence his upbringing. Either Kirk so loved Carol that his agreement to stay away was inviolable to him, or else he was so hurt that he literally blocked thoughts of David from his mind. The latter is probably the most likely, for we never got even a hint, in word or deed, that Kirk knew or even cared that he had a son growing up somewhere.

Now, however, Kirk's overriding desire is to have David's respect. Jim probably believes that it is too late to ever have the kind of love from David that he could have had as a true father, but it would not be too much to hope to gain the boy's respect—even though David philosophically despises much that Kirk stands for.

David, on the other hand, does not even know Kirk, except as "that Boy Scout type" that his mother used to see. (David obviously learned from Carol or, more likely, another family member that she was once involved with Kirk, as he would not have seen Kirk in the flesh.) We do not know for sure when David learns that Kirk is his biological father. We can only assume it is sometime after Spock's death, for there would not have been time for Carol to have told him previously. (Unless, knowing that they could all soon die, and wanting David to know that Kirk was his father, she informed him just before he came to the bridge during the battle in the Mutara Nebula.) It would have been interesting to know exactly how David reacted to this news. Was he shocked, or did he already suspect, having seen his mother and Kirk together? Did he decide to tell Kirk of his regret for Spock's death and his pride before or after he learned the truth? It wouldn't make much difference to Kirk, but it does in the context of David's mindset. It he had gained a new respect for Kirk, and Starfleet, before discovering that they were related, it would indicate that he was admitting to the necessity and value of men such as Kirk and the job that they do. If he was only expressing his pleasure at being Kirk's son, then he may not have learned anything of real value from the situation at all. We shall have to wait until future adventures to see.

The other new kid on the block, Saavik, also piques our curiosity, especially in the matter of her parentage. True, we are given no overt evidence that she is Spock's biological daughter, but we cannot avoid the feeling that she *is* a part of Spock, a larger part than can be explained by just respect and affection. There is that between them, oh yes, respect and affection in an amount and of an unashamed evidence that we never saw between even Spock and Kirk. (In the "old days", that is . . . now, nothing could be plainer or more obvious than the existence of their friendship.) Spock, without doubt, has allowed himself, on the one hand, and Saavik, on the other, to move their relationship far beyond that of teacher and student. In perhaps everything but name, she is his daughter and the spiritual heir of all that he stands for.

Having been raised as an outcast among the harsh Romulan colonies, Saavik probably did not see, or even perhaps feel, any love or affection during her entire childhood. Chances are that she was an embittered and completely recalcitrant child when discovered by Spock and his team. That she has developed into an intelligent and caring person is nothing short of a miracle, and we can only assume that Spock himself was responsible for it. Chances are that he did not, himself, see to her upbringing; an educated guess would have him giving Saavik to Sarek and Amanda to raise. She would have been taught Vulcan lore and educated in the sciences by Sarek; Amanda would have taught her how to act as a civilized Vulcan woman. And also, with or without Sarek's permission, what it means to be a human woman as well, for Spock would have surely explained the difficulties Saavik's dual heritage would cause her in the future. And while human feelings and emotions are not like those of Romulans, they are certainly closer than anything Vulcan ritual could offer. Also, in the loving, safe warmth of Spock's home, Saavik could learn what it means to have a family and a heritage. It worked, for she now thinks of herself as "Vulcan"—but, as Spock undoubtedly told her, thinking of yourself as something and actually being it are two different things.

If the above is true, then it would be more proper to consider Saavik as Spock's "little sister" rather than as his daughter. This is less romantic, but more realistic. Saavik's anger at David for suggesting she is Spock's daughter in the novelization of *Wrath of Khan* pretty much puts that possibility right out of the window. One would have to invent such unlikely scenarios as the Romulan commander's self-fertilization with Spock's semen to otherwise explain his parentage of Saavik. No, Spock, having mellowed and accepted his humanity, responded to the need of a child who must have, almost unbearably, reminded him of himself. And, like any compassionate, caring being, he helped her. Having helped her once, he continued to do so, until he had virtually adopted her. In the sense that he took it upon himself to accept responsibility for a child and to offer her encouragement, training, and even love, then, yes, Spock is Saavik's father.

Now, what of David and Saavik? They exchanged a few bickering lines in the film, but most of the exchanges between them which were to indicate that they were becoming interested in each other were cut out. We are then left with the impression that although they respected and liked each other to a certain extent, they did not immediately fall head over heels in love. Many fans expressed disappointment at this, feeling that a match between Kirk's son and Spock's "daughter" was such a natural outgrowth of the Kirk/Spock relationship that to not allow it to happen would almost be sacrilege. Upon reflection, however, even the most rabid fan would have to agree that such a relationship, while still entirely possible and not disagreeable, *must* grow from within the characters themselves, and not be arbitrarily forced upon them just to satisfy our sense of continuity. As of yet, we know virtually nothing of Saavik's and David's true personalities, and without the kind of week-by-week exposure to them that we had with Spock and Kirk, we never will. Would you expect to introduce two strangers and have them fall in love almost immediately? It is the stuff of bad fiction, and although Star Trek has had its share of bad fiction, it has yet to stoop to such soap-opera tactics.

It is not a new Spock we see in *Wrath of Khan*, simply a Spock who has exorcised his demons and is now free to give and accept friendship and love. He learned, and learned well, from his experience with V'Ger and has successfully applied those lessons to his life. We can expect not only that Spock can now openly and unashamedly call Kirk "friend," but that he also found the words to tell his mother and father of his love for them. The fact that he willingly sacrificed himself is nothing less that we would have ever expected of Spock, but his action affected us all the more because he had now become a richer, more accepted, and, surely, a happier person.

One would hardly expect to find the Khan of *Star Trek II: The Wrath of Khan* discussed in an article about love, but it is Khan who is probably the perfect example Star Trek gives us of how love may be warped and perverted to evil ends. Not since the original series has Star Trek made such a forceful and eloquent statement about love in all of its forms.

Khan, once the noble, if flawed, prince of millions, has been reduced to the leader of a ragtag group of survivors, living in almost subhuman conditions. It is little wonder that he goes quite mad. He still, however, manages to instill in his followers the same fanatical loyalty that he did in the past. Some of them, such as the hapless Joachim, obviously loved him. And Khan has not forgotten his beloved Marla McGivers. Not only does he speak in sadness and anger of her death, he wears a medallion modeled upon the *Enterprise* emblem she wore on her uniform. (It is possible that Marla fashioned this medallion herself in order to remind her—and Khan—of all that she had sacrificed to remain with him.)

Khan, however, represents more: He is the embodiment of all that can go wrong when the aims of science, government, religion, and even love miss the mark, go somehow terribly wrong. Man, as postulated by Star Trek, is a fallible being who does his best to overcome the destructive urges of his humanity, all the while constantly striving to become something more through the acquisition of knowledge. In simple terms, life is a constant struggle to better oneself.

At one time, it was thought that genetic engineering would be the solution to man's problems and faults. Simply design a better man, the scientists must have said, and he will guide the rest of us to paradise. But, Star Trek tells us, the end result of taking human powers to their limit is a being whose failures and faults are also taken to their limits . . . and you end up with a superbeing who is completely amoral, so completely *human* as to be, in a civilized society, inhuman. The first and the most powerful of these beings was Khan. He was the first ultimate male, and, inevitably, the first ultimate failure.

Khan, perversely, is the product of hope and love. Man, utilizing the hard-won knowledge of millions of years, decided he could improve upon nature in a benign fashion and that nature would not object. Nature, however, is an unforgiving force. It cares nothing for high hopes or altruism. Nature simply *is*. And so nature did not cooperate in the experiment. Unconcerned, nature gave the supermen the same animalistic urges and selfishness that she gives the rest of us.

In the case of Khan and the other supermen, love and good intentions were not enough. Yet, in their own smug, superior-minded way, the supermen craved and needed love—not only from each other, but from normal humans as well. Khan's domination of Marla McGivers in "Space Seed" was a means to an end—escape—but there was also a feeling of desperation in it, as if he felt that unless he was loved, even worshiped by someone, he did not exist. And, as mentioned above, Khan, at least, was quite capable of feeling love.

Yet loving individuals is quite a different thing from the kind of love that makes us more than ourselves—love of others, love of freedom, love of diversity. It was this kind of love which Khan and his followers were incapable of feeling, for it requires that one look beyond oneself. Like animals, the "superior" humans could not do this, and thus they were less than human, not more.

With the arrival of Genesis, not only does man now have the power to create not only "superior" humans, but entire worlds may be manipulated and created or recreated to specification. Or whim. Like nature, it matters not to Genesis. *Wrath of Khan* leaves us with the question of Spock's return. Will the power of Genesis revive the Vulcan? But the question is greater than that, yet more subtle. Will the power of Genesis revive humanity's basest urges? McCoy certainly thinks so, and he's always been a pretty good judge of human nature.

Ultimately, however, it comes down to the statement which Kirk made so many years ago: "We are not going to kill today." Mankind can, and must, control itself, its animalistic urges. Any madman could gain control of Genesis and wipe out perhaps dozens of planets before he was stopped, or a would-be dictator would find Genesis a most tempting weapon. Such is the risk of any new technology, whether it be the bow-and-arrow, gunpowder, or nuclear weapons. It is the control of man as a society which must concern us. When the society decides to use Genesis, or any weapon or technology, for sheer destruction and to further its own ends, then the tenets and beliefs of Kirk, of Spock, of Star Trek will have been abandoned.

As stated in the first half of this article (*Best of Trek #5*), Star Trek is based on love. The underlying theme of the series and the films is that man will someday overcome his own humanity and learn to live in peace and brotherly love not only with his own kind, but with myriad other sentient beings throughout the universe. By following Kirk's advice, by admitting to our own humanity and controlling our own inhumanity, we can make that day come all the sooner.

ABOUT THE EDITORS

Although largely unkown to readers not involved in Star Trek fandom before the publication of *The Best of Trek #1*, WALTER IRWIN and G. B. LOVE have been actively editing and publishing magazines for many years. Before they teamed up to create TREK® in 1975, Iriwin worked in newspapers, advertising, and free-lance writing, while Love published *The Rocket's Blast—Comiccollector* from 1960 to 1974, as well as hundreds of other magazines, books, and collectables. Both together and separately, they are currently planning several new books and magazines, as well as continuing to publish TREK.